This book is given
in Memory of
Jane King
by
Jennifer Doyle

Murder
with Honey Ham
Biscuits

Books by A.L. Herbert

MURDER WITH FRIED CHICKEN AND WAFFLES

MURDER WITH MACARONI AND CHEESE

MURDER WITH COLLARD GREENS AND HOT SAUCE

MURDER WITH HONEY HAM BISCUITS

Published by Kensington Publishing Corporation

Murder
with Honey Ham
Biscuits

A.L. Herbert

KENSINGTON BOOKS
www.kensingtonbooks.com

KENSINGTON BOOKS are published by

Kensington Publishing Corp.
119 West 40th Street
New York, NY 10018

All Kensington titles, imprints, and distributed lines are available at special quantity discounts for bulk purchases for sales promotion, premiums, fund-raising, educational, or institutional use. Special book excerpts or customized printings can also be created to fit specific needs. For details, write or phone the office of the Kensington Special Sales Manager: Attn. Special Sales Department. Kensington Publishing Corp., 119 West 40th Street, New York, NY 10018. Phone: 1-800-221-2647.

Library of Congress Catalogue Number: 2020931289

Kensington and the K logo Reg. U.S. Pat. & TM Off.

ISBN-13: 978-1-4967-1801-3
ISBN-10: 1-4967-1801-1
First Kensington Hardcover Edition: August 2020

ISBN-13: 978-1-4967-1805-1 (e-book)
ISBN-10: 1-4967-1805-4 (e-book)

10 9 8 7 6 5 4 3 2 1

Printed in the United States of America

Murder
with Honey Ham
Biscuits

Chapter 1

We are well into May and signs of summer abound in the kitchen of my restaurant, Mahalia's Sweet Tea, in Prince George's County, Maryland. One of my prep cooks, Tacy, is shucking corn, picked fresh from a farm just a few miles away. We'll steam it on the cob and offer it to our customers a dozen different ways—simply buttered and salted . . . or perhaps sprinkled with cayenne and finished with a touch of lime juice . . . or maybe slathered in a black-pepper mayonnaise before giving it a good roll in shredded Muenster cheese—choices . . . choices. To my left, Momma, who makes all the desserts for Sweet Tea, and one of my kitchen assistants are peeling peaches. I can tell they are perfectly ripe from their deep yellow color with just a hint of a pink blush. When they're done removing the skins, they'll slice them, coat them with a thick syrup flavored with sugar, cinnamon, and nutmeg, and pour them into buttery crusts—yes, peach pie with a generous dollop of whipped cream is on the dessert menu.

My cousin, Wavonne, and I are in the middle of it all, standing in front of the stainless steel counter, chopping red peppers for their inclusion in a decadent seafood quiche that will be the highlight of today's brunch selections—meat from local Maryland hard crabs harvested from the nearby Potomac River, eggs whipped to perfection with milk and butter, and soft gouda cheese. The final product will be almost like a savory crab cheesecake. There's also a basket of plump green tomatoes behind me that, as soon as one of us can find the time, we'll slice, season, cover in batter, and fry to a golden brown. Fried green tomatoes fresh from the oil, crisp on the outside, tender on the inside—is there anything better?

This time of year, when the sun-soaked days start early and end late, is my favorite for culinary creations. Everything is fresh, fragrant, and colorful ... and grown from the ground in natural light, the way God intended, rather than in some hothouse.

I'm in the midst of a rare sort of zen moment, one of those times when I can rise above the constant clunk and clatter of my busy commercial kitchen and just take it all in. Everything is running smoothly this morning ... no broken ovens or malfunctioning exhaust fans ... no employees have called in sick ... we're on schedule to open at eleven a.m. with no major hiccups or drama. . . . We're in a *groove*. I've been enjoying taking in the vibrant smells, colors, and textures of the food we're preparing and, right now, despite the wealth of people and noise around me, it's just me, a knife, and a crisp red pepper—that is until Wavonne, who had taken a slight breather from her constant chatter, pipes up to share what's on her mind.

"Remember that guy, Marvin, who I dated earlier this year?" she asks. "That cheap-ass guy that took me to Wing Zone with a Groupon. The one who disappeared ... just stopped returnin' my calls."

"I don't know ... maybe," I say. "Was he the one with the man bun?"

"No, that was Jack."

"Oh ... was Marvin the one with that big mean dog he thought he could bring into my restaurant?"

"No. That was Jamal. And that big mean dog was a cock-apoo, Halia," Wavonne teases. "Marvin was the white guy . . . the one who shaved his head so he didn't have to pay for hair-cuts . . . and had a car but took the bus everywhere to save on gas."

I look at Wavonne with a blank stare as I mull the multi-tude of men she has paraded in and out of Sweet Tea.

"The one who wanted to borrow your Costco card, so he didn't have to buy a membership."

"Oh yes," I say. "He was here for brunch a few months ago and asked if he could have extra bacon instead of the toast that came with his meal . . . and walked off with two sets of my silverware and the salt and pepper shakers. The one that never tipped, right?"

"That's the one. Cheap *and* stupid, but damn is he hand-some," Wavonne coos. "So, yesterday I'm in the city . . . at the wig shop lookin' for a new party wig. And as I'm leavin', I see him walkin' outta the stab-and-grab next door. I was like—"

"Walking out of the *what*?" Momma inquires.

"The stab-and-grab . . . that dumpy little minimart on Good Hope Road," Wavonne clarifies. "Anyway, I went right up to him and gave him a piece of my mind—"

"Not too big of a piece, I hope. There's only so much there to begin with," Momma jokes.

"Very funny," Wavonne replies. "I'm halfway through givin' him a good 'what for' when he tells me he wasn't get-tin' back to me because he was in the slammer."

"Jail?"

"No, Halia. He was deejayin' at some hip downtown club called the Slammer," Wavonne jibes. "*Yes*, he was in jail . . . said he tried to pull a 'dine and dash' at the Carolina Kitchen in Hyattsville. Only, without his car, he could only dash to the bus stop a couple of blocks away. The cops picked him up while he was waitin' for the number eighty-three to

Rhode Island Avenue." She pauses for a moment and takes in my reaction to what she just said. "Don't look at me like that. I told you he was cheap *and* stupid."

"Cheap and stupid . . . *and* a convict? So, when are you going to see him again?" I ask, knowing that Wavonne overlooking cheap, stupid, and a criminal record is nowhere near outside the realm of possibility.

"Friday night. I'm off, and apparently it's six-dollar shrimp night at Bonefish Grill in Brandywine."

"Seriously?" Momma questions. "You're going to date a felon who's not even smart enough to plan a viable getaway? I wouldn't want *Halia* dating a felon, and at her age, her options are far more limited than yours."

"I don't think dinin' and dashin' is a felony, Aunt Celia. If it was, he'd still be in jail," Wavonne says. "And did you not hear me mention what a looker he is?"

Momma takes a deep breath to keep herself from protesting further. Much like myself, she's learned there is nothing she can say to keep Wavonne from doing *anything*—whether it's dating a lawbreaker, spending a week's pay on a purse, or taking on a "second job" by buying into pyramid schemes that mostly involve her constantly annoying her Facebook friends with posts trying to sell weight loss potions, makeup, or jewelry.

Wavonne, who's about fifteen years my junior, is almost thirty years old and has been a handful ever since she came to live with Momma and me when her own mother (Momma's sister) was no longer fit to look after her. We didn't have much luck reining her in when she was a teenager and seem to have even less these days.

"Relax, Aunt Celia," Wavonne says, after Momma exhales with a long sigh. "I'm not gonna *date* him. I'm just gonna string him along until Melva's wedding in September. I wanna show up with a little arm candy, and Marvin will do quite nicely. If I have to look at his fine mug over two-for-one tacos or half-price burgers for a couple of months to be the bridesmaid with the hottest date, so be it."

I'm foolishly about to make a futile attempt to change Wavonne's mind when I hear my name called from behind. I turn and see my hostess, Sondra, poking her head through the kitchen door. "There's a woman here to see you," she says to me. "She was knocking on the glass doors. I told her we weren't open yet, but she wouldn't go away. She looks harmless enough, but she's very persistent."

"Did she say what she wants?"

"No, she just keeps insisting that she needs to speak with you."

"Okay." I untie my apron, hang it up, and exit the kitchen. Once I'm in the dining room I find a tall, lanky woman, who I guess is around or about fifty. She has short brown hair with a few gray streaks and is wearing black flats and a gray tweed suit, which seems like an odd, and highly uncomfortable, clothing choice for the warm weather we are having. As I approach her and take in her sharp edges, the word "severe" comes to mind. She reminds me very much of Miss Jane Hathaway from *The Beverly Hillbillies*.

"Hello," I say. "I'm Halia Watkins. What can I do for you?"

"Trudy McAlister." She extends her hand, which I politely shake. "Do you mind if we have a seat?"

"Um . . . no, I guess not." I gesture for her to follow me to a booth against the wall. "What's this about?" I inquire as we sit down.

"I have an opportunity I'd like to discuss with you."

"Thank you," I say, realizing she is probably selling something. "But I don't need any artwork, I already have an alarm system, I'm not interested in installing an ATM, and I'm really not looking to switch suppliers for anything at the moment."

"Not that kind of opportunity," she says. "Let me ask you: Are you familiar with the program *Elite Chef*?"

"Halia don't watch much TV," Wavonne calls. I should have

known she'd sidle her way to the dining room to see what this mystery lady wants. Wavonne is like a curious cat . . . if cats wore teased-up wigs and too much makeup. She *always* has to know what's going on. "I've seen *Elite Chef* . . . the one with all the cooking challenges and that smokin' hot host, Leon Winfield," she adds, sliding into the booth next to me. "Why?"

Trudy doesn't answer. Instead she shoots a "who the hell is this?" expression in my direction.

"This is my cousin, Wavonne. She's a server here," I say. "*Elite Chef?* No, I'm not familiar with it. I spend most of my time here, and the TV behind the bar is usually on one of the sports channels. What does it have to do with me?"

"Well, as the young"—Trudy stumbles for a moment and takes in all-that-is-Wavonne—"um . . . *lady* said, it's a cooking show . . . a competition to encourage African American engagement in the culinary arts. We started it with BET two years ago when Russell Mellinger was—"

"What do you mean 'we'?" Wavonne, who gets very excited about anything that has to do with television or the movies . . . or just pop culture in general, asks. "You're involved with the show?"

"Yes, I'm Russell's assistant."

"Russell Mellinger? *The* Russell Mellinger?" I ask. "I may not be familiar with *Elite Chef,* but I'm highly familiar with Mr. Mellinger. He owns the Barbary in New York . . . and Honeycomb in Chicago. . . ."

"And Cobalt Blue in Los Angeles . . . and New England Oyster Bar in Boston," Trudy says. "We started the show when he was opening the Barbary—the first season's winner is still the executive chef there. Last year, when he was opening Cobalt Blue, we did a second season to find a head chef for that restaurant. We're currently filming the third season, and this year's winner will be appointed executive chef at

Sunfish, Russell's newest venture—it's slated to open in just a few weeks near National Harbor here in Prince George's County. Russell is also taking his first foray in the lodging business—he's opening a luxury hotel, more of an inn, really, along with the new restaurant. He and his wife are staying there while they're in town producing the show."

"The new restaurant won't be serving soul food, I hope? I *so* do not want to have to compete with Russell Mellinger in my own backyard." I say this like I'm joking, but honestly, the idea would not thrill me. National Harbor is only a few miles from Sweet Tea, and although I trust our food and service would stand up to any competition, from what I've heard, Russell is known for being a businessman first, a chef second . . . and a decent human being comes in a very distant third. I've heard stories of him easily outbidding other entrepreneurs on prime restaurant real estate, pilfering staff from competing restaurants for his own establishments, and using the volume of business done across his many locations to negotiate deals with suppliers that single restaurant owners like myself cannot obtain. Stories abound of employees leaving in tears after one of his tirades, sexual harassment charges that have been quietly settled out of court, and lawsuits from suppliers claiming he owes them money. He's just generally known for being a ruthless, though highly successful, restaurant mogul.

"No," she replies. "It will be a tapas restaurant . . . small plates with a focus on fish and other seafood."

Wavonne groans. "Me and the girls went to one of those tapas places last weekend . . . barely enough food to feed a bird . . . and prices out the wazoo. There were five of us, but each dish only came with four things. . . . Melva's still got fork prong scars on her hand from tryin' to take the last chicken fritter."

"Isn't there *something* you should be doing, Wavonne?" I ask, and don't wait for her to respond before turning my gaze back toward Trudy. "So *Elite Chef* is a television show, and Russell Mellinger is opening a new tapas restaurant and a hotel. I'm still not sure what my connection to any of this is."

"It's been on the QT, but we've been filming the upcoming season here in the DC area. We're actually almost done . . . only two episodes left. We've been taping shows in and around the city—the Kennedy Center, the Botanic Gardens, the National Press Club, Hillwood, the National Portrait Gallery. . . . So many places . . . it's actually been quite the whirlwind. The theme of each competition has been tied to the host location. . . . President Kennedy's favorite foods at the Kennedy Center . . . plant-based cuisine at the Botanic Gardens . . . at Hillwood, we had contestants prepare items Marjorie Merriweather Post served at her grand affairs."

"Very interesting," I reply, wishing she would just get on with it. I have a million and one things to do before we open in two hours.

"So, for the next installment, we'll be filming at the African American museum."

"And you want me to do some catering for the production staff?"

"No, nothing like that," Trudy says. "We'd like you to be a guest judge on the show."

"A judge? On TV?"

"Oh girl, Halia's gonna be on television!" Wavonne exclaims.

"We have two guest judges for each challenge and, of course, Russell serves as a judge in every episode."

"What do the judges do exactly?" I ask.

"Well, ultimately, they evaluate the dishes made by the contestants, but there are usually some other responsibilities as well."

"Like?"

"For the taping you'll be involved in," Trudy says, as if

I've already agreed to participate, "we'll have you tour the museum with the contestants and the other judges . . . get to know them a little bit. Once they're assigned a challenge, you'll be tasked with mentoring one of them . . . with giving them some direction and advice. You'll get a break while they shop for any necessary ingredients. Then we'll all gather again in the evening for the challenge. You'll judge the final creations with Russell and the other guest judge, and the contestant whose dish fails to impress will be eliminated. That's it . . . easy peasy."

"And when is the taping?"

"Um . . . well, that's the thing. It's tomorrow."

"Tomorrow?!"

"Yes. We had an unexpected vacancy on the judging panel."

"So, who you really wanted dropped out," Wavonne proclaims.

"I wouldn't look at it that way, but yes, we did have a judge lined up who can no longer make it."

"Who?" I ask.

"Walter Carnegie."

"The head chef at the museum restaurant? Why did he drop out? Seems like a perfect match for an episode filmed in the museum."

"I'm not sure of the details . . . something about the museum board of directors thinking it was inappropriate. They're letting us film at the facility, but didn't like the idea of the head chef at such a prestigious institution taking part in . . . I believe the term I heard used was 'frivolous.' They didn't want him involved in what they considered a *frivolous* show."

"I'm flattered to be asked," I say, although I'm not sure that's true given that I appear to be a "sloppy seconds" choice. "But touring the museum . . . mentoring . . . judging—that sounds like a full schedule, and there is just no way I can make arrangements to take an entire day off with such short notice. And, honestly, I'm probably not a good fit anyway. I'm just not a 'be on TV' kind of girl."

"Have you gone mad, Halia?!" Wavonne asks. "You have an opportunity to be on *national* television . . . to meet that smoke show, Leon Winfield . . . and you're saying no?"

"It pays one thousand dollars for the day. Not to mention the priceless publicity for your restaurant. We generally average into the hundreds of thousands of viewers."

I'm quiet for a moment as Trudy and Wavonne look at me, both with expressions like a lion about to pounce on a gazelle that fell behind from the herd. I think about what they both just said. The idea of being on TV in front of millions of people makes me very anxious . . . but I guess the publicity would be good for Sweet Tea. . . . Then again, I already have a very loyal and large customer base, and the restaurant is busy all the time. . . . I don't really need it.

Trudy pipes up in the midst of my prolonged hesitation. "I've been authorized to up your fee to three thousand dollars."

"Three thousand dollars!" comes from Wavonne. "Take it, Halia."

"It's really not about the money," I say. "I'm just not comfortable with the idea of being on television."

I'm pretty secure about my looks. I'm on the far side of forty so maybe I don't look as good as I did twenty years ago, but I'd like to think I'm reasonably attractive. And although it would be nice to tone up a bit and drop a few pounds, most of the time I'm fine with being a curvy size fourteen. But that's in real life—this is television we're talking about. I'm not sure I want to put my Rubenesque figure on TV in front of thousands of people. I've seen the comments Internet trolls write underneath online videos—some are downright vicious.

"No need to be anxious. The focus of the show is really the contestants. You won't have a lot of camera time."

Trudy can see I'm still very much on the fence and about to choose the side less preferable to her. "We're in a bit of a bind here," she says. "If I'm honest, at this point, it's either you or we're going to be pulling grill masters from behind the line at the local Red Lobster. I've been—"

"Red Lobster. Yum," Wavonne interrupts.

Unlike myself, Trudy is not used to Wavonne's propensity for unsolicited and in-no-way-pertinent-to-the-conversation remarks, so I throw her a "just ignore her" look to let her know she can continue.

"I've been . . . well . . . because it's really short notice, and we'd really like to have you on the team, not only can I up your fee, but I've also been authorized to make another offer: If you come aboard, Russell will donate ten thousand dollars to the charity of your choice."

"That's very generous." I consider her offer for a moment and let out a sigh. "I guess I really can't turn that down." And I guess I really *can't* turn that down. There are several charities I have a soft spot for that I'd like to see have that money, and if making that happen only costs me a single workday and the possibility of making a fool of myself on national television, I suppose I can live with that. "I'll need to make some arrangements to be sure there's coverage here tomorrow."

"You'd better make some arrangements for me, too, because there is no way I'm missin' out on meetin' Leon and seein' the filmin' of a real live TV show," Wavonne demands. "I'm still bitter over Wendy Williams canceling her tapin' the day I had tickets." She looks at Trudy. "I went all the way to New York to see her, and she canceled . . . said she was 'sick' . . . I have not watched her since."

With my eyes I remind Trudy of her right to ignore

Wavonne as necessary, and she continues. "Russell would like to meet with the judges this evening at the Palm. Are you available at eight?"

"Yes," Wavonne announces.

"Trudy said he'd like to meet with the *judges*, Wavonne."

"I'm sure Wavonne is welcome to come. Shall I tell him to expect both of you?"

I look at my watch and think of all I have to do to get Sweet Tea ready to open this morning, and all I would have to do to be able to get out of here in time to make an eight o'clock dinner in the city. "Why don't I host the team here?" I offer. "It's going to be hard enough to get away tomorrow. I'd really be pushing it if I tried to leave early this evening as well."

"That might work. Let me make a few calls." Trudy gets up from the booth and steps away.

"So Halia's gonna be on TV," Wavonne says as if I'm not sitting right next to her.

"It appears that way," I respond, already feeling the nerves.

"Don't worry, Halia." Wavonne notices my angst. "I got you. I'll do your hair and makeup . . . and I'm already tryin' to figure out what you'll wear for the tapin'. A little MAC Studio Fix foundation on the face, a touch of Black Vanilla Combing Creme on the hair, some Spanx around that midsection. Halle Berry will have nothin' on you." She looks at me and pauses for a moment. "Well, Halle Berry may be a bit ambitious. . . . *Viola Davis* will have nothin' on you."

"Thanks, Wavonne, but I think I can manage on my own."

She has good intentions, but I'm afraid Wavonne's styling help might leave me looking like a contestant on *RuPaul's Drag Race*.

"I've seen you *manage* on your own, Halia. If history is any indication, unless there's some 'dress like a schoolmarm' theme tied to the episode, you'd better let me help you."

I'm about to, once again, decline Wavonne's offer, but then I see Trudy approaching the table after finishing her phone calls, and I realize that in my closet I have both a tweed suit and black flats that are dreadfully similar to hers. I believe I donned both items when I went to church with Momma a few months ago. Considering that I appear to share fashion sense with a woman who reminds me of a character on a vapid 1960s sitcom with less sex appeal than a Catholic nun, maybe a little (just a *little*) fashion advice from Wavonne would not be the worst thing in the world.

"Fine," I say. "But no sequins or rhinestones. And if you start throwing around words like stiletto or miniskirt, the deal is off."

Chapter 2

"How are we doing on the peach pie?" I ask Wavonne, who just stepped out of the kitchen.

"I think I saw two or three whole pies back there. And there's plenty of red velvet cake and a few trays of banana pudding." She notices how fidgety I am. "Look at you all nervous," she says with a laugh.

"I'm not nervous," I say, wishing it were true.

"Mmmhmm." Wavonne says this the same way Momma did when I was a little girl and claimed I had no idea how the crayon marks got on the wall or was not responsible for the missing chocolates in the Whitman's Sampler she was saving for company. "Naomi Campbell's more relaxed when police dogs start sniffin' around her suitcase at the airport," she adds. "You've been runnin' around here like an anxious squirrel all day. We're all used to you bein' a control freak, Halia, but today you've been really over the top—hoverin' over the kitchen staff, checkin' and recheckin' stock, fluffin' centerpieces—and don't think I didn't see you over by the windows earlier makin' sure every shade was hangin' at the exact same length. You do know they make medications for conditions like yours these days?"

"I don't need medication, Wavonne. I just want to make sure everything is in order when Russell gets here."

I'm not usually one to put on airs . . . *really*, I'm not. But ever since Trudy said Russell agreed to meet here at Sweet Tea instead of the Palm, a high end steak house where power deals are struck over sirloins and lobsters, I've been in high gear trying to make sure we put our best foot forward tonight. Of course, I'm really proud of my restaurant—in the general scheme of things, it's hugely successful. I have an abundance of regular customers who have been coming here for years, we regularly make the *Washington Post*'s and *Washingtonian* magazine's top restaurant lists, and most nights, even weekday evenings, we have people waiting for tables. But I can't help feeling like small potatoes in comparison to Russell—the man oversees a national culinary empire and apparently has his own televised show to find chefs to work in his ever-expanding collection of fine dining establishments.

"Well, I hope you're done . . . 'cause it looks like he's here." Wavonne points her eyes past me.

I turn toward the front door and see Trudy, laptop in tow, and Russell, who I recognize from some photos I've seen of him in various magazines, stepping inside Sweet Tea. There's a third person with them who I'm assuming is Russell's wife.

As I walk toward them and get a real-life look at Russell, I realize his magazine pictures must have been heavily retouched. He isn't someone I would have considered handsome from the doctored images accompanying the various articles about him, but in those photos, someone with master Photoshop skills at least took the edge off his coarse appearance, not to mention several inches off his waistline. He's an obese black man with a swollen nose, crooked teeth, and limbs that appear disproportionately small when compared to the rest of his body. . . . And it appears, since the photos I've last seen of him, he's taken a cue from Al Sharpton—his relaxed hair is combed straight back until the ends curl upward behind his neck.

"Hmmm . . . He wasn't 'all that' when I saw him on TV, but he looks even rougher in person," Wavonne says to me as we approach the trio. "Looks like he stole a wig from one of the Supremes . . . and not even a good one."

"Shhh," I say as we get closer to our guests. "Mr. Mellinger." I extend my hand to him. "Halia Watkins. I've known *of* you for years. I'm honored to finally meet you in person."

"Thank you." He grips my hand with his own. "You've met Trudy, and this is my wife, Cynthia." He gestures toward the striking woman of indeterminate age next to him. She has a sort of regal quality about her. Her flawless light brown skin and fit figure might lead one to believe she's in her thirties, but there's something about her eyes . . . a certain wisdom coming from behind them, that makes me think she's much older.

"Lovely to meet you," Cynthia says. She gives me a two-handed handshake, using her right hand to return my grasp while laying her left hand on top of the whole deal. This is when my eyes make contact with a diamond the size of a macadamia nut extending from her ring.

"You too. Welcome to Sweet Tea. This is my cousin, Wavonne. She'll be our server this evening."

Russell and Cynthia, who, if you include her heels, is about four inches taller than her husband, exchange greetings with Wavonne, and I sense a bit of "and we are mingling with the help, *why*?" energy coming from both of them as they shake her hand with a bit less enthusiasm than they did mine.

"Why don't I show you to our table," I suggest. "We're expecting one more, right? Five of us total?"

"Yes," Russell says, "but Trudy has some work to do. If there's a small table nearby that might be the best option for her."

"I'm sure I can arrange that," I say, even though it seems a bit rude to exclude Trudy from sitting with us, but perhaps they see her as "the help," too.

I lead the group to a six top in the back and let Trudy know she can set up at the small two-person booth to the left. While she fires up her computer and slips a Bluetooth thingamajig on her ear, the rest of us take our seats at the larger table.

"Can you get us started with some waters? We can go over the specials when everyone is here," I say to Wavonne before turning to my guests. "Unless, of course, you'd like to start with a cocktail or a glass of iced tea right away."

"Vodka soda," Russell barks while looking at his phone.

"Dry martini for me, please."

"And for you, boss?" Wavonne asks me.

"Just water for now."

"What a lovely place." Cynthia looks around. "Isn't it a lovely place, Russell?" She pokes his arm with her finger.

"Um . . . yes . . . very nice." He barely lifts his head from his phone before looking back down, pecking on the screen, and bringing it to his ear. "Russell here. What's this I hear about a delay in the tile? The tile has to be down before we can move on with other installations."

Although I can't make out his exact words, I hear a male voice on the other end begin to respond, but Russell lets him speak for about a nanosecond before talking over him. "I'm not interested in the 'whats and whys.' You've been hired to handle those. I want that tile down by the end of the week."

The man tries to reply but, once again, Russell talks over him. "I repeat: I *want* the tile down by the end of the week.

Make it happen. I need you to meet deadlines. This is a Russell Mellinger restaurant. If you want to miss deadlines go work for Chili's."

I'm honestly surprised at why he would bother at this point, but I hear the man start speaking again and, to no one's surprise, Russell interrupts him for a third time. "Are we clear?"

The man begins with his excuses yet again, and it's almost painful to hear the vague rumbling of his voice coming from the phone when we all know Russell is just going to cut him off.

"Are we *clear*?" Russell repeats in the harshest tone he's used thus far.

Finally, Russell gets the one word answer he wants and disconnects the phone without saying good-bye. "Idiots," he says. "It's a world full of idiots." He turns to Trudy. "Trudy, put a tickler on my calendar to follow up with Jim about the tile tomorrow . . . and line up some candidates for his job if I end up firing him."

"I'd say, 'forgive him, he's not usually like this,'" Cynthia says to me, "but, unfortunately, he's *always* like this. Can you believe I've put up with him for thirty years?" She turns to Russell. "Can you take it down a notch? You're a guest here, and we need to firm up plans for tomorrow."

"Tomorrow. The show. Yes." He sets his phone down on the table. "As soon as Tilla or Tina or whatever the hell her name is gets here, we'll go over some of the logistics."

"Twyla," Cynthia corrects, and as the name hits my ears I feel the hairs on the back of my neck stand up. *How many Twylas can there be in the local restaurant business?*

"Twyla Harper?" I ask.

"Yes."

Twyla Harper?!" Wavonne says, setting a highball glass down in front of Russell and martini glass down in front of Cynthia. "Of *Twyla's Tips, Tricks, and Tidbits*?"

Wavonne is referring to a regular cooking segment Twyla used to have on the local news.

"That's the one," Cynthia says.

"Is that so," Wavonne replies in a wicked tone. "Things just got *interestin'*."

Chapter 3

"Interesting? How so?" Cynthia asks.

"Well..." Wavonne pulls out a chair and sits down. "Twyla and Halia here have a bit of a sordid history."

"We do not."

"Twyla owns Dauphine in the city," Wavonne elaborates. "Overpriced, mediocre-at-best, Cajun food. Halia worked for her many moons ago."

"Really?" Cynthia looks in my direction.

"Yes. Those were my government job days. I was a loyal civil servant at the Census Bureau for quite some time and worked part time at a bunch of different restaurants around town over the years. Dauphine was the last place I worked at before I quit the bureau and opened Sweet Tea. It was still a happening place back then."

"Dauphine?" Russell asks.

"Yes. It was very popular for a number of years, but I've heard through the grapevine that it has not been doing well for a while... that it's really starting to show its age."

"As is Twyla," Wavonne says. "That old hen must be sixty-somethin' by now."

"Yes, around or about," I say.

"Is that the extent of your history with Twyla?" Russell asks. "That you were once in her employ?"

Wavonne cackles loudly. "That would be a *no*," she answers for me. "Twyla was ridin' high when Halia opened Sweet Tea. She had a good story . . . the same story as Halia actually . . . as a whole bunch of people, I guess. She'd quit a nine-to-five job as a lawyer or a librarian . . . or a lab techni—"

"She was a loan officer," I say. "For whatever reason, when she opened Dauphine, the press ate up her 'leave your humdrum office job and follow your dreams' tale. She was featured in the *Washington Post* and was on the local news . . . and she eventually ended up with a spread in *People* magazine and a guest appearance on one of the national morning talk shows."

"The first year or two Dauphine was off the chain busy," Wavonne says. "Twyla landed a regular cooking segment on the local news that promoted her restaurant and helped pack 'em in. She was great on camera. She has a thick, and if you ask me, overdone, southern accent and knows how to lay on the sugar when she wants to."

"Yes. We're aware of her quasi-celebrity status," Cynthia says. "That's how we ended up casting her as a guest judge. How does Halia factor into any of this?"

"Well . . . like I said," Wavonne replies, "Twyla had a good story and talked a good game . . . got lots of publicity. There was only one problem. Girlfriend couldn't . . . *can't* cook worth a damn. She could get people in the door with all the press and hoopla, but no one came back. A few years after she opened, the place was hurtin' big time, but things started to turn around when she hired someone who actually knew her way around a kitchen."

"Halia?" Cynthia asks.

"Yep. She pretty much saved the joint."

"Wavonne is exaggerating, but I was able to up the

kitchen's game a bit and help her develop a steady clientele. She hired me as a front of the house manager, but the longer I was there, the more time I spent in the kitchen helping her and the line staff. Twyla opened a restaurant with no experience. I'd worked in a dozen restaurants by the time I came on board at Dauphine and had always had a knack for cooking, so I was able to really contribute there . . . improve recipes, change a few work-flows . . . implement some quality control. I also tried an approach to working with the kitchen staff that was somewhat . . . shall we say *novel* to Twyla—I was kind and respectful to them."

"I have a few friends who work at Dauphine. They say she's a total pill," Wavonne says. "My girl Nicki . . . she's a server there . . . calls Twyla 'the Wet Hen.' And Adam . . . he works in the kitchen . . . calls her 'Twyla the Hun.'"

"Wow," Cynthia says. "She seems so nice in the TV clips I've seen of her and has been so pleasant when I've talked with her on the phone."

"She's sweet as molasses when it suits her, especially when she's on camera," Wavonne replies. "But once the cameras are off, or she's in the kitchen out of earshot of her customers, she's suddenly Evillene trying to get her sister's shoes back from Diana Ross in *The Wiz*."

"She's not *that* bad, Wavonne," I defend. "She eventually made me a sous-chef at Dauphine even though I'd never had any formal culinary schooling. I'm grateful to her for that. I learned a lot working for her . . . even if it was more about what *not* to do rather than what *to* do. My experience at Dauphine was immensely helpful when I opened Sweet Tea."

"So how are things between you and Twyla now?" Russell asks.

"They're fine."

"*Ahem* . . . liar . . . *ahem*," Wavonne mutters.

"What? We *are* fine."

"Halia might be fine with Twyla, but Twyla's still got a beef with Halia. I saw her fuming at the Rammys last year when Halia won in the casual brunch category. . . . Bitter as a Brussels sprout, that one."

"Bitter about what?"

"About her restaurant going the way of Mariah Carey's music career. You know . . . still around but not terribly relevant or successful. Even her silly little cooking segments on the local news got canned a few months ago."

"What's Halia have to do with that?"

"She left Dauphine and took all of Twyla's customers with her."

"I did not," I protest. "At least that was never my intention."

"When Halia left Dauphine, the place went back to bein' the second-rate eatery it was before she worked her magic in the kitchen." Wavonne turns to me. "Give me your phone."

"Why?"

"Because you don't let me have mine on me when I'm workin' the floor."

I hand her the phone. "What do you want it for?"

"I bet it's still online," she says, tapping a few keys and scrolling. "Here it is. This is what the *Post* critic said shortly after Halia left Dauphine." Wavonne begins reading. " 'Without the talents of sous chef Mahalia Watkins, who recently left to open Mahalia's Sweet Tea, Dauphine has, once again, become mundane . . . ordinary . . . not awful, but the food has lost that something *extra* that abounded when Ms. Watkins was manning the kitchen. It's unclear whether or not Dauphine will survive Ms. Watkins's exit. Proprietor and executive chef Twyla Harper kept the doors open prior to Ms. Watkins's employ with some good old-fashioned southern charm and a knack for garnering publicity. Without some significant retooling in the kitchen, Dauphine will, once again, have to

rely on Ms. Harper's flair for hospitality and her weekly television appearances—and perhaps a regular supply of DC
tourists who have not already paid a 'one and done' visit to
the establishment to bring in customers and keep the lights
on. It certainly will not be the quality of the food that fills the
seats at Dauphine.' "

"Ouch," Russell says. "That had to hurt."

"Boy, did it ever. This was back when people actually read
newspapers, so having the *Washington Post* tell the entire
DC area that someone else was responsible for the success of
her restaurant did not go over well with Twyla the Hun.
And, not only did the *Post* say Dauphine had gone in the
dumper following Halia's exit, it also told them where to go
to find Halia. The one mention of Halia leaving to open her
own restaurant brought all the Dauphine regulars to Sweet
Tea . . . and they're still comin'."

"You're tempting me to play up this angle during the
show," Cynthia says. "It could be good for ratings."

I laugh. "There's no angle to play. Really. Twyla and I are
fine. Wavonne likes to dramatize everything." I turn to
Wavonne. "And shouldn't you be getting back to work?"

"Yeah," Wavonne grumbles, getting up from the table.

"Interesting dynamic you have with your wait staff," Russell says with raised eyebrows. "Do your servers always pull
up a chair and start gossiping with customers?"

"Not my entire wait staff . . . just Wavonne. She's family . . .
for better or worse. She—"

Before I can finish my sentence, I hear someone calling
from the front of the restaurant. "Yoo-hoo!" I catch someone bellowing and feel little need to divert my eyes from the
Mellingers to find out who just entered my dining room as I
don't know anyone other than Twyla Harper who uses the
word "yoo-hoo," unless they're asking for a chocolate soda.

Chapter 4

"Yoo-hoo" pings through the air again as I turn my head to see a mature woman sashaying toward us underneath a mound of teased platinum-blond hair—your guess is as good as mine as to whether her vivid locks are her own or on loan from some woman with a shaved head in Peru. In my opinion, blond hair on black women isn't always a flattering look, but her golden tresses, like anything that makes Twyla conspicuous, seem to work for her.

As she teeters on three-inch heels in our direction, in a royal blue dress, her face shrouded in heavy makeup, I look past her out the front windows and see that she's still driving the same ginormous white Cadillac Coupe de Ville from 1970-something that she had when I worked for her. Much like her hair and her clothes . . . and her shoes, her car screams "notice me!"

"Twyla," I say, getting up from the table while Russell and Cynthia remain seated. "What a pleasure. It's been forever. How are you?"

"Hi, darlin'. I'm fantastic." She kisses me on the cheek. "Busy busy . . . You know, Dauphine, my volunteer work, trying to stay fit." She looks me up and down. "I wish I could carry extra weight the way you do. You make it work."

I swallow and remind myself to let her petty jibe go. "Thank you. I like to think a little thickness takes a few years off." I scan her from head to toe the same way she did me. "As you get older you can start to look like a bag of bones if you get too skinny." Okay, so I didn't exactly let her little barb go. "Let me introduce you to—"

"I know Russell and Cynthia. I dined at the Barbary in New York last year." She shakes hands with both of them. "You remember me, right?"

"Of course," confirms Cynthia, but her eyes say she has no recollection of ever meeting her.

"Please have a seat," I invite.

Twyla pulls out a chair. "Cleanliness is next to godliness," she says, taking a napkin and sweeping some nonexistent crumbs from the seat before sitting down. "Are the rumors true?" She slides her chair closer to the table. "I heard you were having some money issues and sold out to Cracker Barrel."

I laugh. "No. Sweet Tea is still all mine."

"Hmmm . . . Wonder how that gossip got started. Maybe because Sweet Tea has a similar feel to Cracker Barrel . . . all folksy and informal."

I'm about to respond when I notice that somewhere during Twyla's exchange with me, Russell's eyes lit up. "This is ratings gold," he says.

"What's ratings gold?" Twyla asks.

"The two of you. Like Mariah and Nicki behind the *American Idol* desk."

"Oh, don't be silly," Twyla says. "I love Halia." She puts an arm around me. "And there's plenty to love."

"That's because the food is so good here." I look at her petite figure, up and down. "You have to wonder about the food quality of a restaurant owned by a wisp of a thing."

Twyla is about to speak when Wavonne reappears at the table, hands everyone a menu, and goes over the evening's specials: corn and crab chowder, honey-braised pork chops with homemade applesauce, and a blackberry cobbler for dessert.

After Wavonne takes Twyla's drink order, I ask her to give our guests a few minutes to look over the menu, and once some decisions have been made, Russell starts talking about the show.

"So tomorrow we'll do a little dog and pony thing at the African American museum. We'll get some footage of us walking around with the three remaining contestants, and you can get to know them. Then we'll all meet up in the museum café for lunch and to announce the challenge for this episode. You'll have a nice break while production assistants take the contestants to the store to get any necessary ingredients for the evening's competition. We'll need you at the inn no later than six."

"The inn?"

"Yes, we've been filming all the episodes at my new hotel, the Willow Oak Inn. Sunfish, my latest restaurant, will be on-site there. The lucky winner of this season of *Elite Chef* will be executive chef there."

"Trudy had mentioned you were getting into the hotel industry, but she didn't say we'd be filming at the new property."

"Of course we're filming there. Half the reason I do the show is to get my restaurants . . . and now my hotel, heaps of exposure."

"Trudy said it was near National Harbor?"

"Yes, not far. It's a boutique hotel in Fort Washington. It's on ten secluded acres along the river. Half of the rooms have water views. I had hoped to open something a bit grander, but given the rural preservation ordinances in the area, I could only secure a permit for a smaller venue, so I decided to make the best of it. Thirty rooms on three floors, appointed with the best of everything. I expect five-star ratings all around. We'll be vying for Four Seasons and Ritz-Carlton clientele. My restaurants have always been *destinations* and attract people from all over the country. Now customers will be able to make a weekend out of a visit to Sunfish. And, during the week, we'll cater to smaller conferences."

"I'm surprised I haven't heard anything about it."

"We're not officially open yet. The restaurant is a few weeks away from completion, but we've had a soft opening of the inn while final touches are added. I've invited friends and business associates to stay while we train the staff and finish the build-out . . . and Cynthia and I and the *Elite Chef* contestants have been staying there while we film," Russell says. "You and Twyla are welcome to stay the night as my guests after the taping tomorrow. We tend to go pretty late, and we'd like you on-site the next morning as we see off the eliminated contestant."

"What a nice invitation, but I don't live far from Fort Washington, and I generally prefer to sleep in my own bed."

"Did I hear something about the Willow Oak Inn?" Wavonne says, setting a cast iron skillet filled with sour cream cornbread on the table, before she makes eye contact with me. "And did I hear you turn down an invitation to stay there? For free?" She turns to Russell. "It is free, right?"

"Of course."

"Have you lost your mind, Halia? That place has been the talk of PG County for months. Word is that it's gonna be off the chain luxurious. Melva and I have been watching it come up from the marina when we go there for drinks. Looks like it's almost finished."

"Off the chain luxurious," Cynthia says to Russell. "Maybe that should be the inn's tag line."

Russell doesn't appear to be amused by Cynthia's little quip and doesn't bother to acknowledge it. Instead he looks at Wavonne and says, "Yes, it is almost finished. The rooms on the main floor have been ready for occupancy for weeks—that's where we've been staying, along with the contestants, since we came to town. At this point we're down to just a few final cosmetic projects in the other rooms and some of the common spaces. We'll have a grand opening gala once both the inn and the restaurant are fully ready for prime time."

"Word is the rooms are going to start at six hundred dollars a night," Wavonne says.

"That's about right."

Wavonne looks at me. "You're not seriously passin' on stayin' at an exclusive hotel for free?"

"You really should stay, Halia," Cynthia says. "You'll be on the concierge level. You can get a good night's sleep on a plush-top mattress with thousand-thread count Egyptian cotton sheets. Perhaps after watching a movie on the seventy-inch TV with Bose Surround speakers or taking a soak in your own Jacuzzi tub. You can have your morning coffee on the patio with a view of the river."

"Can she bring a guest?" Wavonne asks.

"I suppose that would be fine."

"Wait until I tell Melva that I'm gonna stay the night at the Willow Oak Inn!"

"Who said anything about staying the night *anywhere*? This is the first mention I've heard of this thing rolling into two days."

"Not *two* days," Cynthia says. "We'd like you on-site the morning after the taping so you can be part of the contestant departure segment. We usually get some footage of the eliminated individual packing their suitcase, offering some final commentary on the patio with the sun coming up in the background, and saying their good-byes to the other contestants and judges. We can have you out of there by seven a.m."

"Seven a.m?" Wavonne says. "I have not been up at seven a.m. since TJ Maxx opened early for a super sale the day after Thanksgiving."

"Wavonne, I think one of your other tables needs some drinks refilled, or some plates cleared, or *something*."

"I'm not really a morning person either with my late nights here," I say, as Wavonne grudgingly walks off. "But if I can be back here by the late morning that should be okay."

"Perfect. So, we're all set."

Right then, Russell's cell phone rings. "Russell here." After giving what sounds like a woman's voice on the other end of the phone a chance to speak, he says, "Okay, I'll be right there." He lowers his phone clad hand. "I have to cut this short. Something has come up at the inn." He looks across the table at me and Twyla. "I'm sure Cynthia can answer any further questions you have." Then, in what appears to be true Russell fashion, he gets up from the table without another word and heads for the door.

Chapter 5

"How will you get back to the hotel?" I ask Cynthia as Russell exits Sweet Tea.

"He'll send the car back for me and Trudy," she says, making me feel silly for thinking that Russell Mellinger actually drove himself here . . . or drives himself anywhere. "Now, what other questions do you have?" she asks, and I wonder if I'm the only person at the table who thinks it's strange that a woman's husband was called away at eight o'clock at night by what sounded like a female voice, said woman's husband leaves with barely a word, and said woman does not seem to be even slightly concerned about his impending whereabouts. Most women I know would have a hundred questions for their spouse and possibly sneak in the car and follow him to make sure whatever answers he gave were actually true. But I guess if it doesn't bother Cynthia, it shouldn't bother me.

"Now that you mention it," I say, "since I've already admitted that I'm not really familiar with the show, may I ask what the challenges, like the one we'll be part of tomorrow, typically involve?"

"We give the chefs a task that they have to complete within a certain amount of time. Last week we visited the

Kennedy Center and the contestants were asked to prepare one of President Kennedy's favorite foods. When the local cherry blossoms were in bloom, we toured the tidal basin and all the contestants thought the challenge would involve cherries. But we like to keep them on their toes, so back at the restaurant we reminded them that DC's famous cherry blossoms don't actually produce any cherries. In recognition of the trees being gifts to the US from Japan, we went with a Japanese food theme."

"So, what's tomorrow's challenge?"

"We like to keep that under wraps, even for the judges. Prior to the competition each judge is paired with select contestants. Since we only have three chefs left, you, Russell, and Twyla will only be paired with one contestant each. You'll be able to offer some guidance to your contestants, so we like you to be as surprised by the challenge as each of them. Russell is not even in on the challenges."

"I find that hard to believe," Twyla says.

"Really. He isn't. Russell has very limited involvement in the production of the show. That's all left up to me and my team. He's got four restaurants to supervise . . . a fifth one opening in a couple of months and a brand new hotel to get up and running. He barely has time to show up for the tapings."

"I guess I have a bit of a leg up—Trudy already told me the episode was going to have a soul food theme."

"Oh, she did?" Cynthia darts her eyes in Trudy's direction and then back at me. "Well . . . let's just say the challenge will involve soul food, among other things."

"Sounds good," I say. "Speaking of soul food, are you ready to order?"

"The braised pork chops special sounds delightful to me and so does that chowder," Cynthia says.

"My crab and corn chowder is one of my favorite soups,"

I say. "This is the best time of year for crab meat. We get it locally and work it into a bath of bacon drippings, butter, pureed potatoes, and half and half. It's divine, if I do say so myself."

"You're making my mouth water, but, sadly, I think I'd better stick with a salad. My metabolism is not what it once was. I'd have to take three spin classes tomorrow if I went with the pork chops," Cynthia says.

"Just a salad for me, too," comes from Twyla.

I signal for Wavonne to come back to the table.

"Twyla and Cynthia would both like the grilled chicken salad."

"The dressing on the side," Twyla says.

"And for you?" Wavonne asks me.

"I'll have the salad, too."

"The *salad*? For *you*?" she questions. "Are you feelin' okay?"

"Yes. I'm fine."

"I ain't never seen you eat a salad in your life. You've been eyein' those pork chops all evenin'." She pauses for a moment, her eyes moving from me to my tablemates and back to me again. "Oh, I get it," she says. "Beyoncé and Kelly are having salads, so Michelle's gotta order one, too."

"Just bring the salads, Wavonne."

"As you wish," she replies sarcastically. She's being a smart-ass, but an honest one. I was planning to indulge in the evening's special—seasoned bone-in chops, seared on both sides before taking a simmer in a bath of chicken broth, honey, and vinegar. But I think I'd feel odd eating pork chops covered in sauce while my guests nibble on salads across the table from me.

I continue to chat with Cynthia and Twyla, and I can honestly say that the energy at the table has changed since Russell left—we are all more relaxed without him barking orders at Trudy or into his phone. When our salads arrive, we eat them with little enthusiasm while Cynthia tells us a bit more about the inn and Russell's plans for Sunfish. We're getting an earful about riverfront dining, arrangements Russell is making with local watermen to ensure a fresh supply of rockfish, and two restaurant designers he's fired, when Wavonne shows up to clear our plates and take a dessert order.

"Can I interest you ladies in any coffee or dessert? Red velvet cake? Peach pie?"

"Would you two be up for sharing something?" Cynthia asks.

"Sure," Twyla says.

"That sounds fine," I respond when what I really want to say is, "No, I don't want to share anything—I'm a grown-ass woman who's practically starving from having nothing more than a salad for dinner, and I want my own freakin' dessert."

"Which one do you recommend?"

"I would probably go with the peach pie. The peaches came in fresh from Georgia this morning."

"Peach pie it is then," Cynthia says.

"With ice cream," I add.

"Sure thing," Wavonne says to all of us before directing her eyes at me. "Remember, Halia. You said I could jet at ten." She looks at Cynthia and Twyla. "It's Reggae on the Roof night at Eden Lounge," she adds, before directing her attention back to me. "Once I bring the pie, can you close out the check when you guys are finished?"

"Sure. No problem."

As Wavonne departs to fetch one slice of pie to be shared by three adult women, Cynthia goes over a few more details about the show until she clears her throat. "So, Halia," she says as if she's about to broach an uncomfortable topic. "*Elite Chef* is not scripted or anything, but we do like our guest judges to be entertaining—you know, have some personality."

"Personality?"

"Yes." She looks at Twyla. "Like how Twyla has this whole sort of southern thing going on. She'll play that up with lots of 'I'm fixin' tos' and 'bless her hearts' and 'hey y'alls.'"

"I'm 'fixin' tos'?" I ask.

"Yes. You know—'I'm fixin' to fry up some chicken.' 'I'm fixin' to go to the movies.'"

"Okay . . . ?" I say, wondering if I look as bemused as I feel. "Surely you don't want me to act like a southern belle?"

"No, but we thought you could be a little more . . . more brash . . . sassy . . . just to keep things entertaining."

"Um . . . I don't think . . ."

"Just throw in a 'Girl!' every now and then . . . or a 'oh no he *di'int*.' Maybe dress a little snappier."

"So, you want me to be Madea?"

"Madea," Cynthia says, like I've just given her an idea. "That's not a bad plan. You adopt a sort of Madea-ish personality—"

"Yeeeah." I cut her off before her ludicrous idea goes any further. "That's not going to happen. With me, what you see is what you get."

Cynthia looks disappointed until her eyes look past me and she smiles.

I turn around to get a look at where Cynthia is staring and see Wavonne coming toward us with a slice of peach pie. She must have put the order in before doing a quick change into her club wear in the ladies' room. Wheels seem to be turning in Cynthia's head as Wavonne sidles toward us in steep black heels, tight jeans, and a low cut sequined top with spaghetti straps.

"This one." Cynthia gives Wavonne a good once-over as she sets the pie and three forks on the table. "Maybe she can be your personality."

"Excuse me?"

"You're lovely, Halia, but you're a bit . . . um . . . *incon-spicuous*."

"Borin'," Wavonne says. "She thinks you're borin'."

"I do not," Cynthia counters. "She just seems very . . . sta-ble . . . genuine. They are great qualities, but they don't ex-actly bring in ratings. What's your name again?"

"Wavonne."

"Wavonne, how about we bring you on with Halia? You're quick with a quip." Cynthia gives Wavonne a long look. "And outfits like that would bring some flash to the show."

"You want me to be on TV?!"

"Yes. We'll just say you're Halia's assistant or something." Cynthia turns to me. "How does that sound?"

"I suppose it's fine, especially since, apparently, I'm less in-teresting than watching paint dry."

"Don't be silly. You two just make a good pair. Viewers will get a kick out of your banter."

"There's my ride." Wavonne looks out the front windows. "Wait until I tell Melva and Linda that not only am I gonna get to stay at Russell Mellinger's new hotel, but I'm gonna be on TV!"

As Wavonne hurries to tell her friends the news, Cynthia, Twyla, and I pick up our forks and begin to share the pie. While we chat a bit more about the plans for tomorrow I find myself eager for them to finish our dessert. I'm tired, and I want to start the closing process so I can get home before midnight. But mostly, I want them to leave so I can make a run to the kitchen for a helping of my pork chops, and my own damn slice of peach pie.

RECIPE FROM HALIA'S KITCHEN

Halia's Corn and Crab Chowder

Chowder Ingredients
4 slices bacon
2 tablespoons salted butter
1 cup chopped onion
2 large potatoes, peeled and sliced into cubes
1½ tablespoons of Sweet Tea House Seasoning
1 teaspoon salt
4 cups chicken broth
4 cups fresh corn off the cob
1 pound crabmeat
1 cup half and half
1 tablespoon finely chopped chives

Sweet Tea House Seasoning
2 teaspoons salt
1 teaspoon black pepper
1 tablespoon paprika
2 teaspoons onion powder
1½ teaspoons red pepper flakes
1 teaspoon garlic powder
1 teaspoon dry mustard

- Fry bacon over medium heat until crisp. Blot on paper towels and chop into small pieces.

- Add bacon drippings and butter to a large saucepan and heat over medium heat. Add onion and simmer for 5 minutes.
- Add potatoes, House Seasoning, salt, and chicken broth. Simmer for 10 minutes.
- Remove 2 cups of the chowder and puree in a blender. (Allow chowder to cool if blender is not heat-safe.) Stir the pureed mixture back into the pot.
- Add corn, crabmeat, and half and half. Stir over medium heat until corn and potatoes are tender, about 10 minutes.
- Serve chowder in soup bowls sprinkled with chopped bacon, chives, and a sprinkle of House Seasoning.

Chapter 6

"This is nice . . . the leather is so soft. I've taken taxis and Ubers, but I've never been picked up by a hoity-toity 'car service,'" Wavonne says as we approach the National Museum of African American History and Culture in the city. We're in the back seat of a black Lexus with our own driver and everything. The show arranged for our fancy pickup this morning, and now we're maneuvering up Fourteenth Street as the imposing building, on five acres of precious National Mall real estate, comes into view. I've passed by the museum numerous times, but it's only now, with immediate plans to view the interior, that I really take it in. Oddly, it looks both ancient and contemporary. The architecture reminds me of artists' renditions of the Tower of Babel. It's as if someone took the bottom third of three pyramids, turned them upside down, layered them on top of each other, and covered the whole thing in a bronze mesh. I have a vague memory of hearing something on the news a while back explaining how the bronze lattice pays homage to ironwork crafted by enslaved African Americans.

The museum has only been open for three or four years. I've always wanted to pay a visit, but you have to get timed tickets in advance and, with all I have to do at Sweet Tea, there is not a lot of time for exploring the city's cultural attractions.

"I'm excited to finally see the inside," I say to Wavonne as I step out of the car.

"*I'm* excited to meet Leon Winfield," she replies, lifting herself from the back seat after her red stilettos make contact with the pavement.

"Are you seriously going to walk around a few thousand square feet of museum in those things?"

"Don't be hatin' on my shoes. They're Tory Burch. Even the bottoms are groovy." Wavonne steadies herself by grabbing on to me, lifts up one foot, and shows me the glitter-covered sole.

"Tory Burch? Isn't her stuff really expensive?"

"I got them 'gently used' off Poshmark. Four hundred bucks."

"Where did you get four hundred dollars to spend on shoes?"

"Outta your purse," Wavonne jokes. "Relax. I charged them. I'll have them back up and sold on Poshmark for three ninety-five before the bill comes."

"I hope so." I take in the rest of her getup. "You do know this is a museum and not a night club?" She's squeezed her size-sixteen figure into a size-fourteen black, knee-length, sheath dress with a red halter neckline sort of crisscrossing her ample chest.

"My flair for style is why they asked me to come along. I'm just trying to keep up my end of the bargain. We're going to be on nationwide television. Maybe I'll be *discovered* . . . become the next Taraji P. Henson. She's a local girl, too, ya know," Wavonne says. "Besides, someone has to show a little flash. You're not going to get any camera time in that . . . What's a polite word? *Nondescript* outfit. It looks like something Whoopi Goldberg would wear to host *The View*. I can't believe you didn't let me help you with your wardrobe."

"Wavonne, you came at me with a low cut purple blouse with feathers on the sleeves. Forgive me if I shooed you away. And what's so wrong with what I'm wearing?" I'm a bit unnerved as I did put a little more effort into my appearance this morning than I usually do. I blew out my hair and even put on a little makeup. My Kasper beige pantsuit isn't exactly haute couture, but I thought it looked nice. And, yes, I'm wearing flats but, considering we're going to do a lot of walking today, it's a wonder I don't have sneakers on.

"Nothing's *wrong* with it, Halia. I don't think anyone would notice it long enough to find anything wrong with it. It's a beige pantsuit. A burka is about the only thing with less style."

"Never mind," I say as we lay our purses on a conveyer belt to be x-rayed and walk through a metal detector. "When did you have to start going through metal detectors to get inside a museum?" I ask no one in particular, but Wavonne takes it upon herself to answer.

"Since always."

"We used to take field trips to the Smithsonian all the time in grade school. I don't remember having to go through Security."

"That was back when the only weapons available were clubs and spears."

"Ha ha," I bemoan as we enter the building, and I catch sight of Cynthia with Russell and Twyla and a few others huddled around her. "There they are," I say to Wavonne, and we approach the group.

"Welcome, ladies," Cynthia says as one of three cameramen turns his camera in our direction. "Don't mind him." She gestures toward the man. "They'll be getting footage all day. We'll only use some of it . . . show a few clips before the competition gets started."

"I didn't know we'd be on camera right away." Wavonne turns to me. "Is Gladys on straight?" she asks, adjusting her wig.

"Yes. Gladys looks fine. You sure teased her up high today."

"What's it they say?" Cynthia asks. "The higher the hair, the closer to God? How did you get it fluffed like that?"

"I'd tell you, but I'd have to kill you," Wavonne quips. "It's a spectacle of curlers, a steamer, a good bristle brush, and about a gallon of hair spray."

"Well, it certainly has . . . um . . . *presence*," Cynthia offers. "Let me introduce you to the contestants. We'll start with Sherry. Sherry Ashbury."

We follow Cynthia toward a striking young woman sipping on a bottle of water. There's something silly to me about using coffee to describe skin tones, but Sherry's is somewhere in the mocha/latte realm. With her warm beige skin, wavy dark hair with golden highlights, and deep brown eyes, she's what one might call 'racially ambiguous.' My guess would be she's half Caucasian and half African American, but she could be a mix of any number of races. She's about five eight, looks about twenty-something years old, and has a figure like a 1950s movie star—ample hips, a small waist, and generous bazoombas—in short, she is gorgeous.

"Sherry, I'd like you to meet one of our judges for the episode we're filming today. Halia Watkins. And this is her assistant, Wavonne."

"Very nice to meet you." I extend my hand.

"You too." She shakes my hand and then Wavonne's.

"Halia owns a local soul food restaurant in Maryland."

"Aren't we in Maryland?" Sherry asks.

"DC," Cynthia says. "We're in DC."

"And DC's in Maryland, right?"

"No. DC's a federal district. . . . It's not part of any . . ." Cynthia lets her voice trail off while Sherry looks at her with a blank glare. "You know what? Maybe it is in Maryland." Cynthia says this in a tone I'm quite familiar with. It's the same tone I use when I start to explain something to Wavonne and, mid-explanation, realize it's just easier to let her go on thinking that the Declaration of Independence and the Constitution are the same thing . . . or stop my explanation short when she wonders out loud why, if *The Sound of Music* was filmed in . . . Austria, there were no kangaroos in it. "Go along with me on this one," Cynthia mutters under her breath to me. "It's just easier that way," she adds before turning her head to speak with one of the camera guys.

"How are you?" I ask Sherry as Cynthia meanders off with her colleague. "All these cameras are a bit daunting. I guess maybe you have gotten used to them by now, though?"

"Yeah. You sort of forget about them after a while. I'm sure they will follow us around as we tour today."

"Have you been here before?" I ask.

"No. I'm excited to see all the exhibits from Africa," she says, with what seems to be genuine enthusiasm. "I've always found those ladies with the saucers in their lips so fascinating. But man, that looks painful! Do you think we'll see any King Tut artifacts or stuff about Amazon tribes?"

"Um, no. I don't think so," I respond. "This is the African *American* museum. Perhaps you're thinking of the Museum of African Art? But I don't think they have a King Tut exhibit . . . not sure about the lip plates." I want to also inform her that Amazon tribes are in South America rather than Africa, but somehow that seems like too much to lay on her all at once.

"Oh." There's disappointment in her voice.

"I'm sure you'll still enjoy it. I've heard there are some really amazing exhibits."

"How about the Pygmies? Will we see anything about them?"

"Girl," Wavonne says. "Pygmies are not in Africa. They're in Austria."

I take a breath and suddenly have a vision of Julie Andrews singing "Do-Re-Mi" in the Austrian Alps to a group of Pygmies while kangaroos hop around in the distance. I'm debating about whether it's worth my energy to educate Frick and Frack about the difference between Austria and Australia and Pygmies versus Aborigines, when Cynthia reappears. "Let me introduce you to Trey," she says.

"It was good to meet you," I say to Sherry as Cynthia nudges Wavonne and me away from her.

"Sherry is not . . . how shall I put it . . . terribly quick witted," Cynthia whispers to me. "But she knows her way around a kitchen. And our audience has historically been largely female—we thought a pretty face and some nice curves might up our male viewership and increase ratings."

If words like "pretty face" and "nice curves" came from a male producer, I'd think it might be grounds for sexual harassment charges, but I'm not sure what to make of Cynthia saying those things. Not that I have much time to think about anything. I've barely escaped Sherry, and now Cynthia is corralling me over to have some forced quality time with the next contestant. Oh well, I suppose, after Sherry, I have nowhere to go but up, right?

Chapter 7

"Trey," Cynthia says to a nicely built young man in a pair of snug jeans and a close-fitting polo shirt. He's quite good-looking in a clean cut, preppy sort of way.

"Hey." He looks up from his phone. "Do you think the camera guys can get some footage of me looking at my phone? When I hold it with my arm bent, my bicep really pops. Look." He shows off an impressive muscle ringed by a tight shirtsleeve.

"I'll see what I can do, Trey," Cynthia replies. "In the meantime, let me introduce you to one of our guest judges for the day, Halia Watkins. She own's Mahalia's Sweet Tea, a highly successful local soul food restaurant. And this is her assistant, Wavonne."

"Nice to meet you." We all trade handshakes. Then Trey pokes at his phone and raises it level with his face. Using it as a mirror, he adjusts the loose curls of black hair hanging over his forehead. "Sorry," he offers, lowering his phone. "Just doing a quick hair check before we go on camera. High def TV can be very unkind." As he slips his phone in his back pocket I notice that he has makeup on his velvety brown skin . . . some concealer or foundation or something. "So, you own a restaurant?"

"Yes. Halia serves the best fried chicken and waffles in town," Wavonne says.

"Nice," Trey says in a subdued manner. "So more basic type stuff then?"

"Basic type stuff?" I ask. "I've had my food called many things over the years, but 'basic type stuff' is a first." I say this in a good-natured way, but I can't say I'm thrilled by some thirty-year-old kid, who probably has delusions of being the next Jamie Oliver or Bobby Flay, saying such things about recipes that took me years to perfect.

"I'm sorry. That was a poor choice of words," Trey says as if it suddenly occurred to him that I'm a judge at this jamboree and maybe he should not get on my bad side. "I just meant . . . you know . . . staples . . . classic American dishes. I've been focused on more complex cuisine since I finished at Le Cordon Bleu in Paris last year." He says "Le Cordon Bleu" in a ridiculously overdone French accent . . . *luh coredawn bluh* . . . and, of course, he pronounces Paris *pah-rhee*. I suspect he thinks it makes him sound cultured and worldly but, mostly, it makes him sound like a jackass.

"Complex cuisine?"

"Yes. I think the next generation of chefs . . . *my* generation needs to really get creative and shake things up. Eventually I plan to open my own place. . . . I'm thinking a fusion of Thai and Middle Eastern—I make a killer hummus with lemongrass and ginger. Or possibly Italian and Indian—I have a recipe for bruschetta made with tandoori chicken that is out of this world."

I'm tempted to respond that if I had a dime for every trendy fusion restaurant, or tapas establishment . . . or celebrity-owned hot spot that has come and gone during the fifteen years that I've been serving "basic type stuff" at Sweet Tea, I'd be an obscenely rich woman. But instead I just say, "Those sound interesting . . . and tasty." I'm not lying when I say this. His fusion ideas do sound pretty good, but I've found that this type of newfangled food is something people only want every once in a while. They are glad to try curry fried chicken and wasabi mashed potatoes, and they may enjoy them, but, when push comes to shove, they want simple fried chicken and macaroni and cheese that remind them of what their grandmothers used to make. And that's why, or at least *one* of the reasons why, Sweet Tea is still going strong after all these years while so many other restaurants have gone the way of the dinosaur.

"Thank you. You have to have fresh ideas to get ahead in this business. The restaurant industry is so competitive these days. That's why I applied to get on this program. If . . . *when* I win, I'll be a household name, do a year or two at Russell's new restaurant, and then open my own place. You almost need to be a celebrity to get a restaurant going these days. It can't just be about the food anymore . . . you need flash and charisma."

"I dunno. Halia's been running Sweet Tea forever, and she's about as drab and borin' as they come," Wavonne teases. "She's outlasted Gladys Knight's Chicken and Waffles in Largo, and the Planet Hollywood on Pennsylvania Avenue . . . and what's the place that Oprah's chef opened by the train station?"

"Art and Soul," I say. "Art Smith opened it several years ago, but I have not outlasted that one. Last I heard, it was still going strong."

"Funny you mention him," Trey says. "Given the circumstances."

"What circumstances?"

"Oh," Trey replies as if he may have said something he shouldn't have. "I thought you knew."

"Knew what?" Wavonne asks.

"Um . . ." he says. "Art Smith was originally slated to be

the judge on today's episode, but there was some sort of emergency at his other restaurant in New York, and he had to cancel."

"I thought it was Walter Carnegie who canceled."

"Yes, but Mr. Smith was supposed to replace him."

"So Halia was their third choice?" Wavonne asks.

"Um . . . well . . . I think they tried for José Andrés when Mr. Smith canceled."

"So, I was the *fourth* choice?"

Trey looks back at me as if he's trying to conjure up a diplomatic response before I hear the words, "fifth choice actually." They come from a full-figured black woman who sort of snuck up from behind me. She appears to be a few years older than me with a plump face and a shoulder length bob of relaxed brown hair. "But you might get a kick out of who their fourth choice was," she adds.

"Really? Who was it?"

"Sylvia," the woman says. "Sylvia Woods of the famous Sylvia's soul food restaurant in Harlem."

"Um," I say. "She's dead."

"*You* know that. I grew up in Harlem, so of course *I* know that. But Russell and Cynthia? Not so much. Cynthia and her team must have made about ten phone calls before they finally figured it out. At one point—I think it was the day before yesterday—Cynthia was on the phone when I walked by, and all I heard was, 'Dead? Are you sure?'"

"If you knew Sylvia had passed, why didn't you tell them?" I ask the woman, who is still a stranger to me.

"What would have been the fun in that?" she responds. "I'm Vera, by the way. I see you've met Vanity Smurf here." She gestures toward Trey, who rolls his eyes but also cracks a smile following her comment. "And I saw you talking to Zendaya earlier." She smiles and waves at Sherry, who is talking with Russell and Twyla. "So, you've met number one and number two. I'm contestant number three."

"Nice to meet you," I say, and introduce myself and Wavonne to her. Unlike Trey and Sherry, she goes right for a hug rather than a handshake. She has a warmness about her that makes this somewhat intimate gesture among strangers appropriate. I suspect it's her age—she easily has twenty years on Sherry and maybe fifteen or so on Trey—and/or her matronly, completely nonthreatening appearance that prompts a smile, rather than a scowl, from Trey when she compares him to a notoriously vain cartoon character. She even manages to let Cynthia making phone calls to reach dead people come off as completely inoffensive. My guess is that she's endeared herself to Trey and Sherry in a motherly sort of way and makes quips like this all the time. Within seconds of meeting her, you get the feeling she's comfortable in her own skin. She speaks her mind, and while Trey has been trying to figure out the best way to flex his biceps for the camera, and Sherry has been touching up her hair and making sure her fake eyelashes are in place, Vera stands before us with a simple, likely drip-dry haircut, no makeup, and an outfit that consists of a pair of "mom jeans," a plain pink T-shirt, and some basic brown walking shoes.

I'm about to ask Vera where she's from when she lets out a loud sneeze, turning her nose in toward her elbow.

"Bless you."

"Thank you," she says. "But you probably only want to do that one time. This time of year, you'll be blessing me all day. My allergies are awful at the moment." I'm only now noticing how congested she sounds. "I think the tree pollen is hanging around late this year."

As I nod my head in agreement Cynthia begins clapping her hands. "Okay, everyone. Let's get this party started. We have three hours slated to tour the museum," she calls over the general clamor of the busy concourse. "We'll start with the lower level first. Let's all head toward the elevators."

Our entire gang—me, Wavonne, Russell, Twyla, Sherry,

Trey, and Vera—follows Cynthia toward the other end of the main hall, where a young man gets Wavonne and I set up with clip-on microphones. Then we step into the elevator, someone presses C3, and as the doors close, Wavonne, much like a 1930s elevator operator, says, "Going down." And, for a quick second, I get an eerie feeling that her words are some sort of omen . . . a forewarning of things to come . . . that something other than the elevator is about to go *down*.

Chapter 8

The elevator doors open to a dimly lit exhibition area, and a young woman in a blue blazer greets us. "Welcome to the David M. Rubenstein History Galleries. These galleries contain three exhibitions, layered one on top of the other. You are starting at level C3: Slavery and Freedom. From here, you will work your way upwards to level C2: The Era of Segregation, and level C1: A Changing America: 1968 and Beyond. From this spot to the third level of the exhibit you'll travel through six hundred years of history. At the end of the History Galleries there is a Contemplative Court where you can spend some time in quiet reflection before touring the rest of the facility. Enjoy your visit."

We thank the young woman and begin to tour the displays. The weak lighting sets a certain tone for this area of the museum, and everyone, even Wavonne, seems to instinctively know to speak in lowered voices and refrain from taking selfies or talking on a cell phone. We take in a video about how, starting in the 1400s, the people of Europe and Africa began to trade with one another . . . and how part of this trade included enslaved individuals. Such trade continued into the 1500s, but only really began to proliferate with

the advent of sugar and tobacco plantations in the Caribbean and the Americas, which created a near endless demand
for labor—this combined with greed and an unimaginable
disregard for human life led to the capture and transport of
more than twelve million . . . *twelve million* Africans, who
were made to cross the Atlantic in squalid conditions aboard
European ships, bound for a life of slavery in the Americas.

"Wow," is about all I can muster to say as the gruesome
video ends, and we move on to view some relics from a Portuguese slave ship. When we come upon actual iron shackles
used to restrain men, women, and children, I begin to find
myself jarred in a way I had not expected. Of course, I studied slavery in school, and I've read the books and seen the
movies, but as we move about the Slavery and Freedom area, I
become increasingly unsettled. There's something particularly
unnerving, beyond anything I experienced reading *Twelve Years
a Slave* or watching *Roots* on TV, about seeing an actual whip
used on human beings who were bought and sold as property,
coins from hundreds of years ago minted with gold generated
from slave labor, and the lace shawl and hymnal owned by
Harriet Tubman.

My general disquiet continues as I come upon a flat stone
the size of my coffee table that, during the 1800s, served as
an auction block just a few miles from here in Hagerstown,
Maryland. My mouth goes dry as I begin to read some of the
names, descriptions, and prices of slaves displayed around
the stone—all of the information lifted from actual bills of
sale—bills of sale for people . . . for *humans*.

The cameras follow us as we continue to tour this dark period of American history, but we really don't say much to
each other . . . or interact with each other at all. A few of us
assemble in front of a 150-year-old slave cabin brought to
the museum, in dismantled pieces, from a plantation in South
Carolina, but no words are exchanged. I think we are all too

deep in thought to speak—picturing in our minds what life might have been like for those who inhabited the structure before us. There are so many "mouthy" people in our group, but Wavonne has not offered a single smart-aleck comment since we entered these halls; Twyla, who uses any excuse to chide me, has been mostly silent; and even Russell, who has been on his cell phone more often than not since I met him, has not made or taken a single call. The subject matter . . . the *people* whose story is being told through all the artifacts . . . and photos . . . and certificates before us deserve some reverence, and we all seem to "get" that.

As we keep moving about, I'm intrigued when I see Wavonne and Sherry, one of whom I know typically doesn't read anything that is not directly related to Beyoncé's beauty regimen or Rihanna's love life, engrossed in a document displayed in a glass case. I shuffle toward them, and see they are reading a small copy of the Emancipation Proclamation. The description notes that it was one of many printed for Union soldiers to read aloud as they advanced in the Southern states in the final days of the Civil War. It does my heart good to see two young women, from a generation often more concerned about where the Kardashians are vacationing or where to get braids like Zoë Kravitz than anything educational, taking an interest in African American history.

As I head up the landing to the next floor, I hear someone sneeze from behind. I'm not surprised to see Vera when I turn around. She catches up to me and reads the signage outside the next section of the History Galleries. "Defending Freedom, Defining Freedom: The Era of Segregation: 1877 to 1968," she recites. "My momma grew up in the segregated South," she adds.

"Really?" I ask, thinking of how my own mother grew up in Washington, DC—not quite the "segregated South," but she's told me stories of segregated lunch counters and depart-

ment stores in which she and my grandmother were allowed
to shop, but not to try on any clothing. Desegregation of private businesses came earlier to DC than in many parts of the
South, but schools did not integrate until the Supreme
Court's infamous *Brown v. Board of Education* decision, so
Momma went to an all-black elementary school until the rul-
ing allowed her to attend classes alongside white students in
junior high.

"Yes. Birmingham, Alabama. She worked in restaurants
after high school in the sixties. She wasn't allowed to eat in
any of them, but waiting tables was apparently okay," Vera
says as we walk through the exhibits about the post-Civil
war years and Jim Crow laws. "She met my father at a
restaurant called Molly's, named after the owner's wife. They
would let black people order takeout, but that was it—we
were not allowed to stay for table service. She and my daddy
decided to leave both Molly's and Alabama when the owner
legally challenged the Civil Rights Act to avoid having to
offer sit-down service to African Americans. They went to
New York . . . to Harlem, where I grew up, and eventually
ended up in DC."

I'm about to ask why her parents chose New York, but before I have a chance to speak, I hear Cynthia's voice from behind. "Can you repeat that for the camera?" she asks Vera,
waving one of the camera guys over.

"Repeat what?" Vera asks.

"The story about your mother working at Ollies and leaving Arkansas or whatever . . . and segregation blah blah,"
Cynthia responds.

"Blah blah?" Vera raises her eyebrows.

"It's a great story," Cynthia says. "Viewers will eat it up."

"Um," Vera says. Not only is an intrusive camera pointed
directly at her but, at Cynthia's direction, someone has also

shown up with some sort of light box and is projecting its beam on Vera. "My momma grew up in the segregated South—"

"Can you say it with a little more feeling?" Cynthia asks. "Maybe don't look directly at the camera . . . look off into the distance . . . imagine your grandmother sweating over a steaming pot—"

"It was her mother," I correct.

"And I don't think she sweated over a steaming pot—she was a waitress," Vera says.

"Oh, for Christ's sake, work with me here," Cynthia says. "Give me a good story . . . and, if you can tear up a bit while telling it, even better."

Vera directs her eyes toward me and throws a look that says, "Is she freakin' serious?" my way before taking a breath, looking off into the distance as directed, and starting again. "You see." She clears her throat. "It was summertime and the cotton was high in the fields," she says, a wicked gleam in her eye. "My rich daddy and my good-looking momma were living easy."

"Wait, wait," Cynthia, who has clearly never seen *Porgy and Bess*, says. "I thought you said your father worked at a restaurant with your mother. Why did he work at a restaurant if he was rich?"

"He was rich in spirit, not money—he was always losing money playing craps on Catfish Row." Vera's allergies are upping the drama of her tale. Her sniffling and stuffy nose makes it sound like she's been crying.

Vera continues to borrow from, and take a few liberties with, the plot of *Porgy and Bess* as she tells a totally made-up story about her parents, complete with a fisherman named Mingo, something called "happy dust," and a tale about how, once during a hurricane, her parents sang "Oh, Doctor Jesus" to drown out the sound of the storm. To her credit, she manages to not crack up, but Cynthia senses something is amiss when I can't help but let out a snicker or two, and the guy holding the light box completely loses it when she talks about how her parents got married on Kittiwah Island and her father's best man was someone by the name of Sportin' Life.

"What? Why is everyone laughing?"

"Because Vera's playin' with you," Wavonne, who apparently crept up behind me at some point during Vera's little spiel, says. "She's been goin' on about the plot of *Raisin in the Sun*."

"*Porgy and Bess*," I correct.

"Whateva' . . . I knew it was some play you made me sit through when I was a kid."

"Very funny, Vera," Cynthia says, clearly not amused. "Can we start from the beginning with the truth . . . or something resembling the truth?"

I listen as Vera talks, honestly this time, about how her parents met while her mother was a waitress and her father was a cook. And how they eventually left Alabama for a brighter future in New York, where they worked in a handful of restaurants before her father landed a job with a bank, rose through the ranks, and eventually moved to DC to take a branch manager position. "He retired from banking about ten years ago, but, fortunately for me, he never forgot everything he learned about cooking in all those restaurants. To this day he can grill a rib eye to perfection and can tell whether it's rare, medium, or well done with just a little touch. . . . He can poach a salmon until it's perfectly pink and flakey and, on Sundays, he fries up some of the crispiest fried chicken you'll ever have—I learned everything I know about cooking from him, and I still use his fried chicken recipe."

"Okay. I think we have usable stuff here," Cynthia says when she feels like she's gotten enough of Vera's family history.

"If you have some Visine, I can make it look like thoughts of fried chicken are making me cry," Vera, ever the smart aleck, offers.

"Get out of here, would you," Cynthia says with a chuckle. "You've caused enough mayhem for the time being."

"I do my best," Vera replies, and Wavonne and I follow her as she steps into the Era of Segregation exhibit.

Chapter 9

"You better be careful. I heard you talkin' about the crispiest fried chicken 'you'll ever have' around this one." Wavonne points toward me. "Halia likes to think of herself as the Fried Chicken Queen."

"I wouldn't go that far, but my fried chicken is from a family recipe as well. I make it the same way my grandmommy did, and it does get rave reviews, if I do say so myself."

"Are you challenging me to a chicken fry-off, Halia?" Vera jokes.

"That's one contest I'd be glad to sign up to judge," Wavonne offers.

"I guess we should focus on the contest at hand for the time being," I say, and turn to Vera. "So how did you end up part of this whole spectacle called *Elite Chef*?"

"I've been watching the show for the past couple of years, and I made a career change recently—I left my job at a health insurance company and opened my own food truck: Vera's Fried Chicken and Doughnuts."

"Fried chicken and doughnuts? Two of my favorite things," I say.

Vera smiles and talks about the trials and tribulations of

getting a business off the ground as we take in the displays about the great migration of African Americans from the South to other parts of the US, the original sign from a bed and breakfast in Maine that catered to black tourists called Rock Rest, and an old COLORED SECTION sign from a segregated train car. The subject matter is not as troubling as the slavery exhibit, but in some ways it hits closer to home as it really wasn't that long ago that events depicted within these walls unfolded. I see the dress Rosa Parks wore when she was arrested for refusing to give up her seat on an Alabama bus and think about how that happened only about twenty years before I was born. I take in an obsolete tape recorder used by Malcolm X and realize Momma was already in her twenties when he gave his powerful speeches. These displays are definitely emotion-evoking but, somehow, when compared to the slavery exhibit, the mood, and maybe even the lighting, are just a tad lighter. No one is clowning around with a selfie stick or talking in raised voices, but unlike the almost complete silence we experienced downstairs, talking among ourselves in a measured tone doesn't seem inappropriate in at least certain areas of this exhibit. We are, however, quiet when we come upon a fragment from the stained glass window of the 16th Street Baptist Church in Alabama that was blown up in 1963 and, of course, we observe a moment of silence when we stand before Emmett Till's coffin. But as we take seats at the interactive lunch counter and begin tapping on the screens, Vera resumes chatting with Wavonne and me. "My daddy helped me a lot when I started my business," she says. "Not only was he an excellent cook, he was pretty knowledgeable about the food service business in general. You'd be surprised how much he learned working in restaurants forty years ago still applies today."

"What's it they say: The more things change, the more they stay the same?" I reply. "We have so much more technology to track inventory and expenses . . . and relay information from the front of the house to the back of the house, but in the end, just like forty years ago, good food and good service at a fair price are what keep customers coming in the door."

"Daddy told me almost the exact same thing when I was debating whether or not to move forward with my venture."

"So, there was some hesitation?"

"Yes. Big time. I had a steady job with an insurance company . . . a regular paycheck . . . medical and dental . . . paid time off . . . a 401K. But boy was I *bored*. I wanted to do something more interesting and more active. I was tired of sitting in front of a computer at a desk all day. I love to cook and have always wanted to get into the restaurant business, so one day, I decided to just take the leap and go for it."

"I'm guessing you're not bored anymore," I say. "That is one thing about the food service business—it's never boring."

"Ain't that the truth. I've definitely learned that since I started my fried chicken and doughnuts venture. From day one it's been a challenge. I thought a food truck would be a way to ease into the business—that it would be less overhead and less of a commitment . . . and require less man power than a full-service restaurant. And I guess that's true, but it's still been so much more difficult than I could have imagined. I found a good deal on a truck, but then it cost me a fortune to make the modifications to meet fire and health regulations, and I didn't budget enough for insurance . . . and the rent for the kitchen I use to do a lot of the prep work keeps rising. As soon as I feel like I'm starting to get ahead, something else comes up. But, at the same time, I love it—every day is different, and people really appreciate my food—they follow me on Twitter to find out where I'm going to park each day."

"So, what happens if you win this whole thing, and Russell hires you as executive chef at his new restaurant? Will you give up your truck?"

"I might try to keep it going on the side. Honestly, I hadn't given it much thought until recently. I never thought I'd make it this far into the competition. I'm a good cook, but we all know how these things go—the people who last the longest are not necessarily those with the highest skill level. The ones who survive the longest are usually the ones who are the prettiest, or loudest . . . or create the most drama. I'm nearly fifty years old and even some of the men in the competition are prettier than I am. And don't get me started with the women—my left thigh weighs more than most of them. I figured my network TV lifespan was one to three episodes. Once I got in the door, I was really only hoping to stay in the game long enough to get some publicity for my truck. I figured they'd send the token frumpy middle-aged lady on her way a few weeks into filming. I would have been happy with an upsurge in business, once the few episodes I was in aired. Being part of the final three is quite a surprise."

"I don't find it that surprising," I say. "You're likable and have a quick wit, and it sounds like you know your way around a deep fryer. Once the shows start to air, I suspect much of America will be rooting for you." I believe every word that just fell from my lips. Vera seems like a kind soul. She has a good story. And it's admirable that she keeps a pleasant demeanor despite obviously not feeling well.

"Thank you. I appreciate you saying that," Vera says before she starts playing around with the interactive screen on the counter in front of her, and I get up to check out an old Southern Railway passenger car with a partition to create separate seating areas for white and black passengers and, later, make my way to the end of this gallery. As I leave the area and walk underneath an actual seventy-year-old plane, apparently called a Stearman PT-13D Kaydet, flown by

Tuskegee airmen during World War II, I think about how I told Vera that America would root for her. I almost told her that *I* was certainly rooting for her, but figured that since I'm a judge and cameras are rolling all around us . . . and there's a microphone clipped to my shirt, I'd better keep that little bit of information to myself.

Chapter 10

As I step up toward the third and final floor of the History Galleries I see Trey and Twyla on the ramp ahead of me.

"Do you mind giving me a little support? These shoes are not meant for inclines," I hear Twyla say as she locks her arm into Trey's and leans into his shoulder. "I should have worn flats but, then again, if I had, I wouldn't have gotten to cozy up to such a handsome young man."

Twyla has a good thirty years on Trey and maybe she meant her words to come across the way a grandmother might innocuously speak to her grandson, but there was a tone or an inflection . . . or *something* in her voice that made her "cozy up" comment sound sort of, for lack of a better word, "unseemly." There's a cameraman next to me, getting the two of them on film from behind. Twyla interlacing her arm through Trey's seems to have caught his attention—he picks up his pace and tries to catch up with them as they enter the A Changing America: 1968 and Beyond exhibit.

I follow them into yet another vast space and try to focus on the exhibits, but Twyla's behavior is distracting. She and Trey are no longer climbing a ramp (that was not that steep anyway), yet Twyla hasn't removed her arm from his as they walk around on a flat surface. I step behind them, and we all view a pamphlet about Soul City, North Carolina, a planned community first proposed in 1969, which was to be open to all races, but placed an emphasis on providing opportunities for minorities and the poor. I'm reading about how the development was sort of a bust and the town never really grew into what it was envisioned to become, when Twyla finally unlocks her arm from Trey's, only to grab his hand. "Look at this," she says, leading him toward a large metal basket used to rescue people caught in the Hurricane Katrina floodwaters. "I remember watching the whole tragedy on the news . . . seeing little children air-lifted in these things . . . so sad," she adds, and leans her head on Trey's shoulder.

As I'm watching this interaction unfold from a distance I hear the *click clack* of Wavonne's heels approach from behind. She edges up next to me and, I'm embarrassed to admit it but, at the moment, we are both finding Twyla's lecherous behavior more interesting than the sweatshirt about the 1995 Million Man March or the boom box carried by Radio Raheem in *Do the Right Thing* . . . or any of the other memorabilia on show around us.

"Oooh, girl." Wavonne's eyes are locked on Twyla and Trey. "Looks like the cougar has come down from the mountain and found herself some prey."

"Twyla's clinginess does seem a bit inappropriate."

"A bit inappropriate?" Wavonne questions. "If a mature man in a position of power was actin' like that—all touchy-feely with a young girl—he'd be 'me-too'd' straight to a courtroom. Seems like an ole crow like Twyla shouldn't be allowed to get away with it either. But, I can see the draw—Trey is quite the little snack."

"He's definitely handsome."

"And definitely *knows* that he's handsome. What's the old song . . . from your generation . . . by that skinny white lady with the giant teeth? 'You're So Vain'?"

"My generation? I'm not even sure I was born when that song came out."

"Whateva'. It's been runnin' through my head since I laid eyes on him. I think he spends more time on his makeup than I do . . . and he's poured into those jeans like Jell-O in a plastic mold. I bet he had to liquify himself to get into them . . . and then go sit in the freezer to become solid again."

"You would know." I give Wavonne's own snug outfit a quick look.

"This dress is supposed to be form-fittin', Halia. If you ever shopped anywhere outside an L.L. Bean catalogue, you might know that."

"I shop L.L. Bean *online* these days, thank you very much."

"Really?" Wavonne retorts. "Did they finally teach you how to use a computer at the senior center?"

I laugh and am about to reply, but I'm stifled when I catch Cynthia out of the corner of my eye.

"Carl, get over here, would you?" she calls to one of the cameramen.

"Can you two do that again? For the camera this time?"

"Do what again?"

"Argue. It might be fun to include a few clips when we air."

"Argue?" Wavonne and I ask in unison.

"That was hardly arguing," I explain. "We do that all the time. I tell Wavonne her outfit is ridiculous. She tells me I have no style. I say her clothes are too tight. She makes a joke about my age. No need to recreate it . . . we'll do it a hundred more times before the day is over."

"I guess I'll take your word for that." Cynthia leans in a little closer to me. "So, we're trying to get judges to spend a little time with each contestant before our tour is over, and we're running behind. I don't think we're going to be able to see the whole museum at this point. We got some footage of you with Vera downstairs, but I'd like you to pair up with

Trey as you explore the next area, and then make some time for Sherry before we all convene in the café."

"Sure," I say. *If I can pry Twyla off Trey.*

"Trey," Cynthia calls in his direction. "The clock's ticking. I think we need to wrap things up here. I'm going to try and gather everyone and usher the group up to the Culture Galleries. We can get some good footage up there. Why don't you head on up with Halia and Wavonne?" she suggests before looking at Twyla. "And, Twyla, I'd like you to spend some time with Sherry. Why don't you come with me and we'll find her?"

"Okay," Twyla agrees, looking disappointed to have to leave her newly commandeered boy toy. "I'll see you later," she says to Trey, playfully poking her finger into his chest before locking step with Cynthia and setting off in search of Sherry, who, based on what little I know about her, may very well have gotten lost. It wouldn't surprise me if she, much like Chevy Chase caught in a London traffic roundabout, is walking in a perpetual circle in one of the displays downstairs and wondering why she's come upon the collection of cornerstones from historically black colleges for the third time.

Chapter 11

"Are you enjoying yourself?" I ask Trey as we exit the History Galleries and make our way through the main concourse to the escalators.

"Enjoying himself?" Wavonne questions, before Trey can answer. "Would you enjoy being pawed by an old lady all morning?"

Trey laughs. "She is a little handsy, isn't she? Not sure what that's about, but it's harmless enough, I guess."

"Spoken like a man who wants her vote when competition time comes," Wavonne says.

Trey laughs again. "I think I can get her vote on my merits alone. I've worked at some of the top restaurants in the country and studied at Le Cordon Bleu." Once again, he pronounces it *luh core-dawn bluh*.

"Yes. You said that earlier about *luh core-dawn bluh*," Wavonne mimics. "I studied at *sir-ah-tays-villay* myself."

"Where?"

"Surrattsville High School," I say. "Wavonne's being a smart aleck," I add before turning to Wavonne. "And *studied* is a bit of a stretch, isn't it?"

"You hush, Halia," Wavonne says as we step off the escalator onto the top floor of the museum and enter the Culture Galleries, where there is an immediate and palpable shift in the energy and feel of this exhibit versus the History Galleries downstairs—the dim lighting is gone, there is upbeat music playing, bright colors abound, and there's a rumble of voices and conversations as patrons finally feel like it's okay to talk freely.

"Cynthia said she wanted me to get some video of you guys at the Foodways sections," a cameraman, the one she called Carl earlier, says. "I think it's over this way."

"I guess that make sense given the culinary nature of the show," I reply, and we follow Carl to the Foodways: Culture and Cuisine exhibit. After all the heavy subject matter we explored earlier it's fun to see things like a wire basket used to catch oysters in the nearby Chesapeake Bay and a pot used to cook greens at the Florida Avenue Grill—opened in 1944 right here in DC and still open today—which bills itself as the oldest soul food restaurant in the country. I can actually feel myself getting a little emotional when we come upon the red chef's jacket worn by the late Queen of Creole Cuisine, Leah Chase, at her New Orleans restaurant, Dooky Chase's. I never met her, but I always sort of considered her, along with Sylvia Woods, to be role models of sorts—*idols* really—they opened and ran highly successful restaurants during a time when women, and black women in particular, did not do such things.

"I just loved her," I say, looking at the bright red chef's coat with two rows of buttons down the middle and her name embroidered on the left side.

"Did you know her?" Trey asks.

"No, but I followed her career. She was amazing."

"I met her a couple of times."

"Really?"

"Yes. New Orleans is a great food city," Trey says in a way

that irritates me a little bit—I mean, I'm well aware that New Orleans is a great food city. "I did some time at Brennan's and Commander's Palace in the French Quarter. I ate at Dooky's a few times while I lived there, and she would walk around and talk with the customers. I loved New Orleans. I got to meet John Besh and Emeril Lagasse . . . and a ton of other celebrity chefs. . . . Bobby Flay, Gordon Ramsey—I tried to get on his show, too."

"I'm gonna need an umbrella for all these names being dropped," Wavonne whispers to me.

I chuckle at her remark before replying to Trey. "I'm jealous that you got to meet Leah. I'm in awe of all she accomplished. Women didn't really open and run restaurants back when she got her start."

"Well, technically, she didn't open Dooky's . . . at least not all by herself," Trey corrects. "Her husband's family originally started it as a corner stand, and several years down the line, she *and* her husband, whose nickname was Dooky, converted it into a sit-down restaurant."

"Interesting." Once again I'm a little annoyed by kid-know-it all, and maybe I'm being overly sensitive, but I feel like he's implying that Ms. Chase could not have gotten her restaurant off the ground without the help of a man. "My understanding is that she was the visionary in the relationship."

I sense that Trey is about to offer a rebuttal when Cynthia steps off the escalator with the rest of the gang. Twyla is chatting with Sherry, and it appears Russell is supposed to get some camera time with Vera but, as usual, he's barking something into his cell phone rather than paying any attention to her.

"Let's take it into the Musical Crossroads section, folks. We need to amp up this party."

Chapter 12

At this point I'm starting to feel like a sheep being herded around by a border collie named Cynthia as she nudges us into the Musical Crossroads section, but I figure that's how these sort of things go, and follow the rest of the group into the music gallery, which is a sea of competing sensory stimulations. When we first walk in we are greeted by Chuck Berry's bright red Cadillac Eldorado, but it's competing for attention with a multicolored costume worn by Jermaine Jackson in the early seventies; a sparkling purple, pink, silver, and gold dress owned by Celia Cruz; Michael Jackson's black sequined jacket; and, yes, even the P-Funk Mothership.

"Wow," Wavonne says. "What's this? It's like *Star Trek* meets disco."

"It's the P-Funk Mothership, Wavonne," I say. "It was legendary when I was a little girl . . . and considered high tech in the seventies. It used to descend, lights flashing, as part of Parliament-Funkadelic's shows."

"High tech?" Trey says in a mocking tone, interrupting the rendition of "Give up the Funk" going in my head. "Looks like a child's school project."

"Well, we thought it was cool," I reply. I'm liking this guy less by the minute when I hear Vera's voice from behind.

"Oh my God!" she says, approaching with Twyla. "Look! The *Soul Train* sign," she offers about the electric dancing train on the wall. "After the cartoons went off, that was must see TV on Saturday afternoons when I was coming up."

I smile. "Me and some of the neighborhood kids used to recreate the *Soul Train* line in my basement."

"I used to pretend I was Madame Butterfly. Remember her? I'd put a butterfly clip in my hair and do the robot to 'Dancing Machine.'"

"What about Don Cornelius and that sexy deep voice?" I ask, thinking how much more fun it would be to tour this exhibit with Vera rather than Trey.

"Of course. He was an early crush."

"He was *fine*," Twyla chimes in before eyeing Trey. "Not as fine as this young man though."

Trey smiles awkwardly while Vera and I exchange glances. "I think *Soul Train* was before my time," he says, and takes a few steps closer to Wavonne and me, in what I assume is an effort to stifle Twyla from touching all over him again.

"I think it ran into the two thousands, but its heyday was definitely the seventies and eighties," Vera says.

Much as I'd like to reminisce about the seventies and eighties with Vera, I catch Cynthia, hovering next to a denim suit worn by Charley Pride, shooting a look of disapproval our way. I suspect it's her way of telling me that I've had my time with Vera, and I'm supposed to be getting to know Trey now.

"How about we meander over to the Taking the Stage section?" I say to Trey before turning to Vera. "Let's catch up on all things P-Funk and *Soul Train* later."

"Sure thing," she says. "Maybe Twyla and I can see what the Neighborhood Record Store section is about."

"Girl," Wavonne says as we stride into the area celebrating all things stage and screen. "They have the costumes from *The Wiz*. I auditioned to play Dorothy when we did a production in high school. Can you believe they didn't give me the part?"

I refrain from saying, "Yes, considering you can't sing, and they probably thought it was unlikely that you would show up to half of the rehearsals." Instead, I offer, "Well, singing was not one of your stronger talents, Wavonne. I remember that production. The lead they ended up choosing did have a really strong voice."

"That was mousy ole Lavenia Monroe. Yes, she could sing, but she didn't have any star quality. What I lacked in singing capabilities I made up for in *presence*."

"Presence?" Trey asks.

"It means she takes up a lot of space."

"You be quiet, Halia," Wavonne counters. "It means people take notice of me. I light up a room when I walk in."

"I think that's more the sequins adorned on practically everything you own, than *you* exactly," I joke.

Wavonne is about to respond when Cynthia appears. "I guess you *were* being truthful earlier. You two *do* bicker all the time."

"I wouldn't call it bickering. We're just playing. Wavonne knows I love her, sequins and all. And I will say she did do a bang-up job with the part she did get in *The Wiz*."

"Don't you tell them about the part I got!" Wavonne orders.

"What?" Trey asks. "What was the part?"

"It was *nothing*, and it was a long time ago."

"Oh, come on, Wavonne. Tell them. After all, it was quite fitting."

Wavonne rolls her eyes and figures she may as well share

the information before I do. "They gave me the part . . . the part of the . . . the Tornado."

Trey and Cynthia laugh.

"The Tornado? I love it!" Cynthia says, and turns to Carl. "You're getting this, right?"

"And she was a damn good tornado, too," I compliment. "Probably the only tornado to swirl around in five-inch platform pumps in the history of the show's production."

"I never once fell on those pumps either," Wavonne brags.

"Walking in high heels is one of Wavonne's many talents," I say to Trey. "Speaking of walking, why don't we head over there." I point toward a display case titled "TV Pioneers."

"Not diggin' any of these outfits," Wavonne comments about a jumpsuit worn by Diahann Carroll in *Julia* and a button-up dress worn by Esther Rolle in *Good Times*. "I didn't realize George and Weezy were so short," Wavonne adds, taking in a suit and dress worn by Sherman Hemsley and Isabel Sanford in *The Jeffersons*.

"Did you watch any of these shows?" I ask Trey. "It would have been in reruns, I guess."

"I'm sorry, what?" he asks.

"*Good Times. The Jeffersons.* Were you a fan?"

"I've caught a few episodes here and there. They were okay I guess." He takes a second to clear his throat. "Sorry, I'm a little distracted. It's interesting and all, but this tour is really dragging on. I thought it was only supposed to be a couple of hours."

So much for my earlier heartfelt joy about young people taking an interest in history.

"Don't get me wrong," Trey elaborates. "I'd love to come back and spend more time here one day, but my mind is on the competition. I wish we could just get started on today's challenge. The more we walk around the more ideas I get about what Cynthia is going to throw at us. At first, I thought they might ask us to prepare some standards from the old South, but when we were looking at Leah Chase's chef jacket I thought they might ask us to prepare Creole food. . . . Then I started mulling over shellfish recipes when we came upon that oyster basket. And now I'm wondering if they may have found out the favorite foods of Motown singers or something and will ask us to prepare those. It's hard to focus."

"I'm sure you'll be fine. You've made it this far."

"I'm not doubting that I'll do well. I'm just strategizing in my head, so I'm prepared later," Trey says, a cameraman getting his every word. "I've studied at one of the top culinary schools in the world and have worked at some of the best restaurants around. I know I can win this, but I'm still trying to stay one step ahead. Maybe I'll go check out that Black Hollywood case. Knowing Cynthia and the production team, they may find some way to tie today's challenge to Whoopi Goldberg in *Sister Act*."

"Pretty boy can get on a sista's nerves," Wavonne whispers to me as Trey saunters toward the display of costumes from *Stormy Weather*, *The Mack*, and as he already mentioned, *Sister Act*. "So full of himself. I think I'm gonna go check out that Diana Ross *Lady Sings the Blues* ensemble we saw in the other room. I bet I can piece something like it together at Marshalls. I'll let you listen to him yammer about how he studied under Julia Child or the Pillsbury Doughboy . . . or that lady in the Popeyes commercials."

While Wavonne heads back to the music display, I rejoin Trey. I'm not that eager to spend more time with him, but Cynthia made it clear that she wanted me to get to know him.

"You're pretty confident in your culinary capabilities," I say, walking up next to him. "I guess that's a good thing. I didn't have that kind of confidence when I was first starting out."

"Where did you go to culinary school?"

"The Learn-as-You-Go Academy for Wayward Chefs," I say with a laugh. "Everything I know I either learned cooking Sunday dinners with Grandmommy or on the job at the handful of restaurants I worked at before opening my own place."

"Maybe that's why it took you some time to be surer of yourself—it probably would have come quicker if you had studied at a top culinary school. But your restaurant serves soul food, right? Like cornbread, and mac and cheese, and fried stuff? I guess you don't really need to do a stint at the Culinary Institute of America to make that kind of stuff, huh?"

My eyes widen in response to his words, and I'm not sure if I'm glad or sad that Wavonne has stepped away. She would be much better than me at giving this cocky little brat a good "what for," but there are also cameras all around us, so it would be hard for her to deny the physical assault charges.

"Well, what we serve at Sweet Tea, a restaurant that, if I may say, has outlasted local venues opened by Richard Sandoval and Wolfgang Puck and Mike Isabella, may not be as ingenious as . . . What was it you were describing earlier? Hummus with lemons and cinnamon or something? But we do okay."

"Hummus with lemongrass and ginger," Trey corrects. "I didn't mean any offense. I think it's great you've had some success without formal schooling, but don't you think—"

"She has had more than *some* success, you little twit." I guess I was distracted by my annoyance with Trey's comments and did not hear Wavonne approaching from behind. I assume she had decided on whatever Diana Ross and Whitney Houston ensembles she might be able to mix and match at the local discount stores and found herself headed back in our direction. Apparently, she caught at least some of what

Trey said . . . and the thing about Wavonne and me (and Momma too) is that we will disparage each other left and right, but the moment someone outside our family does it to one of us, watch out—hell will be paid! "Since Sweet Tea opened many years ago, about a bazillion fusion-nonsense restaurants have come and gone—most of the places opened by young hot-shot chefs who thought they knew it all now have signs for Applebee's and Cheesecake Factory hangin' over the doors while Sweet Tea still has a line of people waitin' for tables."

"Okay, Wavonne," I say, trying to stifle a smile. "That's enough."

"Enough? I'm just getting started."

"If that's just getting started, I better batten down the hatches," Trey says with a chuckle. He seems to be more amused by Wavonne's tirade than unnerved. "But you've made your point. I'm sorry. I should be more respectful of my elders."

"Excuse me?!" I say, unsure if I heard him correctly. At this point, with his little "elders" jibe, I, rather than Wavonne, may be the one facing assault charges. But before I have a chance to say anything, Cynthia, who has been a few feet away making sure this little exchange with Trey is getting on film, steps closer to us.

"Okay," she says in a loud voice. "Maybe it's time for Halia and Wavonne to hook up with Sherry." She looks at Trey. "Why don't you find Russell? Last I saw he was on the phone in the Visual Arts section. Why don't you two mill about the Community Galleries for a little bit, and I'll send the ladies to the Oprah exhibit. Then we'll regroup in the café in a half hour."

"Fine with me," Trey says, and then turns to me and Wavonne. "Ladies," he says in lieu of good-bye, nodding his head at us before departing.

"What a pompous jerk," I say in a low voice once Trey's out of earshot.

"True-dat," Wavonne says, watching him exit the area. The scowl on her face fades as her eyes linger on his backside. "But, *dayem*," she adds, "he's a pompous jerk who looks as good goin' as he does comin'."

Chapter 13

"Cynthia sent me over here to meet up with you guys," Sherry says to me and Wavonne. "How's it going?"

"Good . . . good," I say. "She said something about us touring the Oprah exhibit now, so I guess we head in that direction?" I point to my left.

"Fine with me," Sherry says. "I love Oprah, but I never quite understood her show."

"What's to understand?" Wavonne asks.

"It was just weird how it ran at different times in different cities. It was on an ABC station here at four o'clock in the afternoon, but when I moved to Chicago it was on an NBC station at nine o'clock in the morning."

"The show was syndicated so . . ." I let my voice fade, deciding it will take way too much time to explain syndication to this one. Instead I go with a simple, "Yeah, that is weird."

"Oh-Em-Gee!" Sherry says as we enter the area of the museum dedicated to Her Majesty and see the Harpo Studio sign. "Harpo is Oprah spelled backward! I never noticed that before."

I'm quite certain the cameraman in front of us just zoomed

in on my face to get my reaction to Sherry's comment. I feel like Jim Halpert on *The Office* getting a close-up after one of Michael Scott's zany comments. "Um . . . yes. Clever."

"It's not *that* clever." Wavonne is clearly not trying as hard as I am to patronize Sherry, who starts scurrying ahead of us.

"Look," she calls out. "The 'You-Get-a-Car! You-Get-a-Car!' outfit!" She points to a red suit displayed on a headless mannequin, like a child enthralled with a holiday window display at Macy's. "I remember that episode. I was like ten years old . . . I had just gotten home from school . . . and my mom was on the phone with one of her girlfriends screaming about how 'They all got cars! She gave every last one of them a car!' "

"I remember that, too. Aunt Celia was goin' crazy!" Wavonne says, and turns to me. "She called you at the restaurant. I remember her bein' like, 'Yes! Every single member of the audience got a car!' Then she was like, 'I don't know . . . some crappy Pontiac they probably couldn't sell anyway, but *still*—a new car for *everyone*!' "

"Let me guess, she ended the conversation by reminding me that if Oprah can finagle giving away three hundred cars and still have time to find a man, what's my excuse?"

Wavonne laughs. "I can't remember, but I'd say that's a pretty safe bet."

"My mom is always on me about getting married, too," Sherry says. " 'Your looks aren't going to last forever, Sherry,' " she adds, mimicking her mother. " 'Land a man with money while you can.' "

"You're so young," I offer. "You have plenty of time."

"That's what I tell her. I'm not ready to settle down. I still want to see the world. Did you know there is a Portland, Maine, *and* a Portland, Oregon? I want to go to both!"

"Dream big," I reply feebly.

"And I want to learn to do the hula in the Bahamas and to speak Spanish in Brazil."

"I think Hawaii is where you want to learn to hula."

"Hawaii, Bermuda." She makes a weighing gesture with her hands. "What's it matter? You know what they say: If you've been to one Caribbean island, you been to them all."

And the camera zooms to my facial expression yet again. Listening to this young woman is making my head hurt.

"You know they speak Portuguese in Brazil. Not Spanish," Wavonne says, and notices me looking at her quizzically. "Don't look so surprised. I know stuff. You learn a thing or two when you hang out at Club Rio—half price caipirinhas from five to seven every night."

"Caipirinhas?" Sherry asks. "Those fish that bite you?"

"Those are piranhas, dear. I think a caipirinha is a Brazilian cocktail." I turn my head toward Wavonne. "And, believe me, I know you *know* stuff. But that stuff usually has more to do with wigs and makeup than what languages are spoken in South America."

"Don't listen to her," Sherry says to Wavonne. "People just assume that girls like you and me . . . girls with big boobs . . . that we're stupid. I've been getting it since puberty. Before I started training as a chef and learned more about food, a waiter once asked if I'd like to try the filet mignon. I asked him what sort of fish mignon was, and the whole table laughed at me—everyone at that table has treated me like an airhead ever since. I'm sorry . . . I hear 'filet,' I think fish. If I had been some petite emancipated thing with a flat chest and glasses, they all would have considered my little faux pas a one-time gaffe and moved on. But because I have a killer rack, they label me as stupid."

"I think you mean emaciated, not emancipated." Boy does my head hurt now. "And, I, by no means, think Wavonne is stupid," I protest, feeling like, to be polite, I should probably add that I don't think that Sherry is stupid either, but I'm not sure I can pull that off with a straight face. "Quite the opposite. Wavonne may not be, shall we say, 'academically inclined' or the foremost authority on current events that don't involve Normani or Cardi B, but anyone who can come upon a sign advertising a thirty-five percent discount on a pair of Nine West pumps and immediately calculate the final price in her head is far from stupid. Wavonne's smart as a whip—she just selectively uses her intelligence when the mood strikes her."

"Hmmm," Sherry says. "Maybe that's my problem, too."

Neither Wavonne nor I know how to graciously respond to this, so I just point and say, "Look, the dress Oprah wore to the Legends Ball," and try to move on to a new topic. "So, Sherry, how did you come to be a part of this whole thing?"

"Whole thing?"

"The show. How did you end up getting cast on *Elite Chef*?"

"I just applied through the website, filled out the question-naire, and sent in a head shot. Then I went through a couple rounds of interviews and, next thing you know, I'm packing my bags for DC. It's fun to be back. I worked at restaurants here a couple of years ago, but never really got to know the city. My sister is coming to town this week to watch the fi-nals, and then we'll stay for a few days and do some touristy stuff. She wants to see the Capitol building, and the memori-als, and go to the spy museum. I've been book marking stuff on my phone." Sherry pulls out her phone and starts swiping through photos of various landmarks. "The Jefferson Memo-rial, the Lincoln Memorial, Arlington Cemetery . . ." She slides her finger across her phone again and then turns the screen toward me. "I'm not sure what it is, but this octagon-shaped building keeps coming up when I search on tourist attractions. Looks pretty plain."

"Um," I say, getting a look at the screen. "That would be a *pentagon*-shaped building."

She looks at me, bemused.

"As in *the* Pentagon. It's the headquarters for the Defense Department."

"Oh . . . so it's a pentagon? Not an octagon. Oh well, I never was very good at algebra."

"Geometry, dear. I think you mean geometry." I clear my throat and, once again, change the subject. "So, how long have you been working in the restaurant industry?"

"Just a few years. I studied culinary arts at the Marks Technical Center in Baltimore. They are very selective, you know."

"Yes, the ads they run during *The Price Is Right* and *The Young and Restless* mention how selective they are several times," Wavonne says.

Sherry doesn't seem to get that Wavonne is chiding her and continues. "From there I worked at a couple of restaurants in DC, and then I moved back to Chicago. At the moment, I'm a chef at Comfort Food in Lincoln Park."

Knowing what I know about the Marks Technical Center, I find it hard to believe that Sherry is a *chef* anywhere. I'm guessing she's more of a line cook. The Marks Technical Center isn't really a culinary school, per se. It's more of a for-profit vocational training center—one of those learn to be a chef . . . or bartender . . . or nursing assistant . . . or pharmacy technician in six months or less kind of places. I suspect that it's Sherry's head shot, not her resume, that helped her score some initial interviews to get on *Elite Chef*. And, once whoever made the final casting decisions got an in-person look at the full Sherry-package of hair, and cheekbones, and lips and hips . . . and what she herself described as a killer rack, I'm sure it was a no-brainer to offer her one of the few coveted spots in the competition. Most shows want a va-va-voom factor—Sherry may not bring the smarts or possibly even any real culinary talent to *Elite Chef* but, if nothing else, she definitely brings the va-va-voom.

Chapter 14

"I can't believe you did that!" I say to Wavonne as we walk toward the entrance of the museum café.

"Oh, what's the big deal? I just wanted a photo of me behind the wheel."

"Chuck Berry's Cadillac is roped off for a reason, Wavonne. I leave you alone for five minutes to run to the bathroom and you almost get us thrown out of a federal building."

"I don't know why that security guard got her weave all in a tangle. I was barely in the driver's seat for a hot minute. But look." She turns her phone toward me. "Sherry got the photo!"

I see the snapshot, which Wavonne has already posted to Facebook with the caption: "Check out my ride!"

"I've gotten fifteen likes already."

"I hope your Facebook likes are worth all the trouble you caused. If we weren't with the show, they would have kicked us out of here."

"Maybe not worth fifteen likes, but I bet I'll have over a hundred in the next hour or so—that might be worth a Sweet Tea meal or two," Wavonne says as we walk into the museum café. Once inside, I take a moment to breathe in the fragrant air and all but forget about Wavonne's offense.

"It smells some kind of wonderful in here." I take in the expansive cafeteria as the scent of various spices, simmering brisket, and fresh baked breads and cakes fills the space.

"Buttermilk fried chicken!" Wavonne calls out, looking in the direction of the Agricultural South station. "I think I see some biscuits and macaroni and cheese calling my name, too," she adds as we get closer to the counter. "Braised rabbit, Hoppin' John, slow-cooked collard greens. I may just have to see if the fried chicken and collard greens here are better than yours."

"You say that like it's even a possibility," I quip with a laugh. "Let's check out the other stations before we order."

Wavonne falls in step with me, and we tour the three other stations. I can feel my mouth watering as we take in the gulf shrimp and stone-ground grits from the Creole Coast station . . . and the oyster pan roast from the North States counter . . . and the braised short ribs and skillet cornbread at the Western Range stall. The four stations are a haven of traditional African American cuisine—catfish po' boys, candied yams, smoked haddock and corn croquettes, smothered turkey grillades, and some very interesting empanadas made with black-eyed peas, corn, and chanterelle mushrooms. I find myself wanting to try all of it, but I end up going with the croquettes, some collard greens, and a nice serving of macaroni and cheese while Wavonne partakes of the fried chicken, candied yams, baked beans, and cornbread.

"Do you see the others?" I ask Wavonne while I grab a couple of iced teas, putting one on my tray and one on hers.

"Yeah. They are over there in the corner, underneath that photo of Ben's Chili Bowl."

I look toward an imposing image of Ben's Chili Bowl, a

decades-old DC restaurant (a bit of a dive really) known for its chili dogs, half smokes, and milk shakes. It's been in business for more than fifty years and has become a revered DC institution. Underneath the picture, I see Cynthia and Russell sitting at the middle of a long table. Vera is seated across from Sherry on one side, and Twyla is next to Trey on the other.

"Okay. Let's pay with those vouchers Cynthia gave us and join the gang."

"I know you've lost your mind, if you think we're sittin' down without going to the dessert counter."

"Dessert counter?"

Wavonne points behind me and, honestly, I'm not sure how I missed it—it's like an island of confections rising from the tile floor—red velvet cupcakes, banana pudding, little chocolate Bundt cakes, mini sweet-potato pies, lemon tarts with fresh blackberries, chocolate pudding—it's dessert overload.

I take in all the treats. "I want one of everything."

"One? I want *three* of everything. Hell, maybe I'll hitch the whole bar to the back of Chuck's Cadillac and drive it on outta here."

I chuckle and settle on the banana pudding.

"We've been walking all morning . . . burnin' calories. Why not?" Wavonne says as she takes two desserts—one of the little pies and a cupcake.

"That's quite a trayful," Twyla says to me as Wavonne and I place our food on the table and sit down with the rest of the gang. "A moment on the lips. A lifetime on the hips."

"Ain't nothin' wrong with Halia's big ole birthin' hips," Wavonne says. "They're nice advertisin' for Sweet Tea . . . means the food's good."

I'm not sure if I should thank Wavonne for her words of

defense or give her a smack on the back of the head, so I don't say anything. I just watch as Twyla leans in toward Trey.

"Try this, love," she says to him, lifting a forkful of grits to his mouth.

"Did she just call him 'love'?" Wavonne whispers to me.

We both try not to cringe as Trey lets her put the fork in his mouth, but I hear a faint "Ewe," from Wavonne.

"Delicious, right?" she says in a way that makes it seem like she is talking about more than just the grits.

Another slightly audible "Ewe" comes from Wavonne before we spend the next half hour or so making small talk with the group while trying to enjoy our lunch, which is no easy task given how Twyla continues to fondle Trey while the poor guy tries to eat. Fortunately for us onlookers, he politely declines her second attempt to feed him off her fork, but that does not stop her from leaning against him through half the meal and occasionally managing to touch his hand or upper arm while she talks.

I find myself grateful for a break in Twyla and Trey's little PG-13 performance of *The Graduate* when Leon enters the café, followed by some of the lighting and sound guys. The cameras were on us throughout the morning, but it seems like, just now, they are bringing out the big light fixtures and a team of production technicians.

Cynthia stands up as Leon and his team enter the area of the café roped off for us. "Okay, folks, it's show time. Please sit up straight . . . boobies up, chins down. Don't look directly at the camera. Look at Leon and just follow his instructions."

"I ain't got no problem lookin' at Leon. I just finished one tasty dish"—Wavonne looks at her empty plate—"but that don't mean I'm not up for another."

Wavonne's cackle is met with serious side eye from Cynthia. "Save it for when the cameras are rolling, Wavonne," she scolds before addressing the crew. "Roll cameras."

One of the cameramen says, "Speed."

"That's to let Cynthia know that the cameras are not lagging," Twyla says to us. "I'm familiar with all the lingo from doing *Twyla's Tips, Tricks, and Tidbits* for so long."

A young woman in jeans and a T-shirt steps in front of what appears to be the main camera. "*Elite Chef*, episode twelve, scene one," she says, and clacks the lever down on a slate board.

"Action."

"Welcome back," Leon says to the camera. "As you've seen, it's been a busy morning for our gang of contestants and judges here at the National Museum of African American History and Culture. They've toured the building, learned a lot about history and each other, and just finished a hearty lunch here at the museum café." He pauses, takes a breath, and raises his voice. "I don't know about you viewers at home, but after all that, I think it's time we get down to business! We have three contestants left. The dashing, debonair, and sometimes difficult Trey McIntyre; the beautiful, busty, and bubbly Sherry Ashbury; and last but not least, the sassy, shrewd, and, dare we say, softhearted Vera Ward."

A separate camera zooms in on each one of the contestants as Leon introduces them.

"We have something very special in store for the final three—a challenge that fits the locale . . . a challenge that will test their resourcefulness and creativity." Leon's voice continues to get louder and deeper, but at the same time, he's speaking more slowly, as if he's building up to some grand announcement.

"He remind anyone else of Effie Trinket from *The Hunger Games*?" Wavonne mutters.

Her comment garners a few giggles before Leon continues. "Today we are going to task Sherry, Trey, and Vera with what may be their toughest *Elite Chef* activity to date." Leon looks away from the camera toward the final three. He takes another breath and dramatically asks, "Ladies and gentleman, are you ready?"

Chapter 15

"Okay, folks," Cynthia says as the camera guys take a break. "Sherry, Trey, Vera, I want you guys up here." She directs them to three chairs at the front of the little area we have roped off in the café. "Halia, I'd like you and Wavonne to take a seat at that table." She points toward the table next to the one at which Wavonne and I are seated. She then instructs Twyla to move to the table on the other side. It appears Russell is staying put.

Cynthia then indicates to the crew that she is ready for filming to start again, and a young man on the production team wheels a large, flat screen TV behind Leon. We go through the whole "roll cameras, speed, clapper board" thing before Leon gets going again. "As you viewers at home might have noticed, the museum café is divided into four stations, each representing a distinct region of the country: the Agricultural South, the Creole Coast, the North States, and the Western Range," he says, standing in front of Sherry, Trey, and Vera. There is one camera on him, one on the contestants, and one behind all of us catching some other angles. "We have three tickets in this *toque blanche*." Leon lifts a white chef's hat from the table in front of him and displays it for the camera. "Each one lists a, what you might call, *humdrum* American food staple from one of the regions represented here today. . . . Sherry, Trey, Vera . . ." Leon looks at the three of them with wide eyes, like he's about to send them off to Afghanistan to fight the Taliban. "In a moment you will have an opportunity to draw from the hat. It will then be your job to reinvent the 'oh-so-ordinary' food item listed on your ticket . . . jazz it up . . . give it a 'wow factor.' As I mentioned earlier, there are four regions represented here today, but only three of you. So, we asked Gina Marshall, our first *Elite Chef* winner, to take one of the regions, the Western Range, along with a commonplace food choice, and whip up a little something fantastic to give you some inspiration. Let's go to Gina in New York."

The flat screen behind Leon comes alive and an attractive young woman in full chef's attire appears. From the background you can see she's in a commercial kitchen.

"Hello, contestants!" Gina says. "I hear you're down to one of the final challenges. Believe me, I know how that feels, but hang tight and try to enjoy the ride. I was in your shoes this time two years ago, and no one was more surprised than me when I won the title of Elite Chef and the once in a lifetime opportunity to run the kitchen here at the Barbary in the capital of the world, Manhattan! If it can happen for me, it can happen for any one of you." She pauses for a moment, and I begin to wonder if she is coming to us live via Facetime or Skype, or if the whole thing was prerecorded. "So, when my boss and owner of the Barbary, Mr. Russell Mellinger, the man that made all this happen for me, asked that I prepare a little something to help motivate you guys for today's competition, of course I agreed. I was assigned the Western Range, and get this: *trout fish sticks* as apparently trout, while in streams and lakes all over the country now, is native to waters west of the Rocky Mountains. Who knew. Right?" she asks with a big smile. "How does one reinvent fish sticks?" She throws her hands up in the air as if she'd been tasked with the impossible. "And how do I make them contemporary and interesting? All I knew about fish sticks is that you usually remove them from the freezer, pop them in the oven, and hope they don't taste too processed and bland by the time you take them out. But then I thought of these lovely fish cakes I used to make with salmon when I worked in a restaurant in Anchorage. I figured with a little reworking I could prepare them with trout instead of salmon and shape them into sticks rather than patties. Next thing I knew, I was mincing some fillets in the food processor . . . adding some onion, bread crumbs, eggs . . . a little mustard and mayonnaise and Worcestershire sauce—*everything* is better with some Worcestershire sauce. After a pinch of salt and a few dashes of parsley, chives, and dill, I shaped the whole kit and caboodle into sticks, rolled them in some panko bread crumbs, and fried them in olive oil."

The camera filming Gina in New York pans to a plate stacked with her creations. And, I must say, they do look like they would be quite tasty.

"Not bad, right?" Gina says as the camera zooms out to include both her and the plate of crunchy fried goodies. "But they needed a little something to go with them, so I mixed up a remoulade sauce with mayonnaise, mustard, and some spices."

Gina lifts a fish stick from the plate, dips it in the sauce, and raises it to her mouth. "So, there you go. I hope I've given you a little inspiration for today's challenge. Good luck!" She takes a bite out of her fish stick, and I wonder no more if she is coming to us live. The intense crunch sound coming from the speaker as she bites into the fish stick was clearly added in post-production.

"Didn't give me much inspiration," Trey says as the video fades out. "She essentially rolled some fish cakes into sticks and made the simplest of sauces to go with it. *Yawn*," he adds, folding his arms over his chest and slouching down in his chair.

"They didn't look much better than what you'd get out of a box of Gordon's from Safeway," comments Sherry. "And I thought the Barbary was in New York, but she said she was in Manhattan. Huh."

"I don't know, they looked okay to me," Vera offers. "Maybe not all that creative, but they looked flavorful . . . and nice and crispy. I think the three of us can do better though."

"I guess we are about to find out." Leon excitedly extends the chef's hat to Vera. "Please select your ticket."

Vera retrieves a slip of paper from the hat and unfolds it. " 'Cheese has long been an American staple but is most deeply rooted in the northern states," she says, reading off the ticket. " 'The earliest dairy farms were in the Rhode Island, Connecticut, and Massachusetts colonies. The first large-scale cheese production was started by Jesse Williams in Rome, New York. And, today, Wisconsin has claimed the title of the largest cheese-producing state in the United States, turning out more than three billion pounds of cheese a year.

" 'Your assignment is: the Northern States, grilled cheese, Russell.' " Vera lifts her head and looks at Leon. "Russell?"

"Oh!" Leon feigns surprise. "Did I forget to mention that each ticket also has the name of a judge on it."

"Yes. Yes, you did," Vera replies, playing along.

"I'm so sorry. Let me explain." Leon moves from mock surprise to mock remorse. "Each of the contestants will get a ten-minute consultation or coaching session with the judge whose name is on their ticket. So, Vera, you have a few minutes before we start the challenge to garner some guidance and advice from Russell about giving your grilled cheese a little zing."

Vera seems pleased with her selection and nods at Leon as he moves on to Sherry, who reaches into the hat and grabs a ticket.

" 'Pork, and ham in particular, has always been an important ingredient in Creole cuisine. Who doesn't love Creole Pecan Glazed Ham or Creole Ham, Sausage, and Shrimp Jambalaya . . . or Creole Bourbon Beans And Ham. Your assignment is: the Creole Coast, ham sandwich, Halia.' " Sherry turns toward me, and I can see one of the cameras moving in my direction to capture my reaction to the pairing. "Yay!" she says, all smiles while giving me a double thumbs-up with her hands.

I force a smile back, hoping I didn't audibly sigh when I heard my name. Sherry is very nice, and definitely more pleasant to be around than Trey, but I'm not sure I can really coach or advise her on cooking . . . on *anything* really. I suspect it will be like trying to teach a fish how to climb a tree.

"Your turn, Trey," Leon says. "By process of elimination I guess we know your region and your judge." I see Twyla's eyes light up as the word "judge" leaves his mouth. "But let's find out what food choice you've been assigned."

Trey pulls the remaining slip of paper from the hat. " 'They've been called 'the cement that holds the South together.' Southerners love them. Northerners can take them or leave them . . . mostly leave them. Grits are a breakfast staple below the Mason-Dixon line and more than 85 million pounds a year are sold in the American South. Your assignment is: The Agricultural South, grits, Twyla." The corners of his mouth turn downward. He's clearly less than thrilled about the words on the piece of paper before him, but it's unclear if his annoyance is with his assigned region, his assigned food, or his assigned judge. "Not a lot to work with there, but I guess I will have to make do."

"So, there you have it," Leon says to the camera. "Sherry, Trey, and Vera have their assignments, and now it's up to them to turn some very lackluster food choices into something inventive and fun . . . and, of course, *delicious*." He turns his attention back to the three contestants. "So, as part of this episode, we have a new name for your little trio: the Thrifty Three. 'Why?' you ask." Leon pauses as one of the cameras pans across Sherry, Trey, and Vera. "Because, for this challenge, you will not have access to the *Elite Chef* pantry—for *this* challenge, we are sending you to the grocery store . . . and we're putting you on a budget."

A camera again zooms across the contestants' faces, getting their displeased reactions.

"Shortly, we'll be transporting you to a local grocer and each of you will be allotted a total of thirty dollars to buy all the ingredients you'll need for your competition entry," Leon says to what is now dubbed the Thrifty Three, but I'm not sure any of them are listening at this point. I think they're all inside their heads, thinking about recipes and the price of flour and cheese and ham. "But first, let's have you pair up with your assigned judge at the tables behind you for a quick culinary powwow."

Leon directs Sherry, Trey, and Vera toward the tables behind them where Russell, Twyla, and Wavonne and I are seated.

"How fun! I'm so glad I got you two!" Sherry pulls out a chair across from me and Wavonne while Trey and Vera take seats at the two other tables. "So, I'm thinking maybe I should do some sort of deep-fried sandwich . . . some thick-cut white bread . . . a little ham . . . a little cheese . . . dunk it in some batter . . . fry it up nice and crisp. You know, like a Monte Carlo."

"I think you mean a Monte Cristo," I correct, and try not to groan.

"Ain't nothin' wrong with a Monte Cristo," Wavonne says, sensing my apprehension with Sherry's idea.

"No. Not at all," I reply. "I like a nice deep-fried sandwich as much as the next person, but perhaps we can come up with something a bit more creative."

"Like?" Sherry asks.

"We make these lovely biscuits at Sweet Tea. I call them Salty Sweet Cheese Nips."

"Salty. Sweet. Cheese," Sherry recites. "You've got my attention."

"I use my grandmommy's drop biscuit recipe as the base and add a little cheddar cheese to the dough. After I bake them, I brush them with some melted butter, sprinkle them heavily with salt, and top them with a few oversized sugar crystals."

"She essentially ripped off Red Lobster's Cheddar Bay biscuits," Wavonne says to Sherry.

"I did not! Grandmommy was making her biscuits long before Red Lobster even existed."

"They sound really good, but I'm not sure I get the ham sandwich connection."

"You could use biscuits instead of regular bread for the sandwich. Just slice them in half and place the ham in the middle . . . or, better yet, maybe you can chop the ham and mix it right in with the dough. Then you could make a nice flavored butter or jelly to go with the biscuits."

"You know what would be good on them?" Wavonne asks. "That pineapple–red pepper jelly you made a few weeks ago."

"That would go quite nicely."

"I like the biscuit idea . . . and the jelly, but do you think I can do all that with thirty dollars?"

"A small thing of flour will run you about three dollars . . . a bag of shredded cheese will be another three. Garlic powder can be kind of expensive—I'd factor in at least five dollars for that. I like to use sour cream to hold it all together . . . that will be another two or three bucks. Factor in at least another ten for sugar and salt . . . and, of course, butter."

"That's twenty-four dollars right there."

"See what I mean about Wavonne not being stupid?" I ask Sherry.

"You learn to add numbers quickly in your head when you're at the salon with fifty dollars getting a wet set . . . and want to know if you're gonna have enough left over for a mani-pedi and an eyebrow wax," Wavonne says. "The answer is 'no,' in case you're interested."

"How much are pineapples these days?" I ask, starting to think about the jelly.

"I don't know," Sherry says. "I think you can get one for about three bucks."

"You'll also need a red bell pepper and a lemon . . . some cornstarch . . . and some pineapple juice. All that may throw you over budget. If it does, just buy some honey—you can mix it with the leftover butter for a nice spread." I grab some paper and a pen at the table. "Let's make a list." I start jotting a few things down. That's when I notice Wavonne looking at me with a smirk on her face.

"What?"

"Nothin'" she says. "I'm just getting a kick outta watchin' you do what you do best—take over."

"I'm not taking over," I protest, but the words are barely off my lips when I realize that I am actually doing just that.

I've done it since I was a little girl. Even in elementary school my friends called me "bossy," but as Momma always said, I just had "strong leadership skills." My take charge nature has served me well over the years, and I doubt I'd be running a highly successful restaurant if I didn't have a certain amount of assertiveness, but my role in this situation is supposed to be one of coach and mentor. Sherry is the contestant, not me. "Okay, maybe you're right," I admit, and turn to Sherry. "I didn't mean to commandeer your challenge. Perhaps we should go with your idea for a Monte Cristo."

"Oh please . . . commandeer all you want. Your biscuit idea was much better than mine," Sherry assures. "Why don't we get back to making a list, and then you can go over your recipe with me."

I write out the ingredients for my recipe for Salty Sweet Cheese Nips. I'm about to add the preparation instructions when Leon pipes up. "Okay, folks! That's all the time we have. Contestants, gather up the grocery lists you made and follow me."

"I wish I had time to write down the instructions for you." I hand her the piece of paper that spells out everything she needs to make the biscuits, but nothing about the preparation.

"Thank you." Sherry takes the list from me. "I'll figure it out."

I watch Sherry join up with Vera and Trey and follow Leon toward the café exit.

"I'm not too optimistic about the girl who thought filet mignon was a fish 'figuring out' my recipe."

"I'm not too optimistic about her being able to *read* your recipe."

I laugh. "It's not a complex dish and anything with enough

cheese and butter is bound to be good. I can't imagine she could screw it up," I rationalize. "But, then again, I didn't think there was a grown woman out there who doesn't know Manhattan is part of New York City. I guess all we can do is hope for the best."

Chapter 16

"I could get used to this," Wavonne says. "I feel like a celebrity bein' driven around town in the back seat of a Lexus."

"It's definitely an upgrade from my ramshackle van," I reply.

We just left the museum. After the contestants were taken to whatever grocery store paid a fee to get showcased on *Elite Chef*, we took in a few more of the exhibits and filmed a little interview segment that will be used to introduce Wavonne and me at the beginning of the episode. We're barely out of the city and across the Maryland line when our driver exits the interstate and takes us a few miles down the local highway. We drive by the glittery attractions at National Harbor—the Capital Wheel Ferris wheel, the massive MGM resort and casino, the Gaylord Convention Center, a slew of overpriced restaurants with river views—and make a right onto a side road. We pass a couple of shopping centers and a 7-Eleven before the road becomes more residential. The further we proceed, the tract houses on small lots start to give way to more stately homes on several acres. It's not long before we approach a wide, secluded driveway flanked by decorative stone pillars, each one outfitted with an elaborately carved sign that reads WILLOW OAK INN. An assortment of flowers around the base of the structures provide waves of color offering a cheerful welcome to the property.

"Looks like they are still working on the landscaping," I say as we see some workmen planting shrubbery along the driveway.

"They did say the place has only had a . . . what did they call it? A *lazy* opening?"

"A *soft* opening," I correct as the main building comes into view, and we whirl around into the circular drive in front of a quaint three-story building, clearly designed to have a rustic feel and complement the wooded area that surrounds it. The facade, a mix of gray stones and pale planks of wood, looms underneath a slanted roof the color of clay. An abundance of large picture windows and sliding doors that open to patios or balconies break through the natural exterior. A breezeway connects the main hotel to a one-story building encased almost entirely in glass. The words SUNFISH BY RUSSELL MELLINGER are tastefully etched into the glass.

"I guess that's Russell's new restaurant."

"Yes. I think Trudy said they plan to open soon."

Wavonne and I step out of the car onto a pattern of intricately laid bricks, and the driver removes our bags from the trunk.

"May I take them in for you?" he asks.

"No thank you," I say. This is my first experience being chauffeured around in a company-hired car, so I have no idea if tipping is appropriate, but I give him a few bucks anyway. "They're small. We can manage them."

As we approach the hotel entrance, I can smell the sea air, but it's not until we walk into the lobby that I see the grand view of the Potomac River. We emerge through the main doors to the sight of floor-to-ceiling windows along the back wall of a reception area that showcases what appears to be a not-quite-finished swimming pool at the top of a hillside that rolls into a stunning view of the river.

"I honestly did not know that such tranquility existed this close to the city," I say to Wavonne as we stop to admire a mix of grass and trees and flowing water—things that start to seem somewhat elusive when you spend the bulk of your life tooling around Washington, DC, and its densely populated suburbs.

"It is quite nice, isn't it? That's one of the perks of my job—I get to look at this view all day," a young man behind the counter says to us. "You're with the show?"

"Yes. Halia Watkins, and this is Wavonne."

"Welcome. I'm Mitchell Long, the hotel manager. We have a room ready for you on the concierge level—this level actually. It's the only one with rooms ready for occupancy. The rooms upstairs are still getting their finishing touches."

"Yes, we heard the hotel was open but not quite ready for prime time just yet," I reply, and take another look around. The lobby has the feel of a mountain lodge with lots of rustic paneling, exposed wooden beams, and skylights in the high ceiling. There's a grand fireplace encased in stone and a plethora of dark leather sofas and chairs. To my right is the breezeway that connects the hotel to the restaurant, and to my left is a long hallway, lined with doors, one of which I assume will open up to our room for the night.

"It looks like somewhere they'd film a Hallmark movie," Wavonne says. "Maybe a big city girl comes with plans to tear the inn down but falls in love with the hotel handyman and decides to keep it open."

"Or the inn's owned by her family, and her parents want her to take it over, but she wants to stay at the big New York law firm . . . but she runs into an old high school flame—"

"Who wears flannel . . . They always wear flannel."

"Of course. And she falls in love with Mr. Flannel and decides to stay," I say. "And maybe there's an orchard or a vineyard that needs saving. . . ."

"But it can only be saved by pretty white people," Wavonne says with a laugh. "Maybe one of us could be Candace Cameron or Lacey Chabert's black friend who gets four minutes of airtime."

"I think Kim Fields has a monopoly on those roles," I say. We're both quite amused with ourselves as Mitchell looks on, waiting for his chance to get a word in.

"Maybe not via a Hallmark movie," I say to him. "But I guess this place is going to get on TV, right?"

"I'm sure Mr. Mellinger will make sure we get plenty of exposure on the show, once it's fully camera ready. You do know we're still under construction, right?"

"Yes, Russell said the official grand opening would not be for a few weeks but, looking around, there does not seem to be much left to do."

"Not on this floor. Mr. Mellinger made sure the first floor was ready for guests before the show started taping. He and Mrs. Mellinger have been staying in the presidential suite since they began filming and the contestants have rooms just down the hall from them."

"The presidential suite is on the first floor?"

"Yes. I know, it's on the top level of most, but for this property, it made sense to place it on the first level so it—and all the concierge-level rooms—could have a spacious patio right off the pool rather than a balcony. It's just one of many ways that Willow Oak is unique. We expect to be the choice for exclusive travelers who want a more intimate lodging experience. Mr. Mellinger didn't have the option of building a big tower, so our whole marketing approach is to bill ourselves as the preferred alternative to the over-sized, impersonal hotels over at National Harbor."

"Why couldn't he build a big hotel?"

"Actually, he had trouble building anything at all here. He had a very difficult time acquiring this land for any sort of commercial use. We're in a rural preservation zone, and it took all sorts of wheeling and dealing to secure the approvals and permits. That's why Willow Oak has such a rustic feel. The county board . . . or council . . . or whatever insisted that the building top out at three floors, and that the exterior be made of only wood and natural stone. The board has been trying to lure more upscale businesses to the county for years—you don't get much more upscale than a Russell Mellinger restaurant. So when he was scouting locations in the area for his latest hospitality venture, they did what they could to woo him. They agreed to let him develop protected land, so long as he agreed to construct buildings that would not distract from the natural scenery, and I think he offered to make some investments in the neighboring Fort Washington Park, and hire county residents like myself to staff the resort . . . things like that."

"Sounds like a win-win for Russell and the county."

"Yes. At least it should be once we're fully up and running. As you can see, the pool is still under construction, the rooms on the upper levels are being finalized, and, of course, the restaurant has a way to go before it's ready to seat any diners."

"The restaurant must be somewhat finished, right? We're filming in there shortly, aren't we?" I ask. "I thought that's where all the challenges have taken place."

"The network has outfitted the dining room with cooking stations for the contest, so at the moment it's a mess of cables and hoses and lighting equipment. Once the show is done filming, the contractor will start to lay the carpet and bring in the tables and artwork."

"I wonder if that was the contractor I heard Mr. Mellinger yelling at on the phone the other night."

"Hard to know. Mr. Mellinger yells at everyone. He does not like delays, so the lead contractor, more than anyone, has been getting an earful lately. He and his team have been working really long hours to make sure this place is finished down to the last detail in a few weeks."

"Complete or not, I can tell this place is gonna put the swank in swanky," Wavonne says.

Mitchell laughs. "On that note, here are your key cards." He points to his right. "Your room is just down there . . . first door on your right after you pass the concierge lounge and the presidential suite."

"Concierge lounge?" Wavonne says. "We need to get a photo of me in there for Instagram."

"We serve breakfast in there in the mornings, and there are snacks and a full tended bar available in the evenings. It used to get pretty lively in there at night when we had a bigger group here. But most of the show's contestants have been sent home, so it's been pretty quiet lately."

"Come on, Halia," Wavonne says. "Let's get that photo. I can't wait for all those jealous heifers to see me in the concierge lounge at Russell Mellinger's hotel. Linda thought she was all that with her pictures at the pope's table at Buca di Beppo . . . and let's just see if Melva keeps braggin' about that stupid Carnival cruise she's goin' on for her honeymoon."

"Fine," I say. "Let's drop our bags in the room first."

"Let me get those for you," Mitchell says. "Our bell staff hasn't started yet."

Wavonne and I begin to follow Mitchell to our room, when Twyla emerges from the hallway into the lobby.

"Hello," she says to me and Wavonne. "I was just freshening up a little bit before we start part two." She looks at me and then Wavonne. "Something I'm guessing you two have not done yet?"

I'm about to respond to her rude assumption when I see a large, black SUV pull up in front of the hotel. The passenger door flings open, and I see Cynthia step out. Sherry, Trey, and Vera file out of the back seat and walk around to the rear of the vehicle and start grabbing grocery bags.

"Ladies," Cynthia calls, poking her head through the hotel doorway. "I need you three in the restaurant. There are a few things I want to go over with you before we start taping. Now, please."

"Now?" Wavonne asks. "I was going to switch out my wig and touch up my makeup."

"No time for that," Cynthia calls, stepping back, letting the door close, and regrouping with the contestants outside.

"Better do what the boss's wife says," Mitchell suggests. "I'll take your bags to your room."

"Wait, wait," Wavonne says as Mitchell reaches for her suitcase. "Let me get in there for a second. I need my makeup bag and my wig comb. I've got to touch up all this," she adds, waving her hand from her chin up to the top of her hair, "before we go on TV."

"You look fine."

"Looking *fine* is your thing, Halia. I want to look fabulous."

"I don't think we have time for fabulous, Wavonne," I say. "Cynthia wants us in the restaurant now."

"That's fine. I can multitask and reapply my makeup while she talks to us."

"I think you should give her your full attention, Wavonne. She may have something important to tell us."

"Halia, in high school I used to hot comb my hair, put on my face, and paint my nails durin' first period algebra—I think I can handle a little touchin' up while Cynthia goes over a few things with us. And don't think I didn't learn my algebra either. Just yesterday I figured, if I was averagin' eighteen percent in tips, I needed $888 worth of checks if I was gonna get the $160 I need for those Dolce sunglasses I've been eyein'."

"Maybe I underestimated you, Wavonne."

"Crap. This isn't my makeup," she says, looking into the bag she retrieved from her luggage. "This is my bag of Pringles and Cheez-its in case I get hungry later."

"Then again . . ." I say softly as she scurries down the hall toward Mitchell, "maybe not."

Chapter 17

After Wavonne switches out her bag of salty snacks for her makeup kit, we exit the lobby and walk through the breezeway that connects to the restaurant.

"Wow," I say when we come through the entrance to Sunfish. We're clearly in what will be the main dining room—there's textured beige paper on the walls, squares of smooth oak tiles on the ceiling, and four eye-catching chandeliers hanging overhead.

"They're gorgeous. Aren't they?" Cynthia notices me eyeing the sizable chandeliers made from slats of curved wood bound by dark copper rings. "We had them custom made from the wood of wine barrels."

"Yes. Very chic," I say. "But they don't quite go with all of this." I gesture to the metal counters, makeshift stove tops, sinks, and mixers scattered about. "Are those countertop convection ovens?"

"Yes. We're equipped with everything the contestants need for the challenges."

"I'm assuming, unless this is the most bizarre restaurant ever, that there is a kitchen somewhere. Why aren't we filming in there?" As I ask this I take another look around at what appears to be three stations, each outfitted with a large metal counter stocked with all sorts of supplies and cooking utensils, a sink, a few burners, an oven, and half a dozen small appliances . . . can openers, mixers, blenders, etc. "Oh, I get it. The kitchen is not big enough for this whole . . . this whole production."

"Exactly," Cynthia says. "We need space for all the equipment and then room for the cameras to move about. So we did the build-out here in the dining room."

"Well, I can tell it's going to be a lovely space when it's finished."

"It will be. We wrap filming in a few days, and then we'll lay the floors, start the booth installations, and get the tables and chairs in here. And we commissioned some wonderful artwork for the walls. We expect everything to be in place shortly after we wrap the show for the season."

"And one of those three," I say, nodding my head in the general direction of Sherry, Trey, and Vera as they unpack their groceries, "will be the new executive chef here?"

"Yes. Speaking of which," Cynthia says. "We need to get things rolling. Why don't you take a seat over there with Twyla and Russell."

Cynthia points toward a long table outfitted with three microphones—it looks like something Simon Cowell should be sitting behind with Paula Abdul and Randy Jackson. She follows us as we approach the table and take our seats. Wavonne and I are to the left of Russell, and Twyla is to his right. Both Russell and Twyla are talking on their cell phones.

"Sit tight for a few minutes. We'll get started shortly. You'll spend most of the evening right here observing as the contestants prepare their dishes."

While Wavonne touches up her makeup, I sit back and watch the scene in front of me. The production setup in here is much more sophisticated than at the museum. There are cameras and lighting equipment...and people everywhere. While teams of folks are moving things around, adjusting fixtures, and testing microphones, a young woman with what looks like a tool belt around her waist appears at the table. Only instead of screwdrivers and wrenches, her belt is lined with makeup brushes and tubes of concealer and foundation. Without a word, she begins to apply some of her lotions and potions to Russell's face while he continues to yammer on his phone.

"Oh honey, no," Wavonne says to her. "He'll be creasing in no time with that. We're about the same complexion. Use this." She tries to hand the young lady an elegant-looking glass jar with a shiny metal lid. "Glossier Stretch Concealer."

The woman stares daggers at Wavonne. "Everything I put on Mr. Mellinger's face has been carefully evaluated. Neither he nor I are interested in your drugstore paraphernalia."

"Drugstore? I paid eighteen dollars for this at Sephora."

Russell's makeup artist ignores Wavonne's comment and is barely finished with his face when another woman appears, sprays something on his head, and begins brushing his hair with a big square brush.

"Do you people know nothing?" Wavonne says to the second woman. "That brush leads to split end city. Try my tangle buster." Wavonne pulls the most bizarre-looking hairbrush I've ever seen from her bag. It looks more like a spiked paddle than a grooming device.

"Forgive me if I don't take hair advice from a woman wearing a dime-store wig," the stylist says.

"Dime-store wig?" Wavonne turns to me. "These heifers are mean up in here," she laments. "But she's right. It is a cheap wig. I had planned to switch it out. I was saving my good wig for tonight. I think I'm gonna run back to the room and swap out Gladys for Earnestine."

"You leave Earnestine in her box. We're about to get started."

Russell is still barking at someone on his phone as the woman tending to his hair gives it a final coif and teeters off. He'll never be eye candy, but the makeup artist and hair stylist have made him look . . . well . . . "less unattractive" is about the nicest description I can come up with. I saw the same ladies tending to Leon when we came into the restaurant. I guess it's safe to assume that he and Russell are the only ones getting some professional styling. The rest of us— me, Wavonne, Twyla, and the contestants—apparently, are on our own.

"Okay, folks, quiet on the set. Places everyone. Places," Cynthia calls out as the overhead lights dim.

Some cameramen scatter about, there's a clack on the slate board, and a spotlight comes alive with its beam directed toward Leon. "Welcome back to the *Elite Chef* semifinals," he says, looking at the camera in front of him. "We're coming to you from Russell Mellinger's newest dining spot, Sunfish, the signature restaurant at his soon to be opened hotel, the Willow Oak Inn in Fort Washington, Maryland.

"As you saw earlier, we spent the morning touring the African American museum and, after a tasty lunch in the museum café, our Thrifty Three were given their challenges, put on a thirty-dollar budget, and whisked off to a local grocer to buy whatever they needed for their entry." Leon pauses for a moment and takes a breath. "The stakes are high tonight. We're down to just three contenders for a fifty-thousand-dollar cash prize, a career-defining position to lead culinary operations right here at Sunfish . . . and, of course, the coveted title of Elite Chef." The lights come on over Sherry, Trey, and Vera and their three cooking stations. "Let's check in with our contestants and see what they have in store for us this evening."

Leon walks over to Sherry's station. "Sherry. You were tasked with reinventing a plain ole ham sandwich. What are your plans for making a ham sandwich into something everyone will be talking about by the watercooler tomorrow?"

"I'm making some drop biscuits filled with bits of honey ham and cheddar cheese. When they come out of the oven I'll brush them with some salted butter and top them with oversized sugar crystals . . . the whole salty sweet thing."

"What are these for?" Leon points to the pineapple and red peppers.

"Every biscuit needs a spread, Leon," Sherry says. "I'm going to whip up a pineapple–red pepper jelly to go on the biscuits."

"That sounds like heaven on a plate."

"I hope so," Sherry replies, still managing to look beautiful with her hair pulled back into a ponytail and a chef's coat mollifying her curves. And, just when I think how nice it is that she got through her introduction without sounding like a half-wit, she says, "I figured some pineapple would be a good addition since those voodoo Creole ladies wore them on their heads."

"Did they?" Leon asks. "I'm not sure about that, but whatever the motivation for preparing it, pineapple–red pepper jelly sure sounds good."

Leon moves on to Trey's station. "How about you, Trey. I see grits and eggs . . . and sweet potatoes. What do you have in the works?"

"I'll be preparing a sweet potato–grits soufflé."

"Very interesting. Can't wait to see how that turns out," Leon offers, and saunters over to Vera. "And, Vera, we're excited to see your take on the classic grilled cheese. You've pulled out the waffle iron. I'm intrigued."

Vera laughs. "I'm going to prepare a grilled cheese waffle with avocado and bacon."

Leon starts riffling through the ingredients on Vera's counter. "I see bacon and flour and sugar, but I don't see any cheese."

"Sherry over there"—Vera waves to Sherry—"blew her budget on ham and fancy sugar crystals, so I agreed to share my cheese with her. We went in together on baking powder too."

Sherry holds up a brick of cheddar cheese and mouths the words, "Thank you," in Vera's direction.

"Great to see everyone playing so nice," Leon says. "And what are these for." He starts riffling through more containers on Vera's counter. "Soy sauce? Lemon? Hot sauce?"

"I'm shying away from your typical sweet breakfast waffle. I want it to be more savory and satisfying, so I'm adding a few creative ingredients."

Leon gives Vera a questionable look as if he thinks her ingredients might be a bit *too* creative before moving back to his original spot and talking directly to the television audience again. "So, there you have it. Our final three will get one hour to prepare a dish that makes our judges swoon. And, speaking of judges, let's give our panel another welcome." Some lights are cued to shine on me and the rest of the judges. "Of course, you all know our boss . . . leader . . . captain . . . the reason any of us are here, restaurateur and soon-to-be-hotelier extraordinaire, Russell Mellinger." Russell casually lifts his hand and offers a quick wave. "Next, we have local Washington, DC, culinary legend, owner of the city's top Cajun restaurant, Dauphine, and former host of *Twyla's Tips, Tricks, and Tidbits*, Ms. Twyla Harper." Twyla lights up with a big smile and blows a few kisses toward the camera. "And finally, we have the proprietor of Mahalia's Sweet Tea, Prince George's County's go-to dining establishment for authentic soul food, Ms. Mahalia Watkins, along with her lovely assistant, Wavonne Hix."

"Leon Winfield just called me lovely," Wavonne leans in and says to me as we both smile and wave at the camera.

"So now it's time to get down to business." Leon raises his voice. "Contestants, you have exactly sixty minutes to prep, cook, and finalize your entrée for presentation to the judges. Starting *now*!"

And just like that, a frenzy of activity begins—I see Vera measuring out dry ingredients and dumping them into a mixing bowl, Trey hurriedly cutting sweet potatoes, and Sherry grating cheese like her life depends on it.

"Why didn't she buy preshredded cheese?" Wavonne asks.

"You're asking this about the girl who was just talking about voodoo ladies wearing pineapples on their heads."

Leon walks around as a series of cameras move about, getting the action from multiple angles. He checks in with Trey, who says he'd rather bake the sweet potatoes but needs to chop them for boiling and faster cooking due to the time constraints. Vera laments about how she'd rather cream softened butter into her mix but has to melt it in the microwave to beat the clock. Sherry simply tells Leon she doesn't have time to talk if she's going to get her biscuits in the oven with enough time for them to bake before the buzzer goes off.

It's interesting to have a ring-side seat to all this frantic culinary commotion. Sherry finishes grating the cheese, quickly slaps a piece of ham on the cutting board, and begins chopping it into small pieces. While Trey hastily separates egg whites from the yolk, dumps them into a bowl, and starts to beat them with a hand mixer, Vera pulls slices of bacon from a package and places them in a frying pan. For the next several minutes all three of them are on the move—pots are boiling, mixers are spinning, ovens are preheating . . . and then *it* happens. Vera, who has just removed her crisp bacon from the pan, chopped her avocados, and mixed her waffle batter, walks over to Sherry's station, where she is busy dropping small mounds of biscuit dough infused with ham and cheese onto a cookie sheet.

You're done with the baking powder?" Vera asks, lifting the can of baking powder from the counter.

"It's all yours," Sherry replies.

"Thanks. Can I get my share of the cheese too?"

Sherry gasps, and her face drops. "Oh my God! I forgot!"

"Forgot what?" Vera asks.

"The cheese. I added all of it to my biscuit mix. I just wasn't thinking."

"What?!"

"I was in such a rush. I grated the cheese and just dumped it all into the batter."

"Well, dump some of it out!"

A second cameraman moves in, and two cameras are now on the ladies.

"I don't see how I can. It's all mixed in. I'm about to put the biscuits in the oven."

Vera looks at Sherry in silence, but there is rage boiling in her eyes.

"I'm so sorry. It was an accident. I swear!"

"How am I supposed to make a grilled cheese with *no* cheese?!" Vera shouts at Sherry. Then she turns toward Cynthia, who's off camera. "What am I supposed to do?"

"You'll have to make do with what you have."

Vera returns her gaze to Sherry and that old Heart song from the eighties, "If Looks Could Kill," starts playing in my head as the drama unfolds before my eyes.

"I *really* am sorry. It was a mistake."

Without saying a word, Vera continues to stare daggers at Sherry for another moment or two before turning on her heels and heading back to her station where she picks up a spoon and gives her waffle batter a stir. "So now I get to figure out how to make a grilled cheese with *no* freaken cheese," she says to the camera with a look of desperation and defeat on her face. It's hard to know if her eyes are swollen and her nose is red from the allergies she's been complaining about all day or if they are just a result of her culinary plans going by the wayside. Her eyes hold firm on the camera in front of her while her stirring morphs into more of a heavy whipping motion. "No cheese," she says, her expression becoming more vacant. "The grilled cheese that was going to be my ticket to an executive chef position and a fifty-thousand-dollar cash prize is not going to have any cheese in it." At this point, she is literally stabbing the bowl with the long wooden spoon. "While I'm at it, maybe I can whip up some cheese puffs with no cheese . . . and some macaroni and cheese with no cheese . . . and hey, why not an apple pie with no apples or a . . ." Vera's voice goes silent as something over at Trey's station seems to grab her attention. She lifts her eyes, from whatever she was looking at on Trey's counter, toward the ceiling, as if something of significance has just occurred to her. "An apple pie with no apples," she says again, with a completely different tone than when those words came out of her mouth a few seconds ago. Her vacant, bemused look has been replaced with a more hopeful expression—an expression that says, "Maybe . . . just maybe, I'm not quite out of the game yet."

Chapter 18

The next thirty minutes are full of hurry and bustle. All three chefs are racing around preparing their entries. My cohorts and I at the judging table watch as Sherry minces pineapple and red peppers in a food processor, and Trey pours his fluffy orange batter into ramekins for baking. But, truth be told, all of us seem to be mostly focusing on the whole "no-cheese grilled cheese" saga as we keep our eyes on Vera, trying to figure out what she has up her sleeve.

She managed to convince Trey to let her use one of his sweet potatoes, which she chopped into cubes and dunked into some boiling water. She has since removed them from the stove and, much like Sherry, is taking advantage of the food processor at her station. We look on as she adds some butter, lemon, and garlic to the pureed potatoes and places the whole shebang in a small pot on the stove to simmer.

As the Thrifty Three hurry about their work areas Cynthia approaches those of us at the judges's table and asks us to offer some commentary that they can work in to the final cut of the challenge. Russell and Twyla have television experience, so they offer their remarks with relative ease. I, on the other hand, find myself feeling awkward.

"I'm curious to see what Vera is doing with the sweet potato she borrowed from Trey," I say, feeling like I'm sounding lame. "I wonder—"

Cynthia interrupts me. "What do you think about Sherry using all the cheese? Accident? Or sabotage?" she asks dramatically.

"I'd like to think it was an accident. I mean we all know that Sherry . . ." I struggle with how to finish my sentence. Of course, a slew of tired sayings come to mind: Sherry is not the sharpest crayon in the box . . . dumber than a bag of hammers . . . all foam no beer. But I certainly don't want to say that some village is missing its idiot on national television, so I try to choose my words carefully. "We all know that Sherry . . . well, that Sherry . . ."

"What Halia's tryin' to say"—Wavonne cackles—"is that the only thing Sherry uses her head for is to hold the weave tracks. So it's—"

"That is *not* what I was trying to say," I interrupt. "It's just that Sherry is . . . She's more of a . . . more of a *doer* than a *thinker*." That's about the best way I could spin Sherry's intellect. "I believe it's quite possible that, in the moment, she just forgot that she owed half the cheese to Vera."

Cynthia goes on to prod me for more comments. I assume they will intersperse mine and the other judges' remarks with the footage they are currently gathering of the contestants racing to complete their entries. I come up with some nonsense to say about how I think Trey's sweet potato-grits soufflé is quite a creative idea, how I hope Vera is able to make the best of a difficult situation, and then I offer a few thoughts about Sherry—how the biscuits she's preparing are inspired by Sweet Tea's Salty Sweet Cheese Nips, and how popular they are at the restaurant. Hey, I may as well get a plug in for Sweet Tea where I can.

"We sell out every weekend," Wavonne says. This isn't really true as we don't actually *sell* them. They're complementary as part of our Sunday brunch service, but as Wavonne continues I realize she was just throwing some words out there so she could get on camera. "I know because I'm there . . . at Sweet Tea *every* weekend." She sits up straight and pushes her breasts forward. "Just in case any handsome single men . . . preferably with at least six-figure incomes, want to come by for some . . . some *nips*."

"Thank you for making my brunch biscuits sound vulgar, Wavonne," I bemoan, hoping her comment does not make it to air.

While Wavonne banters a bit more with Cynthia, and I think of how her brash comments and glittery appearance will likely get her more airtime than me (and how I'm perfectly fine with that), the timer hits the one-minute mark.

"One minute!" Leon calls out, and silence falls over the room as Trey, using pot holders, lifts his hot soufflés onto a large plate, Sherry removes her biscuits from a cookie sheet, and Vera spoons a velvety-looking orange sauce over her bacon-avocado waffle. "Thirty seconds!" he yells as the contestants wipe the edges of dishes and add a little garnish.

"Ten, nine, eight . . ."

The clock finally hits zero, and a loud buzzer goes off.

"Time's up!" Leon calls.

Sherry, Trey, and Vera cease movement and stand like soldiers at attention.

"Nice work, everyone. You had a tough task . . . not a lot of time or money to make something to wow our panel of judges," Leon says. "Trey, you are up first." Leon motions for Trey to approach our table with his creation. Trey does as he's directed and lays a serving dish with three ramekins down on the table. They look like desserts you might get at a classic French restaurant.

"So this was my spin on plain old grits," Trey says. "As a

classically trained French chef, I know a thing or two about soufflés, and I figured grits would lend themselves well to such a creation. But, as we all know, grits are pretty shy on flavor. I figured sweet potatoes would add a light touch of sweetness and give the dish some color. I added garlic and other seasonings, just a touch of hot sauce, and topped it off with a little lemon zest."

Leon motions for us to give it a try, so we each take a fork and dig in.

"Very nice," says Twyla after taking a bite. "Much like you, with the orange color and sprinkling of lemon zest, it has quite the visual appeal . . . and it's light and airy. Really well done." She gives Trey a long look. "I just want to eat it up," and your guess is as good as mine as to whether she is referring to the soufflé or to Trey.

Russell also takes a bite. Watching him eat reminds me that being rich and powerful does have its downside—sometimes people are afraid to tell you things you need to hear. Clearly, no one has had the pluck to tell Russell his hair looks ridiculous, that maybe he should spend some of his millions on dental work . . . and, evidently, no one has mentioned to him that eating with your mouth open is not a good look for him . . . or *anyone.* "I agree," Russell says, still chewing. "Great presentation, nice texture, and a perfect mix of sweet and savory. Well done." He says this with little enthusiasm, but given the bright smile that comes across Trey's face, I'm guessing getting a few complimentary words from Russell, even when delivered in his monotone voice, is a win.

"I thought it was really lovely, Trey," I say, glad to be filmed speaking rather than eating. It hadn't occurred to me how peculiar it would feel to be filmed while trying the entries, but I'm finding it makes me quite self-conscious. "It has an almost velvety quality, and there's something very decadent about it. It's flavorful, but no one seasoning is overpowering.

And the lemon zest is a really nice touch. I never would have thought of adding that, but it's a unique taste. Great job!"

"Thank you," Trey says, quite pleased with himself, and steps away.

Leon nods at Sherry, and she walks toward us with a tray of three biscuits, a glass bowl filled with red jelly, and a small dish with a square of what looks like cream cheese on it.

"So, I need to thank Halia for helping me concoct this take on the classic ham sandwich. I was thinking about making a Monte Carlo . . . I mean Monte Cristo, but Halia helped me come up with these biscuits and even gave me the idea to chop up the ham to include in the biscuit mix, but it was my idea to use buttermilk to give it some tang. And who doesn't want a little something to go with their biscuit?" Sherry asks, eying the bowl of jelly. "The pineapple–red pepper jelly was also Halia's idea—"

"*Ahem!*" Wavonne loudly clears her throat into our shared microphone.

"Oh wait," Sherry says. "I guess it was Wavonne's idea, but it was me that thought combining it with some cream cheese would drive the whole thing home." Sherry steps over to the table, lifts the bowl, and pours the jelly over the square of cream cheese.

As she steps back, we each take a turn hand-splitting the warm bread, slicing off a wedge of jelly-coated cheese, and spreading it on a biscuit.

"Oh my! That is divine!" Twyla says after giving Sherry's creation a taste. "I mean . . . it's quite nice." She purposely lessens her enthusiasm. "It's good . . . really, but I'm not sure all the flavors work. I think maybe both the rock sugar crystals on top and the jelly make it a bit too sweet. But still . . . great effort," she says, and then sends a wink in Trey's direction.

"Perfection," Russell announces, while Twyla proceeds to

take another bite of the biscuit she spoke so coolly about just moments ago. "It reminds me of some scones I had at the Savoy in London, although your biscuit may very well be superior. At some point during my culinary studies I learned that our primal instincts lead us to sweet *and* salty foods—that a sweet or salty taste meant that food was healthy and nutritious while sour or bitter foods were an indication for avoidance. We are wired to like salty foods . . . we are wired to like sweet foods. Sherry, I do believe you've found the perfect mix of both." There is an uncharacteristic kindness and maybe even a little excitement in his voice. I guess women who look like Sherry can make men do anything.

"Very, *very* nice, Sherry," I say as the camera pans to me, and I notice, out of the corner of my eye, that Twyla has just shoved the last of her cream cheese and jelly laden biscuit in her mouth. "I'm glad I was able to offer some guidance, but you're really the one who brought it home. Your biscuit was light and airy. The buttermilk was a nice touch, and the concept for the jelly and cheese spread really worked. Well done!"

As Sherry smiles, pleased with the feedback she got, Leon motions for her to return to her station, and Vera steps forward with three plates on a serving platter, each holding crisp bacon and avocado slices sandwiched between waffles—the whole thing topped with a silky orange sauce.

"I'm not sure I want to say or hear the word 'cheese' ever again but, as you know, my assignment was to make a grilled cheese with a swank factor. As you also know, my assignment took a bit of a turn when Sherry"—Vera swings her head around, gives Sherry a look, and then returns her gaze to the panel of judges—"breaking an agreement I was kind enough to make with her, used *all* of my key ingredients. I had planned to infuse my waffle with shredded cheddar, but with no cheese to be had, I was forced to get creative.

"You might remember that, at one point when I was vocalizing my displeasure with my predicament, I mentioned something about making an apple pie with no apples. This gave me an idea. I thought about how my mother used to make a mock apple pie with crackers instead of apples. I figured if my momma could make a mock apple pie maybe I could make a mock grilled cheese. Then I saw Trey's stash of sweet potatoes, and my wheels really started turning. I worked at a restaurant years ago where we used to make a vegan nacho sauce with sweet potatoes. I figured I had nothing to lose, so when Trey agreed to give me one of his precious spuds"—Vera looks in Trey's direction and gives him a thumbs-up—"I whipped up a faux cheese sauce . . . some mashed sweet potatoes, a little milk, soy sauce, a touch of lemon, and some hot sauce. I hope you like it."

My cojudges and I pick up a fork and slice off a portion of Vera's entrée. We all make sure we get some waffle, avocado, bacon, and sauce on our forks.

"Hmmm," Twyla says after swallowing. "It's . . . I'm not sure how to describe it," she adds.

"The look on her face seems to be describing it just fine," Wavonne whispers to me.

"It's . . . well, if I'm honest, it's . . . it's . . . underwhelming. The faux cheese sauce is actually not bad and complements the other flavors, but I'm afraid your waffle is a bit chewy and flat. I'm sorry, dear."

"I have to agree with Twyla," Russell says. "It was a viable recipe and could have worked with the improvised cheese sauce, which is actually quite nice. The bacon and avocado were also pleasant additions, but the waffle . . . the *waffle* is definitely subpar . . . rubberlike. This one is not a winner, Vera."

Vera's eyes go from Russell to me, and my heart drops as she awaits my comments. I'm fond of her and have been sort of rooting for her all along. Trey and Sherry are so young, have plenty of time to make their marks, and let's face it, their youth and good looks will open many doors for them. Vera is older and, while by no means ugly, she's definitely not a looker—this could be her last chance for a big break. But, much as I like her, I can't say the same for her waffle, which has a toughness to it. It's too dense and a little bit soggy.

I let out a sigh. "Vera." I say her name, mostly to just stall for time and try to think of some sort of positive opening remark. "I admire your spirit and your can-do attitude. You were thrown a curve ball and you found a way to swing at it, but I'm afraid you missed. It was a valiant effort. Really! The idea was solid, and the flavors worked, but the waffle . . . the waffle was not good. You didn't forget to add baking powder, did you?"

"No. I distinctly remember adding it . . . a whole tablespoon."

"It wasn't old, was it?"

"No. I didn't look at the date, but I just bought it today and . . ." Vera's voice trails off, and her eyes veer in Sherry's direction and then back to the judging table. "Actually, Sherry . . . Sherry grabbed it for me at the grocery store. I forgot it when I was in the baking aisle. Time was getting tight, and I needed to hit the produce section for my avocados, so Sherry said she'd get it . . . she suggested that we share that too." Vera quickly walks back to her station, flips over the can of baking powder, and lets out a long, loud groan before flipping the can so the bottom faces the camera. "It expired two years ago!" she bellows, swinging her head in Sherry's direction. "You sabotaged me! You *totally* sabotaged me!"

There's rage and disbelief . . . and maybe confusion in Vera's eyes—eyes that are fixed on Sherry as an eerie quiet comes over the room.

"I just grabbed the first can on the shelf," Sherry finally says, breaking the silence. "I was in a hurry, too. I didn't have time to look at dates. I used it in my recipe as well. Why would expired baking powder even be on the shelf to begin with? It was an accident!"

"Another accident?" Leon says to the camera. "Or another 'accident'?" he adds, doing the air quote thing with his fingers when he says "accident." "And, if Sherry and Vera used the same expired baking powder, why did Sherry's entry turn out so tasty while Vera's fell flat." He moves his gaze from the camera to the judging table. "Judges: I guess it's up to you to figure it all out. Did Sherry just make some simple mistakes or was she out to get Vera all along . . . and does it even matter? Either way, we ask that you decide now who is going home, and who is going to make it to the final round of *Elite Chef*."

I confer with Russell and Twyla, but we don't chat long. We all seem to agree that, while it was unfortunate that Sherry's errors (whether accidental or on purpose) affected Vera's entry, it was Vera's choice to be trustful and work out a cheese-sharing deal with Sherry. And it was also Vera who did not check the expiration date on one of her key ingredients. And, while her waffle would have been good had she used fresh baking powder, and even better if she'd gotten her share of the cheese, it likely still would not have been as tasty as Trey's soufflé or Sherry's biscuits.

"Have you reached a decision?" Leon asks.

"Yes," Russell says.

"And who is it that will be leaving us this evening?"

Russell, with no feeling, no hesitation, no perfunctory kind words, simply says, "Vera."

"Vera, please step forward," Leon instructs.

"You gave it a nice try, Vera," Russell says, and I think he is actually trying to sound regretful but, honestly, I'm not sure it's in him. "There is no one at this table that was happy to choose you for elimination, but you, like any chef, have to be ultimately accountable for your food. Your lack of one key ingredient and the expiration of another may have been the result of Sherry's errors, but chefs have to take responsibility for the decisions they make and the consequences of those decisions. In the end it was *your* decision to leave tasks to others and not check up on them that made your entry a loser. I'm sorry, Vera. Please hang up your apron and go."

RECIPE FROM HALIA'S KITCHEN

Halia's Salty Sweet Ham & Cheese Nips

Ingredients
6 ounces sliced ham
1 tablespoon olive oil
1 tablespoon brown sugar
2 cups all-purpose flour
½ teaspoon salt
2 teaspoons baking powder
½ teaspoon baking soda
2 teaspoons sugar
½ cup buttermilk
¼ cup sour cream
½ cup melted butter (and another ¼ cup melted butter to
   top baked biscuits)
¼ cup water
1 cup shredded sharp cheddar cheese
2 eggs
1 tablespoon of turbinado sugar
1 tablespoon coarse sea salt

- Preheat the oven to 450 degrees Fahrenheit.
- Sprinkle ham with brown sugar and fry on both sides in
  olive oil until slightly crisp. Chop ham into small pieces.
- Sift flour, salt, baking powder, baking soda, and sugar
  into bowl. Mix on low speed until combined.

- In another bowl, combine buttermilk, sour cream, butter, and water. Stir the dry ingredients into the wet with a spoon or spatula until well combined.
- Fold in shredded cheese and chopped ham.
- Drop dough onto a parchment-lined cookie sheet in ½-cup-size mounds.
- Beat eggs and, using a brush, lightly coat each biscuit with the egg wash.
- Sprinkle the tops of the biscuits with equal amounts of turbinado sugar and sea salt.
- Bake for 15 to 20 minutes or until golden brown.
- Immediately after removal from the oven, brush each biscuit with melted butter.
- Serve immediately.

Chapter 19

"Champagne," Wavonne says, helping herself to a glass of bubbly from a silver tray Cynthia is passing around in the concierge lounge at the inn. "Nice."

"Thank you." I take a glass as well.

"Attention please," Cynthia calls after passing out all the crystal flutes. "As has become a tradition following each challenge, we'd like to toast the chef leaving us." She turns to Vera, who is standing next to her. "Vera, your time in the competition may be over, but you're still definitely a winner. Out of ten contestants you made it to the final three. Everyone involved with the show, on and off camera, enjoyed getting to know you and learning from you. I have no doubt that you will have great success in the culinary world when you leave." Cynthia looks around at all of us. "Cheers to Vera!"

"To Vera," I say, raising my glass along with the rest of the gang. . . . Well, most of the gang—Twyla apparently declined the invitation to stay overnight and went back to her restaurant. Leon and the crew, and their cameras, are nowhere to be seen either. And, I must say, it's nice to get a break from being filmed. Today has been quite the experience, but I think one stint on television is enough for me.

"I can't say I miss the cameras," I say to Wavonne.

"Me either." Wavonne takes a sip from her champagne glass. "My shoulders are sore from trying to hold my girls up all day. I don't want any viewers at home saying I've got saggy bazoombas."

"What's this about saggy bazoombas?" Vera asks, approaching us from the side.

"Nothing. Wavonne is just . . . just being Wavonne," I respond. "How are you holding up? I'm so sorry things didn't go your way this evening."

"I'm fine. You win some. You lose some. And maybe Sherry did sabotage me, but like Russell said, my food is ultimately my responsibility. I had a good run and, if nothing else, hanging in there for eight episodes will be great publicity for my food truck."

"You're bein' an awfully good sport," Wavonne says. "If Dorothy Dandridge over there"—Wavonne eyes Sherry—"had messed me up like that, my earrings would've been off and someone would've had to hold my wig while I gave her a good what for."

"I'm sure it was an accident," I say, even though I guess I'm not really certain it was. It seems extremely unlikely that Sherry would mistakenly use all the cheese *and* saddle Vera with expired baking powder, but at the same time, I'm not sure Sherry is smart enough to come up with even the simplest of schemes to eliminate her competition. A few minutes ago, I saw her walk into a mirror and then apologize to her reflection for bumping into it. Or at least I'd give her the benefit of the doubt. Sherry's not the brightest or most focused person I've ever met. It's not inconceivable that she really did forget that she was supposed to share the cheese, and that she didn't check the expiration date on the baking powder. I mean she . . . um . . . how to say this politely . . . her . . ."

"Her cornbread is not quite done in the middle?" Wavonne

offers. "She left the relaxer on too long, and it seeped into her brain?"

"While that's not exactly how I would put it . . ." I reply, "but, yes, that's the gist."

"Maybe her elevator doesn't exactly go to the top," Wavonne says, "but it doesn't take a criminal mastermind to pretend to forget something or slip Vera some bobo baking powder."

"It doesn't matter at this point," Vera says. "What's done is done. So I've lost my chance at fifty grand and the job of a lifetime at what will likely be a Michelin-starred restaurant. I have my health . . . yeah, my health and . . . and . . ."

"And some new friends in me and Wavonne." I give her a hug.

"Thank you," she says. "I'm really not feeling well. I guess I'll go back to my room and pack up. They'll want to get some footage of me leaving with my suitcase tomorrow as the sun comes up. If getting eliminated is not bad enough, they have you get up at the crack of dawn to document your humiliation," she adds with a laugh. "But then again, this is *my* send-off. Am I supposed to stay until everyone leaves?"

"I'm not sure. This is my first time at this sort of rodeo."

"Oh well. I suspect this little shindig will wrap shortly. They used to get a little crazy at the beginning of the competition when there was a big group and a lot of rabble rousers, but Sherry's about the only late-nighter left. I tend to turn in early, and Trey does, too—you know, Mr. GQ needs his beauty sleep. Without anyone to party with, I imagine Sherry will call it a night early, too."

"Speaking of calling it a night, I think I'm about ready to go find my room." I turn to Wavonne. "What's our room number again?"

Wavonne looks at the little folder our key card came in. "Room two."

"That's just down the hall," Vera says. "You're right next to me, on one side anyway. Russell and Cynthia are on your other side in the Presidential Suite."

"I guess we are all on the first floor? The manager said they are still working on the other floors."

"Yep. Trey is on the other side of me . . . and Sherry's room is next to his further down the hall."

"Are the rooms off the chain *schwanky*?" Wavonne asks.

"They are very nice. Aside from the Presidential Suite, I think all the rooms are the same. They're quite spacious and comfortable with some great freebee shampoos and soaps in the bathroom. And we all have patios by the yet-to-be-completed pool . . . and nice views of the river."

I'm about to excuse myself and retire for the evening when I see Vera tense up as she catches sight of Sherry headed in her direction.

"Vera," Sherry says in a soft voice.

Vera gives Sherry her attention but says nothing.

"I really am sorry about the mishaps today. I swear on my life that I didn't—"

"You didn't what?" Vera cuts her off. "Mean to slip me expired baking powder? Use up all the cheddar? Not even think about offering some of your cream cheese to me once you used all the cheddar?" Vera lifts her hands and shakes her head. "You know what? It's fine." She takes in a long slow breath, clearly trying to not lose her temper. "What's meant to be is meant to be. Maybe there is some ridiculous chance that all the accidents today really were *accidents*. But, if they weren't, it will all just come back around to you one day. Karma's a bitch," Vera says, and you just know she wants to add, "And so are you."

"They really were," Sherry says. "Accidents I mean." She fiddles with the buttons on her chef's coat. "I really am sorry." When Vera can't be bothered to respond, Sherry turns to me and Wavonne. "It was really nice to meet you both and thank you for all your help today."

"You're welcome," I say as Wavonne looks at her suspiciously.

"It's been a long day, and I'm exhausted. So, if you'll excuse me . . ." She looks back at Vera, perhaps hoping that Vera will say that she doesn't blame her for anything or that she forgives her . . . all's well that ends well. But Vera continues to offer nothing but silence and a stoic expression.

"Well, this isn't awkward at all," Wavonne says.

Sherry stands in place, nervously waiting for Vera to say something . . . *anything* to her, but if Vera's talking, it's only with her eyes.

After what feels like a lifetime of silence, Sherry simply says, "Okay then," and turns to leave.

Vera watches her exit the concierge lounge, and as I look on, I wonder if the karma that Vera was talking about—the karma that Vera called a bitch and said might come back around to Sherry—might show itself sooner rather than later.

Chapter 20

"Girl, this place is lit!" Wavonne gives our room a good once over. "Plush linens." She rubs her hand around on the bed. "Giant screen TV, surround sound, fancy bathrobes . . ." She opens a little refrigerator next to the desk. "Minibar!" she exclaims. "Russell said it's *all* complimentary—I may just have me a five-dollar bag of M&Ms." She bends over and looks inside. "It's all computerized and stuff." Wavonne eyes the red digital numbers underneath each row of tiny twelve-dollar bottles of liquor and six-dollar cans of Pepsi before getting distracted by the sights outside the sliding glass doors. "Look, Halia. We can walk right outside our room to the pool. Shame it's not ready yet."

I join Wavonne by the doors and look out. Straight ahead is the pool with a wooded area behind it and, slightly to the right, a charming view of the river.

"It really is quite nice," I say, before looking away from the window at the interior of our room. We have two queen beds, a dresser, a contemporary sofa, a sleek desk covered with all sorts of local magazines and tourist guides, and a table with two leather chairs at each end. "This carpet feels like it has three inches of padding underneath it. I'm not sure I'm going to be able to stay at a Holiday Inn after first-class lodging like this." I grab my suitcase from the bed where Mitchell laid it, move it to a luggage rack, and unzip. "I don't think I'll bother unpacking since we're just here for one night."

"Me either." Wavonne sets her suitcase down on the floor, pulls the spread back on the bed closest to the sliding doors, and plops down on the crisp white sheets. She grabs the remote control for the TV and starts pressing buttons. "All this Ritz, and there's no Netflix on this TV," she groans, as I walk into the bathroom with a few toiletries and set them on the counter. When I come out Wavonne has found something to watch, but is only half paying attention to it as she rubs lotion on her arms.

"What's this?" I ask, looking at the TV.

"*Nappily Ever After*. It's about a sista who shaves off all her hair and finds inner peace or somethin' . . . I dunno. . . ."

"Can you turn it down a bit? I'm going to change and then crawl in bed and call it a night."

Wavonne lowers the volume on the TV while I grab an oversized T-shirt from my suitcase and return to the bathroom. I change clothes, brush my teeth, and give my face a quick wash before heading back into the room, turning off the overhead lights, and getting into bed.

"How late are you going to stay up?" I ask, hoping Wavonne will turn the TV off shortly, so I can sleep in peace.

"It's not even eleven thirty, Halia. Most nights you've barely left the restaurant by now."

"True," I say. "But for some reason, I found today to be particularly exhausting."

"I think you're just gettin' old, Halia. Maybe you need to get some of those Suzanne Somers creams or vitamins or somethin'."

"I'll get right on that, Wavonne," I reply. "In the meantime, can you turn that lamp off?"

Wavonne clicks the little knob on the light fixture, but the

TV is so big, its glow still lights up the room. Despite the lack of darkness and low hum of whatever nonsense Wavonne is watching, I close my eyes and, after a few minutes, I can feel myself starting to doze off. I've lost awareness of the sound coming from the TV as my body unwinds from a busy day, and my mind starts to dissolve into sleep. Wavonne's occasional laughs next to me sound low and distant. I'm probably seconds away from full slumber when . . . *BANG!* An ear-splitting sound pierces the air.

I bound from my near sleep state and look at Wavonne, whose eyes are just as wide as mine, but we don't have time to say anything or get up from our beds when a second, equally loud *boom* comes roaring through the room.

"What the . . . ?" Wavonne hops off the bed.

"It sounds like . . . it can't be . . ." I quickly jump out of bed as well.

"Can't be what? Gunshots?" Wavonne says.

"I'm sure it's not gunshots." I hurriedly slip on my pants and tuck in my nightshirt. "Maybe a pipe burst or a car backfired or something."

I walk over to the door, open it just enough to stick out my head, and see Trey emerging from his room. He has some sort of pink paint or cream on his face. Then I hear a door opening to my right and see Cynthia hurry in my direction from the concierge lounge with the attendant following. As they scramble past Wavonne and me, Mitchell appears at the end of the hall and rushes in our direction.

"The gunshots came from Sherry's room," Trey calls down the hall to Mitchell.

"Shots?" I say to Wavonne as we step into the hallway. "Don't you think it's a bit hasty to be talking about gunshots? It could've been any number of things," I say to Trey as we join the group outside Sherry's door.

"It was gunshots all right. My bed was nearly shaking from the vibration."

"I think you're overreacting," Mitchell says, and knocks on Sherry's door. "It sounded like something popped or burst. This is a brand new building and still under final construction. Something probably just came loose or . . . or I don't know. . . ."

Mitchell knocks again. "Ms. Ashbury? Is everything okay in there?"

"Nothing is okay in there!" Trey says. "Unless Sherry was lighting firecrackers, there was just gunfire in there."

We all look at Trey like he's hysterical—maybe because the idea of gunshots at an upscale resort just doesn't seem plausible, or maybe because his face looks like an ad for Mary Kay.

"What's all over your face?" Wavonne asks.

"It's a Himalayan salt mask. It's very good for your skin." He's distracted and clearly annoyed with the question. "I hadn't planned on being seen in public the rest of the night, but don't we have more pressing matters to discuss? Sherry could be dead in there."

"Ms. Ashbury?" Mitchell calls again, and really gives the door a good pound. "I'm going to use my master key and enter your room, Ms. Ashbury," he calls. He waits just another second or two to see if there's any response. Then he slips a key card in a slot, a little green light comes on, and he pushes the door open. As it swings inwards, an acrid scent enters the hallway. My pulse quickens and I immediately tense up. I have never actually smelled gunfire, but it seems highly likely that the part metallic, part smoky, part just plain rank odor drifting into the hallway is, indeed, from gunfire.

Chapter 21

Mitchell pokes his head in the door and gasps. "Oh my God!" he says as he steps inside. I can't help but follow him into the room, and apparently Trey can't either as he trails in behind me.

I gasp in the same way Mitchell did as my eyes take in the sight before me—Sherry, lying dead on the bed with two distinct wounds—one in the chest and one in the stomach.

"I'm calling from the Willow Oak Inn in Fort Washington," I hear Mitchell say into his phone. "A guest . . . a guest has been killed . . . shot."

While Mitchell continues to offer details to the dispatcher on the phone, I try to collect myself. This is certainly not the first dead body I have come upon, but that doesn't mean I'm not seriously rattled by it. The sight of a once lovely young woman with fresh wounds that proved fatal is making me dizzy and nauseated, but I manage to keep it together enough to give Sherry and the room a quick visual inspection.

Sherry is lying on her back with her eyes closed and, as I didn't hear her scream prior to the shots being fired, I imagine she was asleep when she was killed. The sliding door to the pool area is slightly ajar, which leads me to believe that the murderer came from the patio leading to the pool.

I try to get closer to the bed to get a better look when Mitchell, still on the phone, waves me away. "They're telling me to keep everyone out of the room." He points to his phone. "I need you guys to leave," he says to Trey and me.

We both do as we are told, but as we exit the room, Cynthia, who up until now has been observing from the hallway, steps inside.

"Mrs. Mellinger. I have to ask you to leave and—"

"I own this place." She cuts him off. "I'll do what I please," she adds curtly. "Has it occurred to anyone that she might still be alive?"

Cynthia approaches the bed and places the tips of her fingers to Sherry's neck. As she checks for a pulse, I hear Russell's voice from behind. "What's all the ruckus about?" he calls in a casual tone from down the hall behind us. "What? What happened?" he asks when no one answers his question. "What?!" he says again, clearly getting the idea that something serious has gone down.

Instead of answering him, Wavonne points toward the threshold dividing the hallway and Sherry's room. Russell turns away from us to step inside. When he catches sight of Sherry an unrecognizable noise comes from his throat . . . more of a roar than a gasp or a groan. His eyes are narrow and his mouth is hanging open as he approaches Sherry and lifts her hand in his. "Oh my God!" comes from his mouth, his voice cracking as he grasps her limp hand in his. From where I'm standing, with an obstructed view from the hallway into Sherry's room, I can no longer see Russell's face, but I can see Cynthia's, and there is a certain look in her eyes as Russell quivers over Sherry's dead body—it's a look I've seen before, at least in varying degrees . . . on a customer's face when Wavonne has messed up their order for the third time, on Momma's face when her car was mistakenly towed from the Sweet Tea parking lot, on Susan Lucci's face when she lost the daytime Emmy for the eighteenth time. I know that look. It's a look of pure, seething rage.

Chapter 22

"What's going on?" Vera walks into the concierge lounge. She appears shaken and disoriented. "Sherry's been killed?" As she asks me this, it only now occurs to me how glaringly absent she was immediately after the shots went off.

"Come here, sweetie," I say, and give her a hug. "Yes. I'm afraid so."

"I heard the gunshots and immediately went to the tub."

"The tub?" Wavonne asks.

"That's what we always did when we heard gunshots. I grew up in Harlem, when Harlem was *Harlem*. Momma always said the safest place when guns were going off was the bathtub."

"You're smarter than any of us," I say. "The rest of us bozos couldn't get out of our rooms fast enough to find out what happened. In retrospect, that was a really stupid decision, but we . . . or at least *I* didn't think the noise was gunfire. I figured there had to be another explanation. You don't expect gunfire in places like this."

"I grew up in the hood and when you heard shots, you cowered in the house until the police came . . . and even then, you stayed inside and tried not to get involved. I only came out of my room because one of the police officers knocked on my door and told me to wait in here with everyone else."

"Why don't you sit down," I say. "We have some coffee on, and I'm sure something 'stronger' from the bar could be arranged if you want a drink to settle your nerves."

"Maybe a coffee."

I'm about to make my way to the coffeepot when a familiar face enters the lounge.

"Well . . . if it isn't Prince George's County's answer to Miss Marple. What are you doing here, Ms. Watkins?!" Detective Hutchins, who arrived at the inn about an hour ago, says to me. The detective and I have a bit of history—even though I have helped him solve more than one murder case, he still seems to mostly think of me as a busybody who just gets lucky . . . when I'm not getting in his way. When he got here, a barrage of squad cars and crime scene vans in tow, he offered a few cross words to Mitchell for letting anyone in the room and then instructed all of us to get out of the way and wait in the concierge lounge until further notice. For the last several minutes Russell, Cynthia, Trey, Wavonne, and I . . . and the lounge attendant, whose name is apparently Jerome, have been sitting in the lounge watching police officers and men and women in white jumpsuits with cameras and masks over their mouths and noses hurry past the door. Some coming, some going, some coming back again. Moments ago, we saw Sherry's body being wheeled out in a zipped black bag.

"It's a long story."

"What's the short version?" the detective asks.

"I was hired the last minute to be on Mr. Mellinger's show, *Elite Chef*, as a guest judge. We were filming here . . . over in the restaurant earlier in the evening. He kindly let Wavonne and I stay overnight as we were supposed to film another segment in the morning. I was in bed about to fall asleep when the shots were fired. Wavonne was watching TV. It must have been about eleven thirty. We hurried out of the room to see what was going on and—"

"There may have been an active shooter in the building and instead of immediately calling the police and barricading yourself in your room, you essentially sprinted into harm's way? That seemed like the smart thing to do?"

"Well, when you put it that way, not so much." I feel like I'm six years old and Momma just caught me writing on the wall with a permanent marker. "But I didn't think the noise came from gunshots. This place is so . . . so . . ."

"Bougie," Wavonne says.

"It's just not the kind of place that makes gun violence come to mind when loud popping noises go off. But, you're right, we should have stayed put and called the police."

"What's done is done at this point, I guess," the detective says. "Did you see or hear anything unusual before the shots were fired?"

"No, not a thing."

"You didn't hear any commotion or Ms. Ashbury scream . . . anything like that?"

"No, it was perfectly quiet and then *boom* . . . two *booms* actually . . . just a second or two apart."

"What happened when you left your room?"

"Trey said the shots came from Sherry's room. He had just stepped into the hall when I opened the door to our room. We joined him and the others outside Sherry's door."

"The others?"

"Cynthia and Jerome, the bartender or attendant or whatever, were there. . . . They were in here when Sherry was killed and scurried down the hall just ahead of me and Wavonne. And Mitchell . . . he passed by our room and ran ahead of us as well. Russell showed up a few minutes later."

"How many minutes?"

"I don't know . . . two or three maybe."

"Mitchell told me that you and Mr. McIntyre"—Detective Hutchins looks in Trey's direction—"entered the room before we got here."

"Um . . . yes."

"Because?"

I refrain from saying that I wanted to get a firsthand look at the crime scene and search for clues. Instead I offer, "I guess curiosity got the best of me." I rock back and forth on my feet nervously. I know my questions and comments will annoy him, but I decide to go ahead with them anyway. "The brief time I was in there I saw her eyes were shut. I thought people's eyes typically opened when they died."

"Not always," he says. "Often if people die in their sleep their eyes remain shut."

"Yeah . . . I figured that meant she was asleep when she died. She had wounds to the chest and stomach, right? You saw the sliding glass door was ajar, right? The killer must've entered from there, don't you think?"

"We are *not* doing this, Ms. Watkins."

Wavonne laughs. "Not doin' this?" She's still laughing. "Because you've been so successful at keepin' Halia out of your bidness in the past? You know when TV One remakes *Bewitched* with an all-black cast, Halia is on the short list to play Gladys Kravitz and nose around and nose around and nose around."

"Who?" the detective asks.

"No one," I say. "I was just asking a few questions, thinking I might be able to offer some help since I was here when the gun went off and got a firsthand look at the crime scene right after." I look around the room. "And know a thing or two about everyone in here."

"My officers and I will be interviewing everyone, but I think I've gotten all I need from you." He hesitates for a moment. "Well, almost everything. That woman sitting down over there"—he nods his head in Vera's direction—"Ms. Ward. My understanding is that she's the only one who remained in her room after Sherry was killed. Is that correct?"

"Yes. As far as I know."

He looks at Vera and then back at me. "Okay. Well . . . thank you. Unless either one of you has anything to add, you're free to go."

"Okay . . . but maybe we'll stick around for a bit and—"

"I'm sorry. Perhaps I should rephrase that," he says. "Please go now."

"If you don't mind, I'd like to stay and . . ." I let my voice fade as the look on his face tells me he absolutely minds. "Okay, we're going."

I usher Wavonne out of the concierge lounge, annoyed that I won't be able to hear Cynthia, Russell, Trey, and Vera answer the detective's questions.

"Let's pack up our stuff and get out of here. The Willow Oak Inn has sort of lost its luster."

"Yeah . . . a dead body will do that to a place," Wavonne says, and the two of us head down the hall to gather our things and go home.

Chapter 23

"Stop eating the marshmallows," Momma says to Wavonne. "They go in the cakes. Not in your mouth."

Momma removed a few of her chocolate butter cakes from the oven a few minutes ago, and Wavonne is helping her finagle some marshmallows into them—you have to poke little holes and insert them after the cakes are baked, or they will just melt into the batter in the oven. Once they get some marshmallows dotted throughout the cakes, Momma will frost them with a milk chocolate icing and dust them with graham cracker crumbs . . . and voilà, we'll have a supply of s'more cakes for the dinner service.

"I'm just eatin' one here and there . . . makin' sure they're fresh," Wavonne replies, and I must say it's a nice change of pace to hear someone talking about marshmallows instead of murder. It's been a day and a half since Sherry was killed, and it's all anyone—me, Wavonne, Momma, my customers, the people on the news—has been talking about.

"You keep tasting food for freshness, you're going to burst out of those pants," Momma says, and looks in my direction. "Wouldn't kill you to drop a few pounds either, Halia."

"How did this become about me?" I'm at the other end of the kitchen, organizing some utensils, minding my own business . . . and now, wondering if it's time to go back to talking about Sherry's murder. At least it would move the conversation away from my weight.

"I met this new pharmacist over at the CVS when I was filling one of my prescriptions. He was so nice and handsome . . . and didn't have a wedding band on." She says this as if this should somehow answer my question. "Bet he makes well into the six figures . . . good benefits, too. He's about your age, but he's a small fellow . . . almost petite. He might look like a little munchkin next to you. But, if you lose a little weight, it might work."

"What might work?" I ask, even though I know the answer.

"You and him . . . that's what might work. Lord knows I could use a family discount at the drugstore. Let's make you up an illness so you can go to the doctor and get a prescription for something. Then, when you fill it, and the clerk asks if you have any questions for the pharmacist—"

"I can ask him for some psych meds for my looney mother?"

"She don't need a prescription, Aunt Celia," Wavonne offers. "She can just go over there and ask him where they keep the over the counter menopause supplements . . . like Estroven or whatever. Good way to start a conversation as any."

"I was thinking more along the lines of a basic antibiotic or high dose vitamin D . . . something benign that won't scare him off."

"I should take the two of you along . . . tell him I'm a package deal . . . that Heckle and Jeckle come with me. That would scare him off." I hop up from the stool I was sitting on. "I've got a few things in the dining room to take care of . . . one of which is getting away from the two of you."

Momma and Wavonne laugh. "Oooh . . . I think Aretha needs a Snickers bar," Wavonne cackles.

"Maybe we can get her a script for some Paula Abdul–happy pills, so she's not so testy,"

I roll my eyes at the two of them and exit the kitchen. We just opened for dinner a few minutes ago, so there's only a handful of people in the restaurant when the kitchen door swings closed behind me. I'm about to say hi to some regulars when I'm sidetracked by a familiar face standing at the hostess station.

"Hey there," I say to Vera when I reach the counter. "Are you okay?" Throughout most of the competition, at least until the cheese and baking powder mishaps and . . . well . . . the murder of course, Vera always looked, for lack of a better word, "pleasant." She smiled a lot and exuded positive energy. She had a face and an aura that made people feel comfortable. But, at the moment, those looks and feels are nowhere to be seen—she looks distraught and frightened.

"No . . . not really."

"Come over here and have a seat." I put my hand on her shoulder and lead her to a small booth along the wall. She sits down on one side of the table, and I take a seat on the other. "What's going on?"

"I've been at the police station in Landover all morning. They had me in one of those windowless rooms like you see on the TV crime shows and were asking all sorts of questions. They honestly think I may have shot Sherry."

"Why?"

"I was the only one who didn't come out of my room immediately after she was killed. They kept asking me where I was over and over again. And I kept repeating the truth, that I was in the bathtub waiting for an all clear. From the questions they were asking I could tell what they were thinking. They asked me if I owned a gun . . . if I knew how to shoot a gun . . . if I had changed clothes or showered after the gunshots went off. They think I snuck into her room and killed her. And, while everyone was hovering around the crime scene, I was ditching the gun and changing clothes and showering to get any gunshot residue off me. I can't prove I was in my room the whole time, and the police know I had it in for Sherry after her so-called mistakes ruined my entry for the competition. They have no one else with a motive."

"Aren't there some security cameras around that would have shown you leaving your room or entering Sherry's room?"

"I asked the same thing. They said there are cameras in the hallway and lobby and even the concierge lounge . . . and the restaurant, but they have not been installed yet around the pool."

"Geez . . . It feels like we're under surveillance 24/7 these days, but when you really need a camera there isn't one."

"You don't think I killed her, do you?"

"Of course not," I say, and I guess I mean it. Vera hardly seems the murdering kind, and I know people have killed for more ridiculous reasons, but I seriously doubt anyone is going to risk life in prison to settle a grudge over cheese and baking powder.

"Of course, I was upset that Sherry messed up my entry for the competition, but the idea that I would kill someone over losing a cooking contest is absurd. When they finally let me go, with instructions to not leave town without permission, I sat in the car and started Googling everyone at the hotel—I wanted to see if anyone else might have a beef with Sherry. I came across some information about you solving some previous murders. I'm hoping you might be willing to look into this one. I'm afraid if they don't line up another suspect, it's only a matter of time before they arrest me."

"Oh sweetie, I don't know. I'm not sure there is much I can do, and Detective Hutchins gets a little irritable when I start poking around in his cases." I see Vera's face, which I didn't think could go any lower, drop even more, so I try to soothe her. "They can't pin a murder on you that you didn't commit. Clearly, they don't have enough evidence to charge you with anything, or they wouldn't have let you go."

"I guess," she agrees, but she's still clearly troubled.

"They must be looking for other suspects," I reassure. "You said you were poking around online about some of the others at the inn. Did you find anything interesting?"

"No . . . nothing that made me think anyone would want Sherry dead."

"Sherry had good relationships with everyone on the show as far as you know?"

"Yeah . . . possibly one *very* good relationship."

"What do you mean by that?"

"There was some gossip going around that Sherry had a thing going with Russell."

"Really? He's a good forty years older than her."

"And a few million dollars richer than her if you want to talk numbers. She wouldn't be the first young woman to go after a rich older man."

"True."

"I never really saw anything, but there was talk . . . talk that someone saw them canoodling in the pantry . . . that someone saw him stroking her hair or patting her behind when he thought no one was looking. It was just rumor mill stuff."

"It wasn't just rumor mill stuff. Of course, Russell and Sherry were doin' it," Wavonne says, suddenly appearing at the table.

"Where did you come from? And how do you know?"

"I was gettin' some tea, and I saw you with Vera, so I came over to say hey. And I *know* because there was just a certain way they were lookin' at each other all day at the museum . . . or *not* lookin' at each other. They were both starin' at one another a lot throughout the day, but if their eyes actually met they would immediately look away—they didn't want anyone to catch them makin' eye contact. He also smelled of her perfume when he sat down next to us at the judgin' table. Not to mention he had a couple strands of long brown hair on his suit jacket . . . way longer than Cynthia's hair."

"Why didn't you tell me?" I ask, annoyed that I, amateur sleuth that I am, didn't notice all the things she mentioned.

"Tell you what? That some hot young thang was bangin' some old troll for his money? It's not like that's anything new or interestin'. Besides, I thought it was obvious. You want me to also tell you the next time the sky's blue or the pope's Catholic? You do know there are seven days in a week, right?"

"All right, all right," I say. "If Russell and Sherry were having a fling, that opens a whole world of motives. The affair could have gone south and been a motive for Russell to kill Sherry. Cynthia could also have found out about the two of them, which would have given her a motive, too. And, if you think about it, as long as we're throwing out hypotheticals, even Trey could've done it just to eliminate his final competitor. He and Cynthia had the same opportunity you did," I say to Vera. "All of our rooms were on the same side of the inn—we all had doors leading to the pool area. Both of them could have exited from their patios, entered Sherry's room from her outside door, and killed her. If they were fast enough, they both would have had time to shoot her, run back to their rooms, and act like they'd been there all along."

"But Cynthia wasn't in her room, right?" Vera says. "She was in the lounge when the shots were fired, and the police said there was a camera in there. They would know if she was lying."

"Hmmm . . . I guess you're right," I agree. "And then, of course, there's Russell. Do you know where he was when Sherry was shot? He didn't appear in plain sight for several minutes after the gun was fired."

"I don't, but I'm sure he had to tell the police. He's a rich, powerful guy, but I think the police would have taken him in if he hadn't been able to account for himself, don't you?"

"I would hope so," I say. "Well, you've given me a few things to think about," I add, and realize the inevitable is happening—I'm dipping my toes into this investigation.

"Does this mean you'll help me?"

"Yes . . . a little at least. I think we need to find out for sure if anything was going on between Russell and Sherry . . . and what Trey and Russell were doing when Sherry was killed."

"I already told you that Russell and Sherry were gettin' busy."

"I know, Wavonne, but it is possible that there are other explanations for him smelling like her perfume and having strands of hair on his person." I turn back to Vera. "Is there anything else . . . anything else you're aware of . . . any thoughts or ideas that might be helpful?"

"I guess I have more of a *question* than a thought or idea." Vera shifts around in her chair. "The cops said I was the only one who didn't emerge from my room right after the gun-shots, but it just occurred to me that when I did finally come out and went to the concierge lounge like the detective told me, I didn't see Twyla. Where was she?"

"She wasn't there. She didn't have a room at the inn. She said she had something to take care of at Dauphine, so she didn't stay over."

"Really? You're sure?"

"Yes."

"That's weird."

"Why?"

"I saw Twyla milling about by the pool about forty-five

minutes or so before the shots went off. I figured she was just cutting across the courtyard from the lobby to her room. But you're saying she didn't have a room?"

"No . . . I mean yes, she didn't have a room. I actually saw her drive off after we finished filming. You can't miss her in that big white Cadillac."

"She must have come back at some point. I'm one hundred percent certain I saw her out there."

"Okay . . . so now you've given me even more to think about. I'll mull it over tonight and come up with a game plan to start trying to figure all this out in the morning. I definitely need to talk to a few folks tomorrow."

"Thank you." Vera gets up from the table. "Um . . ." She wavers for a moment.

"What?"

Vera's quiet, like she's not certain she wants to share whatever is going through her mind. "I'm not sure. It had been a long day. I was tired and had had a few glasses of champagne. I think maybe my eyes were playing tricks on me, but I think . . . I mean . . . I *know* I saw Twyla, but *maybe* I saw someone else, too."

"Who?"

"I don't know. I'm not even sure if it was a *who* . . . may have been more of a *what*. He . . . or *it* was in the woods behind the pool, almost like . . ." She stops talking, cautious about saying anything further.

"Vera, I can't be helpful without all the information. What did you see?"

She sighs. "It was sort of like a . . . like a Sasquatch."

"Bigfoot?" flies from Wavonne's mouth.

"I know . . . it sounds crazy, and I only got a quick glimpse of it, or him, before he disappeared behind a tree, but he was super tall . . . like almost seven feet . . . and had long, shaggy hair and a beard."

"Sista girl is seein' Jason Momoa in the woods," Wavonne says to me under her breath.

"Why didn't you call Security?"

"Because I was exhausted, a little tipsy, and had just been eliminated from a competition that would have given me the opportunity of a lifetime. I figured I was just seeing things. And I don't think there was any Security other than Mitchell at the front desk."

"Honestly, I have no idea what to do with that."

"Well," Wavonne says. "Maybe we can try to find out if Sherry, at some point, double crossed Chewbacca—maybe he came down from the Death Star and did her in."

"Cool it, Wavonne," I say, and turn to Vera. "Forgive the question, but I have to ask, and I promise I will not judge you based on your answer. But prior to seeing this . . . this *creature,* you hadn't, by chance, indulged in any recreational drugs beyond the champagne you had in the lounge with us? Pot or something?"

"No. I'll be the first to admit that it sounds nuts. That's why I was hesitant to mention it at all." She looks down at the ground and back up at me. "There's one more thing."

"I gotta hear this. Did you see the Loch Ness monster in the river, too?" Wavonne asks. "You know I'm just teasin' ya, girl," she adds, and puts an arm around Vera's shoulders when it becomes clear how unsettled she is by whatever it is she thinks she saw. "What? What's the one more thing?"

"The creature . . . I think he was wearing . . . I know this sounds bonkers . . . but I think he was wearing a Hawaiian shirt."

"Maybe Bigfoot missed his flight to Honolulu," Wavonne says. "I'm sorry. I couldn't help myself," she adds. "Seriously, maybe you were just tired or had a little too much bubbly. One time, after a few too many peach bellinis, I thought I saw Idris Elba at the Olive Garden in Waldorf. Turns out he was just one of the guys who dunks the precooked noodles into the boiling water before they sauce them. I went home with him anyway. He said he'd fake a British accent and let me call him Idris, so I figured what the—"

"Wavonne, Vera is not interested in hearing about your Olive Garden hookups." I turn to Vera. "But maybe Wavonne is right. Maybe it was just a combination of being fatigued and a little tipsy." I get up from the table, too. "I've got a few things to take care of, but I'll give everything you've told me some thought and check back in with you tomorrow. Honestly, Vera, if you didn't kill Sherry, and I don't believe that you did, I don't think you have anything to worry about."

"Thank you," she says, and turns to leave. "I hope you're right."

RECIPE FROM HALIA'S KITCHEN

Celia's S'mores Cake

Cake Ingredients
2 cups all-purpose flour
1 teaspoon salt
1 teaspoon baking powder
1½ teaspoons baking soda
1¾ cups sugar
¾ cup unsweetened cocoa powder
½ cup whole milk
½ cup sour cream
1 stick of salted butter (½ cup)
3 eggs
1 teaspoon pure vanilla extract
1 cup strong hot coffee
1 cup mini marshmallows

- Preheat the oven to 350 degrees Fahrenheit.
- Generously grease and lightly flour two 9-inch round cake pans.
- Sift flour, salt, baking powder, baking soda, sugar, and cocoa into bowl. Mix on low speed until combined.
- In another bowl, combine milk, sour cream, butter, eggs, and vanilla. With the mixer on low speed, slowly add the dry ingredients to the wet until well combined.

- With mixer still on low speed, add coffee, and mix until well combined.
- Pour batter into the prepared pans and bake for 25 to 35 minutes, until a toothpick comes out clean.
- Cool in the pans for 20 to 30 minutes, until cakes are still slightly warm.
- This is where things get tricky :-). Using a knife, cut slits into the cake. Insert marshmallows, one by one, using a toothpick and the knife, throughout the cakes.
- Turn cakes onto racks to cool completely.
- Be sure to keep the side with the slits on the bottom and spread icing over the opposite side.

Milk Chocolate Frosting Ingredients
1½ cups softened salted butter
1 cup cocoa
5 cups powdered sugar
⅓ cup whipping cream (then 1 tablespoon at a time until desired consistency is achieved)
½ teaspoon vanilla
1 6.8 ounce melted Hershey's Milk Chocolate bar (Recommend melting in the microwave on the defrost setting)
1 cup crumbled graham crackers

- Cream butter in a mixing bowl with an electric mixer on medium speed until soft and fluffy.
- Gradually beat in cocoa and powdered sugar.
- Beat in whipping cream, vanilla extract, and melted Hershey's bar.
- Frost cake and top with crumbled graham crackers.

Chapter 24

"So, what are you gonna do about 'coo-coo for Cocoa Puffs'?" Wavonne asks.

"Who?" I ask. We've just gotten home from the restaurant. Wavonne is sprawled on the living room sofa, and I'm in a chair researching a few things on my phone.

"Vera."

"I don't know. I'm poking around on the Internet now."

Wavonne sits up. "Find anything?"

"Not really. I've been running a couple checks on Twyla. I figured I'd look into her first—"

"Because you don't like her?"

"I like her just fine, Wavonne," I say. "It's just odd that she came back to the hotel. She could have a good explanation and, unlike Trey and the Mellingers, I can't think of any reason she'd want Sherry dead. But still . . . why was she outside by the pool so late? After we wrapped the taping, she said she had to go back to her restaurant and would meet us in the morning to film Vera's send-off."

"What are you looking at now?"

"Dauphine has a Facebook page. I'm just scrolling through

it. So far all I see are photos of dated decor and bland food. Although her brunch beignets do look pretty good. At least she . . ." I go silent as something catches my eye.

"What?" Wavonne asks, watching me raise the phone closer to my eyes.

"Look." I hand the phone to Wavonne.

"That's Sherry."

"Sure is." I take the phone back and look at the photo in question again. "It was posted two years ago." In the photo, Sherry's wearing a short apron with a few pens clipped to one pocket and a leather-bound check presenter in the other. "Clearly, she was once a server at Dauphine."

"They didn't act like they knew each other at the museum or the inn."

"Yeah . . . more weirdness." I continue to scroll through the page to see if I can find any other photos of Sherry.

"You know," Wavonne says, "my friend Nicki works at Dauphine. She's been waiting tables there on weekends for years. She might have a little four-one-one."

"Can you call her tomorrow?"

"I can call her now."

"It's almost midnight, Wavonne."

Wavonne grabs her phone from the coffee table. "You can call Nicki at midnight—she's in the restaurant biz like us. Call her at nine a.m. though, and she'll jump down your throat. As far as she's concerned, nine a.m. is middle of the night." Wavonne taps her phone screen a few times and puts it on speaker.

"You still have my black sweater, Wavonne . . . and you owe me forty-two dollars for when your credit card was declined at Cloak and Dagger," Nicki says instead of hello.

"Hey, girl," Wavonne says, doing what she always does

when people say things she doesn't want to hear—ignoring them. "How you doin'?"

"I'm okay. Watching Hulu and painting my nails. I just sent James a booty text, but I haven't heard back yet. If he doesn't come over, I'll probably put some conditioner on my hair and try that clay mask I bought at Ulta the other day. I was thinking . . ."

Wavonne presses the mute button while Nicki keeps rambling. "Girlfriend is nice and all but, damn, she talks way too much."

Wavonne often complains about people who talk too much—mostly because, if someone else is talking too much, *she* can't talk too much.

"I'll let her blather for a few minutes." Wavonne lays the phone on the table and gets up from the sofa. "I'm gonna grab a Dr. Pepper from the kitchen. I doubt she'll pause, but if she does, just say 'uh-huh.' Once she wears herself out, we'll ask her about Sherry." Wavonne unmutes the phone and walks away.

While she's in the kitchen, I get an earful about what was on sale at Ulta last night, how the burger Nicki got from McDonald's had pickles on it when she asked for no pickles, how she might order something from DoorDash because she didn't like the hamburger with the pickles, and how she'll have to go if James texts her back as she hasn't shaved her legs since Friday.

"But he still hasn't gotten back to me. He might be asleep. Sometimes he goes to bed early. I could call him and block my number to wake him up, so he sees my text but doesn't know that it was me who called. . . . Calling him would seem desperate. I—"

Wavonne comes back into the room and picks up the phone. "Nicki, honey, take a breath. I don't think James is in the picture tonight," she says. "Listen, I got a question for you. How long you been workin' at Dauphine on the weekends?"

"Almost four years. I started after they fired me at Jasper's. They said I talked too much and—"

"So you must remember a girl named Sherry . . . Sherry Ashbury?"

"Sherry? That little hustler?"

"Hustler?"

"She left a couple of years ago, when Twyla caught her stealing."

"Stealing?"

"Yeah . . . she had some sort of scam going with the bartender. I don't know all the details. I came in one day and both she and the bartender had been fired. Twyla didn't talk about whatever went down with us low level wait staff, but word is Sherry took her for a nice chunk of change."

"Interesting," I say.

"Who's that?"

"That's Halia. My cousin. She's here with me."

"Hi, Halia," Nicki says to me. "Why are you guys asking about Sherry?"

"She applied for a job at Sweet Tea, and we found out on the sly that she worked at Dauphine . . . so sort of a reference check," I lie before Wavonne has a chance to respond. I don't feel like mentioning the murder and all the questions it will raise. I would think Nicki would have heard about Sherry's murder by now as it has been all over the news, but maybe she doesn't stop talking long enough to find out about much of anything.

"I thought she was nice enough before I learned she was robbing Twyla blind. She liked my hair, so I used to give her tips about salons and hair products. Her hair was a different texture than mine though, so—"

Wavonne mutes the phone again. "I'm gonna brush my teeth and get ready for bed. I'll be back in a few minutes. You know what to do." She unmutes the phone, and I prepare to pretend I'm listening and offer the occasional "uh-huh" if necessary, which is not hard to do—I've been doing the same thing with Wavonne for years.

Chapter 25

"This place looks like somewhere the vampires in *True Blood* would eat," Wavonne says as we step into Dauphine. The door closes behind us, and all evidence of daylight disappears.

"Yeah . . . it's not exactly bright and cheery, is it?" I respond. "It's been a hundred years since I worked here. I guess I'd forgotten how dark it is in here. Feels like we're in a church from the Middle Ages."

We stand just inside the entrance and take in all that is Dauphine. The only windows are at the front of the building, and Twyla had them covered in stained glass, so the place gets next to no natural light. If I remember correctly, when Twyla designed the decor, she was aiming for a 'night time al fresco dining' vibe—she wanted customers to feel like they were on the patio of some New Orleans restaurant after the sun went down. Strings of lights meant to give the impression of twinkling stars in an evening sky and dimly lit metal chandeliers with faux candles provide the only illumination. The gothic furniture with all its contours and ornaments gives the restaurant a sense of heaviness. There are no booths, only tables that surround a lengthy oval-shaped salad bar designed to look like a Mississippi steamboat. It even has a paddle wheel at the far end behind the canisters filled with thousand island and ranch . . . and blue cheese.

"Ladies," Twyla says, sashaying toward us. She looks out of place in this dreary restaurant in her tailored yellow pants, floral print shirt, and bright smile. "What a nice surprise." She looks around her at the small number of diners dotted throughout the place. "We're a bit slow today with the weather and all."

It's not a picture-perfect day—a bit overcast and a little humid, but it's certainly not the kind of weather that would keep anyone from going out to lunch. I think Twyla's just embarrassed for me to see how past its heyday Dauphine is, so she's coming up with a reason . . . *any* reason for why the clientele is so sparse.

As we mentioned to Cynthia a few days ago, Dauphine opened to great fanfare and lots of press many years ago and was a hot restaurant on and off for several years. Twenty years ago, its garish interior seemed campy and fun. But now, after decades of wear and tear, the place looks like an eating venue you might find at a low-end amusement park or a dinner theater in the Poconos putting on a second-rate production of *Wicked*.

"Really. Yes, Sweet Tea was quiet today, too," I lie. "That's why Wavonne and I thought we could sneak out for lunch. Seeing you made me realize I haven't been here in forever, we thought we'd swing by for a little gumbo or jambalaya . . . and see how you're doing since . . . well, you know. It's so awful what happened to Sherry."

"Yes, terrible." Twyla says this with a finiteness that implies that's all she wishes to say about the matter. She then turns, grabs two menus from the counter behind her, and motions for us to follow her. "Let me find you a table."

We follow Twyla and take a seat at a table next to a wrought iron column with some fake green ivy looping through its intricate design.

"What can I get you guys to drink?" She runs her eyes from my head to my toes. "A *Diet* Coke?"

Seriously you're just going to take a drink order? We're not going to talk about Sherry's murder? "Maybe just an unsweetened iced tea for me." I want a sweet tea, but I'm afraid she'll look at my midsection and say something like, "Are you sure that's a good idea?"

"Sweet tea for me, please . . . heavy on the sweet."

"Sure."

"This place smells like 'dirty mop,'" Wavonne says in a hushed tone as Twyla walks away.

"It does sort of have that vague ammonia-mixed-with-mildew smell." I open my menu. "I don't think she wants to talk about Sherry. She kind of shut down my attempt to bring her up over by the door."

"If I killed Sherry, I probably wouldn't want to talk about it either."

"Let's not find her guilty just yet." I give the menu a look and start running down the list of items. "She has crab soup, spicy pecan-crusted haddock, shrimp and crab étouffée, crawfish and shrimp beignets," I read aloud to Wavonne. "Well, it all *sounds* good. I doubt it *tastes* good, but . . ." I don't finish my sentence when I see Twyla approaching with two glasses of tea.

"Here we are." She sets them down on the table. "Have you had a chance to look at the menu? We have a few lighter items on this side"—she points to the salad section on my menu—"if you're still hoping to get swimsuit ready before the end of the summer."

"Halia doesn't have time to swim," Wavonne says. "*Her* restaurant is busy." As I mentioned earlier, while giving me a hard time is a full-fledged hobby of hers, the moment anyone outside the family chides me, Wavonne's the first to come to my defense.

"It all looks so good. I remember a lot of these dishes," I

say, truly surprised that Twyla has not made a single update to the menu since I left. "I think I'll go with the jambalaya."

The Oysters Rockefeller and the crawfish with red beans and rice, please," Wavonne says.

"Excellent choices. I'll put those orders in," she says, and turns to walk away.

"Twyla," I call to her back, and she turns around. "Are we really not going to talk about Sherry's death . . . her *murder*?"

"What's there to talk about? I'm mean it's disturbing and very sad for Sherry and her family, but I barely knew her."

"But you did know her a little, right?"

"Of course. We'd spent the day at the museum and the evening at Russell's restaurant."

"But you knew her before that . . . when she worked for you."

"How did you know about that?"

"The restaurant business is a revolving door, Twyla—you know that. Some of my staff have worked here. Some of your staff have worked at Sweet Tea. They all gossip with each other at the bars after work."

"I guess." Twyla looks antsy, like she can't get away from the table fast enough. "It was years ago that Sherry worked here."

"And years ago that you fired her?"

"I *had* to fire her. She was stealing from me." For the first time since we got here, Twyla's weird semipermanent smile fades. "Did you come here for lunch or to give me the third degree?"

"Maybe a little of both," I reply. "If I may ask, what was she stealing from you? Money? Liquor? Food?"

Twyla sighs as if she's annoyed by the question. "I'm not sure it's any of your business, Halia, but she had a scam going with one of my bartenders, Malcom. She got him to ring in well drink prices when charging customers for top shelf liquor and split the difference with him. Sometimes she got him to leave drink charges off her checks altogether, so her customers might give her a bigger tip. She even worked with him to bring in their own bottles of wine for cash-paying customers—they would give the customer their bottle so none of mine would be missing from inventory and pocket the entire charge, which was usually more than double what they paid at Total Wine or Costco or wherever they got their stash. Malcom kept them hidden behind the bar."

"How did you catch her? Did you press charges?"

"I didn't catch *her*. I caught *Malcom*. The police said I only had enough proof to make a case against him as he was the one I busted for short-ringing drinks and with his own stash of wine. Sherry was careful not to leave any paper trails that pointed to her . . . at least any that would stand up in court. I fired both of them, but I could only press charges against Malcom."

"She made the bartender her fall guy, eh?" Wavonne asks.

"Yes. He ended up doing time . . . like four months."

"How much did they steal?"

"I'll never know. Enough." Twyla adjusts her weight on her feet as if she's preparing to turn around again. "What's it matter? Sherry and Malcom were not the first employees to steal from me, and they won't be the last. I seriously doubt her exploits with my bartender have anything to do with her murder."

"I'm sure not," I say. "But why didn't you tell anyone that you knew Sherry when we were at the museum?"

"What was I supposed to say when Cynthia introduced us to each other? 'This is the little thief who robbed me blind?' Sherry pretended to not know me, and I just followed her lead. And I don't have any actual proof that she stole from me. I suppose she could've sued me if my talk of her thieving ways affected her standing on the show."

"Did you tell the police that Sherry used to work here?"

"I haven't talked with the police. What would they want with me? I wasn't even at the inn when she was killed."

"I guess that makes sense," I say. "I'm sorry for all the questions. I'm just trying to piece a few things together. The police are looking at Vera as a suspect in Sherry's death, and she has sworn up and down that she didn't do it, and I believe her. I was just curious if there are any other leads the police should be following up."

Twyla looks at me curiously, as if she's trying to figure me out. "Well, let me go put those orders in for you."

"Okay, but one more question," I say. "I know you left the inn shortly after we wrapped filming...at about eight thirty."

Twyla nods.

"You didn't come back later that night, did you?"

"What? No. Of course not."

"You're sure? You weren't out by the pool around, say, ten forty-five?"

"No. Why would I have been by the pool?"

"I've asked myself that same question." I give her the same curious look she just gave me. "Oh well...no matter... Maybe Wavonne and I should just get down to the business of having lunch." I offer Twyla a smile in hopes of lightening the mood.

"Yes, that sounds like a good plan," she replies. "I'll get the oysters out first."

"Perfect." I turn my head toward Wavonne as Twyla approaches one of the ordering stations. "You believe her?"

"I don't know," Wavonne says. "Someone who thinks she saw Bigfoot in the woods ain't exactly the most reliable source for seein' Twyla outside her door."

"True."

"So, what now?"

"I'm thinking we should go back to the inn and poke around . . . see if we can catch up with Russell and Cynthia . . . and maybe Trey. I'd like to ask all of them a few questions."

"Can we start with Trey?"

"I guess. Why?"

"I want to ask him about the Himalayan salt mask he was wearing. . . . Boy Wonder is sort of obnoxious, but he's got nice skin."

"Seriously?"

"Yes," Wavonne says. "You have your questions you want to ask and I have mine."

Chapter 26

"You think he's still here?" Wavonne asks as we walk down the hall toward Trey's room.

"I'm not sure. I assume they halted production of the show given recent events. If they didn't, there's no one left for Trey to compete against anyway. He may have gone home."

I knock on the door and hear someone rummaging around inside before it swings open.

"Hi," Trey says. "What are you guys doing here?"

"We were just wondering if we could chat with you for a minute."

"Um . . . sure." He opens the door wider and signals for us to come in. "This is about Sherry, I assume?" He motions for us to sit down on the little sofa.

"Yes." Wavonne and I take a seat, and I notice his room has the same layout as Sherry's and the one I shared with Wavonne the other night. "I probably shouldn't be, but I'm trying to do Vera a favor, and see what I can find out about the night Sherry was killed."

"A favor for Vera?"

"The police find it suspect that she waited so long after Sherry was killed to come out of her room."

"I think they wonder if she was in her room at all . . . at least when Sherry was killed," Wavonne says.

"They think Vera killed Sherry?"

"They are looking at her as a possible suspect. That's all."

"Seems silly. Vera's not a murderer."

"I don't think so either, but sometimes the cops do things in a hurry and try to get cases closed as fast as possible. I figured it couldn't hurt for me to follow behind them and see if I can find out anything they may have missed."

"I'm not sure I can be of much help. I told the police everything I know."

"Which is?"

"I was on the bed on my laptop when the shots went off."

"Did you hear anything unusual before all the noise?"

"You can't really hear much between the walls here," Trey says. "My TV was on, and I was brainstorming for the final competition when I heard the gun. I knew we were filming at the Museum of American History the next day, and I heard Cynthia talking with one of her assistants about the Julia Child kitchen exhibit. I figured the next challenge would likely be related to some of Julia's recipes or classic French cooking. I had just put on my salt mask and was looking up duck à l'orange recipes when I heard the shots. Like you guys, I immediately ran out of my room to see what was going on."

"Probably not the brightest thing to do on any of our parts. Vera had the right idea about staying in her room until the police got here," I say, before adding, "So, these walls are pretty soundproof?"

"I wouldn't say soundproof. I couldn't really hear voices, but when Russell made late night visits to Sherry's room there was definitely some racket over there."

"So the rumors are true? Russell and Sherry were having an affair?"

"I told you," Wavonne says.

"Unless they were playing whack-a-mole on Sherry's headboard, yeah, I'd say that's a pretty safe bet. I may not have been able to hear voices, but her bed ramming up against the wall . . . yeah, that came through pretty clear."

"Did you tell the police about Russell and Sherry?"

"Yes. Like I said, I told them everything I know."

"As long as we are talking about things you know," I say. "Do you know if Cynthia was aware of Russell and Sherry's affair?"

"No. I don't know if she knew, and I certainly was not going to be the one to tell her." Trey sits down on the edge of the bed. "But I suspect that she did, and I think she found out recently. Cynthia's attitude toward Sherry changed about a week ago . . . and not in a good way."

"How so?"

"When we were taping the first few episodes, Cynthia was very cordial with her. I might go as far as saying that Cynthia paid special attention to her. She was always chatting her up and, here and there, she loaned out Russell's hair and makeup girls to her. We, the contestants, that is, didn't get hair and makeup. Only Russell and Leon got that. So, some attention from Russell's stylists was a treat for Sherry. But about a week ago, their relationship seemed to sour. Cynthia started speaking to her only when necessary, and when it came to hair and makeup, Sherry was left to her own devices. There was just a coldness from Cynthia that was not there before."

"Seems odd that the police would have a focus on Vera when it seems that Cynthia likely had a motive too," Wavonne says.

"Yeah, but Cynthia was in the lounge when Sherry was killed . . . and word is that not only is she on camera in the lounge, but the bartender or attendant or whatever you call him can vouch for her being in there as well."

"Maybe Cynthia didn't know about the affair, and Sherry threatened to tell her. That would put Russell on the suspect list," Wavonne says.

"I was standing next to Russell when he talked to the police," Trey offers. "He said he was in the restaurant with his contractor when Sherry was killed, so he has an alibi, too."

"What was his contractor doing here at eleven thirty at night?"

"I don't think Russell making his contractors burn the midnight oil was anything unusual. He's known for being pretty hard-nosed, and he was anxious to get Sunfish open in a few weeks."

"So, we know what Russell and Cynthia were doing when Sherry was killed, and they both have alibis." I want to add, "But what we don't know is what *you* were doing." Even though Trey told us what he was up to when Sherry died, unlike Russell and Cynthia, he has no witnesses or cameras to prove it—nothing to verify he didn't dash out of his room, into Sherry's through the patio door, and shoot her. Then rush back into his room in time to come out into the hallway looking as if he was as surprised as anyone by the gunfire.

"My guess is Sherry's death had nothing to do with anyone involved with the show. I don't think anyone is going to commit murder over a cooking contest."

"I hope you're right, but it certainly was one way to eliminate the competition," I say, and look for any changes in his facial expression . . . to see if my words about eliminating the competition unnerve him, but I see nothing unusual or telling.

"The only *competition* left on Monday was me." Trey looks at me like I'm accusing him of something. "I can assure you that, as much as I wanted to win and be named Elite Chef, it is certainly not something I would kill anyone over. Besides, I don't even know how to shoot a gun."

"She was shot at very close range. I don't think whoever

did it had to know much about shooting guns. But that's neither here nor there. I wasn't accusing you of anything, Trey. Like I said, I'm just asking questions . . . seeing what I can find out." I get up from the sofa and Wavonne follows my lead. "We should be going. I appreciate you sharing with us." As I say this, it occurs to me that Trey seems significantly less obnoxious than he was during our earlier encounters. He hasn't pronounced anything in a pretentious French accent or mentioned where he went to school . . . or belittled Sweet Tea the whole time we've been here. "It was nice talking to you," I say, and for the first time I really mean it.

"You too." He turns his head and looks me in the eye. "And, listen, I hope you'll forgive me for making cracks about your restaurant serving . . . what did I call it, 'basic type stuff'? I've actually known of your restaurant for years and have always wanted to try it. But since I started on the show, I've been borrowing from the Omarosa playbook. You can't just be a great chef to win this thing. You really have to be some sort of entertaining character, someone who brings in viewers, if you want to keep from being sent home. Everyone loves a villain and the more obnoxious I am, the more I find Cynthia sending the cameramen my way. Outside this circus I don't belittle other chefs or talk in overblown French accents while constantly reminding people of my credentials. I was just playing a role."

I can't help but laugh. "You played it very well."

"You sure did," Wavonne says. "If you played it any better I may have punched your lights out."

"Although there was one little nick in your armor," I say while Trey laughs at Wavonne's comment. "I knew you weren't all bad when you let Vera have one of your sweet potatoes, so she'd actually have a chance during the last challenge."

"How could I say no to Vera? She's such a nice lady. I can't believe the police would think of her as a killer, even for a second." He gets up from the bed. "So, we're good?"

"All is forgiven," I reply, and Trey follows Wavonne and me to the door. And it's only now, when I'm walking back toward the hallway, that I see something—a door along the wall shared with Sherry's room—a door that, when unlocked and opened on both sides, would connect Sherry's room to Trey's.

Chapter 27

"I'm assuming you saw the door," I say to Wavonne as we walk down the hall toward the hotel lobby.

"What door?"

"The one that connects Trey's room to Sherry's."

"There was a door to Sherry's room?"

"How did you not see it? It was to the right as we were walking out of his room."

"I was asking Trey about his mask when we were walking out of the room. I wasn't paying attention to doors," Wavonne says. "He said it's just coconut oil, pink Himalayan salt, and a little grapefruit oil. Do you think they sell all that at Wegmans?"

"I don't know . . . probably . . . but I can't say I'm terribly interested in Trey's beauty mask at the moment."

"I don't know, Halia. I'm looking these masks up online now." Wavonne is swiping on her phone as we walk. "Says here it hydrates, soothes, and detoxifies. Maybe we can pick up the stuff tonight and whip up one for me . . . and maybe one for you, so you look nice and fresh when you meet Aunt Celia's pharmacist."

"Momma's pharmacist is the least of my concerns at the

moment," I say as we step into the lobby. "That connecting door to Sherry's room really bothers me. Trey could have maneuvered between his room and Sherry's much faster via that door than if he had to go via the patio. I mean he could—" I stop talking and almost lose my breath. For a quick second I think I see Sherry, back from the dead, at the front desk talking with Mitchell. I begin to wonder if Vera is not the only one seeing strange sights . . . until we get closer to the lobby, and I realize it's only someone who looks an awful lot like her.

"You must be related to Sherry," I say to the young woman after we approach the counter, and there is a break in her conversation with Mitchell. "You look so much like her."

"I'm Angela, Sherry's sister. I'm here making some . . . some arrangements."

"It's nice to meet you. I'm so sorry about Sherry. Such a lovely girl. We got to spend a little time with her shortly before her . . . her . . . the *incident*."

"Thank you." You can tell Angela has been crying but seems to be keeping it together at the moment. "Let me guess," she says. "You're Halia." She shifts her head in Wavonne's direction. "And you're Wavonne."

"How did you know?"

"I talked to Sherry shortly before she . . . you know . . . and she mentioned both of you. Said you helped her come up with an amazing biscuit recipe. . . ." Angela starts getting teary eyed. "I'm sorry. She was just in such a good place when she told me about you guys. And that was the last time I talked to her . . . the last time I'll *ever* talk . . ." Her teary eyes morph into full-fledged crying.

"Please don't apologize. It's okay." I put my arm on her shoulder. "Cry all you want."

"I just can't believe it." Angela wipes her eyes and tries to collect herself. "She sounded tired when I talked to her, but she was so happy to be part of the finals and was looking forward to me coming to visit to see the final taping. I had just gone to bed when I got the call that she'd been . . . that she'd been killed."

"Why don't we go have a seat." I keep my arm on her shoulder and lead her to a sofa by the fireplace. "I'm sure this is an incredibly difficult time. And there's always so much to do after someone passes."

"She didn't pass. She was *murdered*."

"Yes," I say quietly. "And it's horrendous. You didn't come to town by yourself, did you?"

"I did. Our parents were too distraught to travel. Someone needed to come and arrange to transfer her body and collect her things, and I already had a ticket booked."

"That's a lot to handle all by yourself. Are you managing okay?"

"As good as can be expected, I guess. I spent the morning talking with the police, and then I had to go to a local funeral home, so they can help arrange her transfer back home once the county releases her body. At least it's kept me distracted."

"Were the police able to tell you much? Are they any closer to finding out who is responsible for Sherry's death?"

"They said they are following up a few leads, but they don't have enough evidence against anyone to make an arrest."

"Do you know anyone who would have wanted your sister dead?"

"No. Sometimes Sherry operated in what I call the 'gray area,' but I don't think she'd ever done anything that would make anyone want to kill her."

"What do you mean?" Wavonne asks. "The gray area?"

"Sherry was always looking for a quick buck or some sort of hustle to make some fast money. Sometimes her schemes were legal and sometimes they weren't . . . and sometimes they were just more unethical than illegal—like this whole thing she had going with Russell. I assume everyone knows about that by now."

"It seems to be the worst kept secret in PG County," Wavonne says.

"It does appear to be pretty out in the open at this point, but we don't know any real details about their affair. Was she in love with him?"

Angela looks at me like I just asked her if unicorns exist. "She was in love all right . . . with his money." She pulls a tissue from her purse and dabs at her eyes. "Sherry was my baby sister. She was very dear to me, but she could be a shady character . . . always scamming. She was determined to be Mrs. Mellinger Number Two. She'd been plotting the whole thing for months . . . getting cast on the show, studying up on Russell and what he likes, ensuring she got some alone time with him to make her moves. Her goal all along was not to win the contest, although that would have been a nice plus. . . . It was to win Russell."

"Forgive me for saying so," I offer, "but that seems like a lot of . . . I don't know . . . a lot of *maneuvering* for someone that . . . How do I say this? For someone who was not . . . overly mentally endowed."

Angela sighs. " 'Not overly mentally endowed'? That's the politest way I have ever heard anyone called stupid in my life," she says. "But, thing is—"

"She wasn't stupid, was she?" I ask, suddenly thinking about what Trey just told me and Wavonne about how he was playing a role to be a favorite among the viewers.

"Sherry was so *not* stupid. The whole dingbat routine was an act."

"So, just like Trey, she was hamming it up for the cameras to ensure her survival on the show?"

"She was 'hamming it up' even before the show. She knew

she needed a shtick to get a spot in the competition, so she adopted a whole Jessica Simpson–Chicken of the Sea thing. I went with her when they were doing the casting interview. She mentioned how her neck was hurting because her head was so heavy, and that she hoped they weren't shooting in New Mexico because her passport had expired. Believe me, you had to be smart to pull off pretending to be as dumb as she did. And it worked. She was the multiracial answer to Chrissy Snow. We talked almost every day over the past few weeks, and she said the producers were eating it up. She was confident that, even if her culinary skills were subpar, they wouldn't eliminate her if they thought her airhead antics would draw ratings."

"So her whole, 'Oops I forgot and used all the cheddar and grabbed expired baking powder by mistake,' thing was a farce? She purposely sabotaged Vera?"

"Of course, she did," Angela says. "Well at least she did with the cheese. She said she just got lucky with the baking powder and, when I talked to her last, she wasn't sure why her biscuits rose and Vera's waffle didn't—they both used the old baking powder"

"That part is strange," I say. "But so many other things make sense now that we know Sherry didn't share an IQ with a dodo bird."

"Like what? What things?" Wavonne asks. "I thought it was odd that someone as dim-witted as we thought Sherry to be had managed to pull off the scheme she had going at Dauphine a couple of years ago."

"Oh, that one," Angela says. "That was when she was working at that tacky Cajun restaurant that looks like Catwoman's lair. I think she made enough cash off pilfered liquor to buy her Lexus."

"If she made enough money to buy a luxury car, she must have taken Twyla for tens of thousands of dollars."

"Twyla?"

"The owner of Catwoman's lair," Wavonne says.

"Twyla owns Dauphine," I clarify. "She made it seem like Sherry's exploits were not such a big deal . . . maybe worth a few hundred bucks or something."

"You don't think this Twyla would have murdered Sherry?" Angela asks.

"I don't think so, but it wasn't that long ago that someone was stabbed to death over a Popeye's chicken sandwich, so people have certainly killed for less. I know Detective Hutchins at the police department. I'll make sure he's aware of Sherry's history with Twyla," I say. "Other than her antics with Twyla and her affair with Russell, is there anything else that might be useful to know . . . that might offer any leads?"

"I don't think so, but I was worried about her because of the whole Russell thing. Last week she told me she thought she had him where she wanted him and had given him an ultimatum—he was to tell Cynthia about them and ask for a divorce, or she was going to end their relationship."

"Do you know if Russell told Cynthia?"

"No, but Sherry said that Cynthia came by her room before she called me the night of the murder. She thought Cynthia had come to confront her about the affair, but it turned out she only came by to tell Sherry that they had moved up the scheduling for the following day, and Sherry needed to be ready by seven a.m. instead of eight a.m. Come to think of it, she said Trey came by as well, claiming to just want to wish her luck . . . a sort of 'may the best man win' kind of moment."

"She didn't mention anything about having any sort of cross words or conflict with either one of them?"

"No, she mostly just mentioned their visits in passing . . . in between talk of how good the red velvet cake was at the museum cafeteria, and how she was liking the new moisturizer she was using on her elbows. We just yammered about nothing on our phone calls. Most nights we did this for about an hour while we got ready for bed, but that night, the day had really taken a toll on her. She said she was calling it a night early, so we only talked for about ten minutes. Little did I know, a few minutes after we hung up she'd . . ." Angela starts to lose her composure again. "No." She straightens herself on the sofa. "I've cried enough for one day, but I am really tired. I got a room at the Gaylord, so I think I'm going to call an Uber and head over there. Russell offered to let me stay here, but that would be too weird."

"No need to call an Uber. We'll drop you off." I get up from the sofa. "If there's anything else we can do for you while you're in town getting things settled, please let us know."

"That's nice of you, but honestly, I prefer to ride over there alone."

"Girlfriend's sick of your questions, Halia," Wavonne says.

Angela almost cracks a smile. "Maybe . . . just a little. But you've been very kind. Thank you."

"You're welcome," I say. "Really, if we can do anything . . ."

Angela nods, and Wavonne and I turn to go as she pulls out her phone and starts tapping on the screen to order her ride. As we head for the door I start to mull everything over in my head: Russell and Sherry's affair, Sherry insisting that he tell Cynthia about said affair, the money Sherry stole from Twyla, the door adjoining Sherry's room to Trey's. I'm wondering why, with all these red flags, Vera is the only one the police have brought in for questioning, and that's when I see Russell emerge from the hallway that leads to his suite. I watch as he says something to Mitchell at the desk and then moves on toward the breezeway that leads to the restaurant.

"Hey," I say to Wavonne. "Why don't we—"

"Go talk to Russell?"

"Am I that predictable?"

"I saw that look in your eyes as soon as you caught sight of him . . . like a kid in a candy store."

"Only, instead of candy, I want information."

Chapter 28

"Hello?" I call after Wavonne as I walk into Sunfish. We saw Russell walk in ahead of us, but now he's nowhere to be seen. The dining room looks kind of spooky and surreal. With most of the lights off, the remnants of the competition—the cooking stations, the mixers, the pots and pans—seem like they're lurking in the shadows.

"Over here," a voice calls from inside a doorway on the other side of the room.

Wavonne and I follow the sound and find Russell seated behind a desk in a little nook of an office.

"Hi," I say.

"Hello," Russell replies. "What can I do for you?" He asks this in such a way that it's clear he'd rather not do *anything* for me.

"Um . . . nothing," I say. "We were here talking to Trey, and we saw you head this way. Just thought we'd say hi and see how you're doing."

"I'm fine. Thank you." He says this in a "You said you wanted to see how I'm doing. I've told you. You can leave now," sort of way.

He clearly is not interested in having a rap session with us, and given the little use he has for niceties, I figure I'd better get a few questions in before he just flat-out tells us to skedaddle.

"I see all the sets or stations or whatever for the show are still up. Are you planning to resume taping sometime soon?"

"I haven't decided what we are going to do about the show, but we'll need to close it out somehow. Perhaps when an appropriate amount of time has passed, we will default back to Vera, and she and Trey will compete in a final challenge."

"I guess whatever happens, it will be a less interesting show with Sherry gone though."

"Agreed." He looks at me suspiciously. "What is it you want, Halia? I have work to do."

"I've been trying to piece a few things together from the night Sherry was killed. That's why I was here speaking with Trey. I guess I'm hoping you might be able to help some with that, too."

"Why? Isn't that a job for the police? That Detective Hutchins fellow?"

"Yes, but so far, the only suspect they seem to have any interest in is Vera."

"Sherry's mistakes, if they were in fact *mistakes*, caused Vera to lose a high stakes competition, and she was nowhere to be seen after Sherry was killed. Doesn't seem odd to me that she would be on their list."

"Maybe not, but other people certainly had dubious relationships with Sherry as well."

"Other people?"

"Yes. Turns out she worked for Twyla years ago and stole from her, and it's not out of the realm of possibility that Trey could have taken Sherry's life to eliminate his competition. Word is also that her relationship with Cynthia appeared to sour over the last week or so. And . . . well . . . I'm sure you're aware, at this point, that most everyone is in the know about your relationship with Sherry."

"My relationship?"

"That the two of you were . . . were . . ."

"Gettin' jiggy wit' it," Wavonne says.

"Okay, we are done here, ladies," he says abruptly. "My relationship or lack of relationship with Sherry is none of your concern."

"We'll be on our way," I reply. "But just one question, if you don't mind."

Russell looks back at me, neither confirming nor denying if he minds.

"You mentioned how Vera was nowhere to be seen after the shooting. But you were decidedly absent for a few minutes after the shooting as well. Were you—"

"I was right here in the restaurant with my contractor when Sherry was killed. I was on my way out to take a walk and smoke a cigar—it's sort of a nightly ritual to relax and clear my head, but I made a pit stop in here to see the progress my contractor was making. I heard the gunshots when I was showing him how I wanted the molding finished. I figured there must have been some benign explanation for the noise, so I didn't exactly rush to check it out." He gives me that same suspicious look he gave me moments ago. "I suspect what you really want to know is if I have an alibi, and the answer is yes. Not only do I have a witness, but the dining room is under 24/7 surveillance. Both my contractor and I were on camera when the shots went off."

"I'm sure you understand that, given your relationship with Sherry, it's not unreasonable to think—"

"I believe I already told you my relationship with Sherry is none of your concern. I also already told you I have things to do." Russell turns about thirty degrees in his chair, so he's now more facing his computer screen than Wavonne and me.

"Thank you for your time, Mr. Mellinger." When he continues to stare at his computer screen rather than acknowledge my comment, Wavonne and I turn to leave.

"Well, he was just a breath of stale air," Wavonne says as we walk through the restaurant.

"Yeah . . . not exactly sunshine and rainbows, but he's not the most pleasant person to be around when he isn't grieving, so I guess him being a little curt was to be expected."

"Do you think he's grieving? Do you think he saw Sherry as anything other than a side chick?"

"Maybe. There was something about the look on his face, and the groan that came out of him when he saw her on the bed . . . and the way he held her limp hand that makes me think he had real feelings for her . . . assuming Russell Mellinger can have real feelings for anyone."

Wavonne and I walk outside the restaurant. We've barely stepped off the sidewalk onto the parking lot when I see a gangly figure emerging from a little Toyota Corolla.

"Is that Trudy?" I ask Wavonne.

"Unless Billy Bob Thornton threw on a tweed skirt and a pair of flats, my guess is yes."

"Trudy," I say as she approaches us with a laptop bag over one shoulder and a couple of manila file folders in her hand. "How are you?"

"I'm okay. Such a weird few days. I'm still trying to wrap my brain around it all." She turns her head from left to right, taking in the scenery around us. "This is such a lovely property. Who would have thought something so ugly . . . so *awful* would ever happen at a place like this."

"I know. I think this being such a beautiful and exclusive hotel is why most of us were convinced the sound we heard the night Sherry was killed wasn't gunfire—at a place like this, it *had* to be something else."

"We're not sure what it all means for the inn. There has

been so much publicity about what the press has dubbed the 'Elite Chef Murder,' Russell is afraid the whole place might be done for."

"I'm sure it will be fine. People have short memories, and this property is too beautiful for people to stay away."

"Maybe," Wavonne says. "But I bet they repurpose Sherry's room into a storage closet or somethin'. I don't think anyone is gonna want to spend the night in the 'Murder Room.'"

"Oh my," Trudy says. "Murder Room? Are they using that term now, too?"

"I think Wavonne just made that up now."

"I hope so." Trudy starts rustling the folders in her hand. "I should be on my way. I need to go over a few things with Russell."

"We just saw him. He's in his office in the restaurant," I say.

"I'm sure he was glad to see you."

"Yeeeah, not so much."

Trudy narrows her eyebrows at me. "Really?"

"I guess he thought I was asking too many questions."

"About what?"

"About Sherry and his relationship with her, and what he was doing when she was killed."

"I can see how those might be unwelcome questions."

"He must be well aware by now that *everyone* knows that he had a thing goin' with Sherry," Wavonne says.

"Of course. Or at least that everyone involved with the show knows, but so far, the press has not picked it up. I'm sure he doesn't want to confirm or deny anything about their relationship in hopes that he'll be able to keep it off the news until interest in the story dies down." Trudy pulls the strap on her bag higher up on her shoulder. "I really better get moving. Russell is waiting for me. I don't want to be late. He's not the most genial person to be around when you're on time."

"Okay, but one last thing."

"What?"

"Do you know of anyone who might have wanted Sherry dead?"

"No. She was a reasonably pleasant young lady even if she was dumb as a box of hair. I know she had a conflict with Vera at the last taping but, from what I heard about it, it was nothing anyone would kill over."

"What about Russell . . . and Cynthia? Did you have any knowledge of Russell and Sherry's affair going south recently?"

"No, Russell is pretty selective about what he shares with me. You've seen him around me. . . . He mostly just barks orders."

"And Cynthia? Do you think she may have found out about Sherry and Russell's affair?"

"I don't know, but some things have certainly been going on with Cynthia."

"What sort of things?"

"I'm not sure I should say anything. . . . It's yet another thing Russell's afraid might make the papers." Trudy takes a breath and seems to contemplate for a moment or two about whether or not she should share whatever information she has. Fortunately for me, she seems to decide on divulging. "Cynthia has a bit of a problem with pills."

"Pills?" Wavonne asks. "Like tranks? Codies? Roofies? Sobos? Purple drank?"

"I have no idea what any of those are," Trudy says. "Opioids. I think OxyContin is her drug of choice."

"Really?"

"Yes. We thought she had beat it, but it seems she went to buy some pills a few days ago. Russell said that over the last week or so, she'd been distant and irritable. He was afraid she may had fallen off the wagon, so he asked me to keep tabs on her . . . to follow her when I could. She was pretty busy when the show was filming, so mostly I only ended up following her on the occasional trip to the hair salon or the Neiman Marcus across the bridge in Virginia. But late last week, things got weird."

"How so?"

"I followed her to the rental car counter at that big hotel over by the bridge. She parked her Mercedes and rented a little Kia Rio. When she got inside, she put on a short curly wig and a pair of oversized sunglasses. She clearly did not want to be recognized."

"Where did she go?"

"She went into the city . . . to an apartment complex called Brentwood Manors."

"Brentwood Manors?" Wavonne says. "There's a shooting there like once a week."

"Yeah . . . it looked like a rough area," Trudy agrees. "Cynthia parked the little Rio, went into one of the apartment buildings for a short stay, and came out a few minutes later. And then, as if things were not odd enough, she got back in the car, drove about two blocks down to another building, and did the same thing."

"You think she was buying drugs?"

"Why else would someone of Cynthia's means go into a crime ridden neighborhood? She hurt her back a few years ago . . . started on some OxyContin . . . and got hooked. She was essentially a junky for months. Before she went into rehab, she used to doctor hop to get her drugs. . . . She would even go to the emergency room with various contrived illnesses to get her fix. But, as far as I know, she's been . . . or *had been* clean for over a year. Controls are tighter at doctors' offices now. If she's fallen off the wagon, she may have no choice but to get her pills on the street."

"When she left the apartments she went into, did she come out with anything? A bag or a package?"

"No, but she had a nice size shoulder bag on her when she went in. I'm sure she would have just put any pills in there."

"Has Russell confronted her about it?"

"He doesn't know."

"What?"

"It all went down the day before Sherry was killed. It wasn't something I wanted to tell him over text or e-mail, and I hadn't gotten a chance to speak to him privately before Sherry was shot. He's had enough to deal with the last few days without being told his wife is back on the sauce. I suppose I have to tell him soon though, maybe tonight. Hopefully, he can intervene before Cynthia spirals completely out of control again. If she hasn't already. She did some crazy stuff when she was hooked last time."

"You think she might have already done something crazy? Something like off Sherry?"

"If she's back on the pills and found out about the affair, anything is possible."

"But she has a witness *and* was caught on camera in the lounge when the shots were fired."

"Yes. That's what I heard. But perhaps rather than killing Sherry herself, she arranged to have her killed and made sure she had an alibi when it happened. It's awfully convenient that she just happened to be somewhere with a camera at the exact time Sherry was killed, no?"

"Maybe. But why kill Sherry? If Cynthia did find out about the affair, why not just divorce Russell?"

"Maybe they had a prenup, and she wouldn't get any money if they divorced," Wavonne says.

"They do have a prenup, but Cynthia would get plenty of money if they divorced. I manage all of Russell's important papers. I've seen the prenup and, in the event of a divorce, Cynthia would get eighty thousand dollars a month for the rest of her life."

That figure makes me swallow hard. "What does one even do with all that money?"

"I wouldn't know," Trudy says. "I don't make that in a year."

"You and me both," Wavonne says. "*Two* years."

"With this talk of earning a living, I guess Wavonne and I should get back to Sweet Tea. Thank you for the information, Trudy."

"You're welcome. I hope it helps. Please don't tell anyone, especially Russell and Cynthia, what I shared with you. I shouldn't be spreading gossip, but Cynthia's behavior has me worried, and I can't help but think it might be connected to Sherry's death. Do you think I should share what I know with the police? I'm generally pretty respectful of my employer's privacy, but someone's been killed."

"Of course we won't tell anyone, but yes, I think the police need to know what Cynthia has been up to. Even if it's just via an anonymous phone call or something."

"You're probably right. Maybe I will give that detective that's been coming around a call tomorrow."

"I really think you should," I say, and decide I've taken up enough of Trudy's time. "I guess we'll be going. Have a good night," I say, while at the same time wondering if it's even possible to have a good night if that night is going to be spent with Russell.

Chapter 29

"She said she would come?" Wavonne asks, scooping ice from the cooler into some glasses before filling them with sweet tea and dropping in a lemon wedge.

"Yes. I thought I might have to go to her, but when I called and asked her if she wanted to come by for lunch, she quickly agreed. She said she has a lot of downtime now that the show is on hiatus. I think she's bored."

"I guess spendin' your husband's money gets dull after a while?" Wavonne places the glasses of tea on a tray. "I'm happy to carry her burdens if she wants to send some coin my way."

"I'll let her know. There she is now," I reply as Wavonne trots off to make a drink delivery.

"Cynthia," I say as I move closer to her. "How are you?"

"As well as can be expected, I guess."

As usual, she looks lovely. Her hair is pressed bone straight and falls just past her shoulders. She's dressed casually, you might even say simply, in a pair of fitted plaid pants, a white blouse, and a beige blazer, but somehow she still looks as elegant as someone in a designer evening gown. I have a vague memory, from when she was here last, of her saying she'd been married to Russell for thirty years, which makes me think she must be at least in her late forties even though she doesn't look a day over thirty-five.

"I'm sure it's been a taxing few days. Maybe I can take your mind off things with some fried chicken and waffles, or we have a crab and sweet-corn quiche on special this afternoon."

"That sounds really nice, but I eat pretty light at lunch," she says, following me to a table by the front windows.

"We have some nice salads on the menu, and our homemade chicken noodle soup is pretty low calorie. Why don't you take a look at the menu while I get you something to drink. Iced tea? Coke? Glass of wine?"

"A glass of chardonnay would be delightful." She takes a seat. "You'll join me, I hope?"

"Sure," I say, grateful she asked me to sit with her, so I didn't have to invite myself.

After fetching Cynthia's glass of wine and an iced tea for me, I find Cynthia looking at the menu when I return to the table and take a seat.

"Anything catching your attention?"

"This Cobb salad sounds nice."

"Is that what you'd like?" I wave Wavonne over.

"Wavonne," Cynthia says when Wavonne reaches the table. "How are you?"

"I'm okay," Wavonne answers, and cuts right to the chase. "It's awful what happened to Sherry and all, but Halia and I are still goin' to be on TV, right?"

Cynthia smiles. "I'm pretty sure we'll air the whole season in the fall, but we're still figuring out how we are going to end the competition and wrap up the final episode."

"Okay . . . good to know. I was—"

"Wavonne," I interrupt before she starts asking if she can be in the final episode or get a free weekend at the inn or a gift card for Sunfish. "I think Cynthia was eyeing the Cobb salad."

"Salad? She does know we got fried chicken back there?"

Cynthia laughs. "That's a bit heavy for me. I think I'll go with the salad."

"Suit yourself. You want the house dressing that comes with it?"

"It's quite nice. We make it here," I say. "Some shallots, red-wine vinegar, olive oil, and a little garlic and Dijon mustard."

"That sounds perfect."

"Got it," Wavonne says, and looks in my direction. "Since you're pretendin' you eat salads these days, should I put a Cobb salad order in for you too?"

"Yes, please."

"So, are things calming down a bit since the . . . the *incident*?" I ask after Wavonne has left the table.

"I suppose. Sherry's sister came to town to make arrangements to transport her body back to Chicago and collect Sherry's things from the inn." Cynthia takes a long sip of wine. "One of those crime scene clean-up companies came and did some clean up in the room, but I think we're going to completely gut it . . . pull up the carpet and replace the furniture. So far, despite all the bad press, no one has canceled for our official opening weekend next month. I'm a little surprised."

"I don't know. I guess people are used to all sorts of things going down at hotels. I have *so many* stories from just owning a restaurant, and no one stays overnight here."

"I'm sure you do. We've seen our share of antics at Russell's restaurants as well. My favorite was the server who was running a prostitution ring from Cobalt Blue. Men would ask for her to be their server, and when she took their order they would ask if we had any Pepsi Blue and—"

"They stopped making that years ago."

"Exactly. That was the code word to let her know they were there for something other than smoked salmon and tuna tartare . . . or *anything* that was actually on the menu. It seemed odd that so many men who were dining alone would specifically ask for her, but she really tipped her hand when she drove up one evening in a car nicer than mine. Russell's restaurants are high-dollar, so our servers do well, but not show-up-to-work-in-a-Mercedes-E-class kind of well."

I laugh. "Yeah . . . I'm not sure who's done worse . . . my employees or my customers. I had a customer who wanted to bring his emotional support iguana in here one day, and another guy who offered Wavonne fifty dollars for her underwear—"

"Don't think I wasn't tempted." Wavonne sets down a pan of piping hot sour-cream cornbread. "Fifty dollars is fifty dollars. A sista's got bills."

"Thankfully you chose your dignity over fifty dollars."

"Good thing he didn't offer me a hundred. My dignity is only worth so much."

Cynthia chuckles. "So much for eating light," she says, looking at the cornbread.

"Sorry, it's complimentary. I'm used to bringing it out to all the tables. I can take it—"

"No, no," Cynthia says. "It's here now. I'd hate to see it go to waste." Cynthia looks up from the cornbread to me. "It smells heavenly, and I'm sure we could trade stories about the restaurant business for days, but somehow, I don't think you invited me to lunch to eat cornbread and talk about support iguanas and Wavonne's underwear."

"Was it that obvious?"

"Russell said you grilled him last night, and Trey said you came by his room as well. I figured I would probably be next, and if I didn't come to *you*, you'd come to *me*. Besides, Detective Hutchins told me not to talk to you, and I don't like people telling me what to do or not do."

"He did *what*?"

"He said you might start asking questions . . . that you had a bit of a . . . what did he call it? A 'Columbo complex.'"

"A Columbo complex? Oh, he's going to get an earful the next time I talk to him."

"I don't know about Columbo. I've always thought of her more as the African American answer to Velma on *Scooby-Doo*. Velma was sort of frumpy with no fashion sense, too," Wavonne says. "And I'm Daphne, because, you know, she was the pretty one."

"Don't you have other tables, Wavonne?"

"They can wait."

"Columbo, Velma," Cynthia says. "Either way, I clearly didn't listen to Detective Hutchins, or I wouldn't be here. If you're able to find out anything he isn't, I'm all for it. It's creepy knowing that whoever killed Sherry is still out there, especially when you're sleeping a few doors down from the scene of the crime." Cynthia helps herself to a slice of cornbread and spreads a dollop of whipped honey butter on it. "So, what is it you want to know, Halia?"

I take a moment to collect my thoughts and try to find a diplomatic way to ask her such a sensitive question. "Um . . . well . . . lots of things I suppose. But first and foremost I guess I'm wondering if . . . ?" *Gosh, how do you ask a woman, who may or may not know about her husband's infidelity, if she knows about her husband's infidelity?* "It's a difficult question to ask, but . . . did you know . . . were you aware that—"

"Did you know Russell was doin' the horizontal bop with Sherry?" Wavonne blurts.

"What?! What does that have to do with anything?"

"I'm sorry Wavonne, who clearly has some other tables

that need tending to, asked the question so callously." I give Wavonne a "beat it" look and continue as she walks off. "But it's important information. If you knew about the affair, and honestly, I'm not sure how you couldn't, given that everyone else seemed to know about it, that knowledge would give—not that I'm accusing you of anything—but it would give you a motive to kill Sherry."

"Me kill Sherry?! Maybe you're not as good at this detective stuff as you think. If you'd done your homework, you'd know that I was in the lounge when Sherry was killed. I have proof on video, and Jerome, the attendant, was in there with me when the gunshots went off, so I have a witness as well. So, whether or not I knew about my husband's philandering is not relevant."

"Isn't it though?" I ask. "Again, I'm not accusing you of anything. I'm just exploring possibilities. But, hypothetically, just because you didn't kill Sherry yourself doesn't mean you were not involved in her death some way."

"Oh my. I came here because I thought I might be able to offer you some help in finding out who did actually kill Sherry. I had no idea *I* would be a suspect in your little inquiry."

"I'm just trying to cover all the bases, that's all. A wife suddenly finding out about a husband's affair could provoke her to do almost anything."

"Let me ask you this, Halia." Cynthia sits up straight in her chair. "How could I have suddenly found out about something I engineered?"

"What do you mean?"

"I mean *I* set up the affair between Russell and Sherry."

I'm quiet for a moment while I try to make sure I heard her right. "I'm sorry . . . *what*?"

"If you must know, every season of *Elite Chef* I find a little . . . a little *playmate* for Russell. This last time it just happened to be Sherry."

"You purposely set your husband up to have an affair?" I ask with disbelief. "Why would you do that?"

"Um . . . you've seen him, Halia," she says. "He's *disgusting*. Every night he's on top of some little dim-witted hoochie is one less night he's on top of *me*."

She's waiting for me to say something, but I'm too stunned to respond. I've seen a lot of crazy stuff in my day, but I've never heard of anyone setting up extramarital affairs for their own husband.

"You looked so shocked, Halia. Like you've never met Russell." She casually takes a bite out of her cornbread as if what she just told me should make perfect sense to anyone who has met her husband. "And it's not just that he's hard to look at with those jagged teeth and that belly hanging over his pants . . . and that *ridiculous* hair. He's about as interesting and fun to be around as a wet cat and sometimes he even smells bad. The less time I have to spend with that man, the better. Let me tell you, any night I do not have to share a bed with Russell Mellinger is a good night. If he isn't gross enough already, he smokes a cigar every evening before bed and gets under the covers smelling like a musty tobacco barn. Let him get in Sherry's bed smelling that way." Ms. I-Eat-Pretty-Light-At-Lunch slathers some more honey butter on her cornbread and takes another bite. "I thought he was out smoking his cigar when Sherry was killed, but I guess he got sidetracked talking to the contractor."

"If you find him so distasteful, why not divorce him?"

"Being Mrs. Russell Mellinger comes with a lot of perks, Halia. I say 'jump' and people ask, 'how high?'" Do you think I'd really be the producer of a national television show if I was not his wife? If staying married to a hobgoblin gets me treated like royalty, I can put up with a fat belly and cigar breath."

"Well, this is certainly not the information I expected to get today."

"Maybe not, but it should be useful in clearing my name. Why would I kill someone who was doing me a favor and taking my husband off my hands a few nights a week?"

"I don't know," I say. "But let me ask you about something else."

"What was I doing at Brentwood Manors last week?"

"How did you know that was going to be my next question?"

"Because I saw you talking with Trudy, that meddling old marm, in the parking lot last night before she went to see my husband. Funny how right after talking with her, he comes back to the room and starts asking what I was doing in the city last week at a rough and tumble apartment complex. He wouldn't say how he found out I was there, but I'm sure Trudy had something to do with it. She either followed me or had someone follow me."

"So why were you there?"

"I'll tell you the same thing I told Russell," she replies. "Given all your digging around, you may or may not know that I used to have a problem with prescription drugs, but I've been clean for over a year. Last week I had a bad spell. I'd fallen out of touch with my sponsor, and I let the cravings get the best of me. I got a tip that I could get some OxyContin from a dealer in Brentwood without having to go to the doctor and get the third degree, so I went and made a purchase." Cynthia shifts around in her seat. "But there's something about scoring drugs in a seedy neighborhood that makes you take stock of things and realize you don't want to go down the addiction rabbit hole again, so I called my sponsor, and she convinced me to flush them as soon as I got home, which I did. As of today, I'm still one year, three months, and two days sober."

"I'm glad to hear that. But one more question," I say as I catch sight of Wavonne coming in this direction with our salads. "Word is that you went into two of the apartment buildings in the community. Why did you go into two different places?"

"The guy I was told to meet didn't have what I was looking for. He sent me a couple of blocks down the street to someone he called an 'associate,' who had what I wanted."

Wavonne places the salads down in front of us.

"This looks very nice, but I'm not really hungry anymore."

"Please stay and have your salad." I take a look at our plates laden with avocados and bacon . . . and chopped eggs and blue cheese . . . and want to chuckle at the idea of Cynthia thinking they're something "light." They probably have as many calories as a cheeseburger. "You said you wanted to find out who killed Sherry, and that's all I'm trying to do. Now that we've gotten the difficult conversation out of the way, you can enjoy your lunch."

Cynthia looks down at her salad, and while it may not be fried chicken or smothered pork chops, it does look reasonably appetizing.

"Try some of the dressing." I hand her the little metal gravy boat with my house dressing in it that Wavonne set down with the salads.

Cynthia reluctantly takes the container from me and lightly pours it over her salad, spears some greens, avocado, and bacon on her fork, and takes a bite. "The dressing's good," she says, going back in with her fork for another mouthful.

"The red wine vinegar gives it the tartness, and we roast the garlic before mincing it—that makes it nice and sweet," I reveal, glad a tasty salad seems to be getting me back in Cynthia's good graces. "So earlier, before I, perhaps needlessly, started asking you about what you knew about Russell and Sherry's affair, you said you came today because you thought you might be able to offer some information that might be helpful. Did you have anything in particular in mind?"

"Not so much *anything* . . . more *anyone*," Cynthia says.

Chapter 30

"What do you mean by 'more *anyone*'?" I ask Cynthia.

"I mean *Vera*. Russell said you were concerned about her being the only suspect the police were investigating. Maybe she shouldn't be the only one on their list, but when she came to see me shortly before Sherry was killed, she certainly seemed like someone who might be capable of . . . well, *anything*."

"When exactly did she come to see you?"

"After we finished taping, but before we all gathered in the concierge lounge for her send-off. She begged me for a redo, and said it was only fair given that Sherry clearly sabotaged her. She was highly agitated and, no matter how many times I said no, she would not let it go. Our suite has two rooms, and I thought we were done when I said good-bye to her to take a call in the bedroom, but when I came back out she was still in the living area . . . and still insistent that I give her another shot. Finally, she threatened to sue if I didn't right what she thought was clearly a wrong."

"What did you say?"

"I told the silly woman the truth—that justice is for the rich, and she'd go bankrupt trying to sue the Russell Mellinger machine. Only then did she finally leave." Cynthia takes a bite of her salad and puts her fork down. "I feel bad for her. She got a raw deal, but that's how competitions work—there are winners and losers. I told Vera she needed to accept what happened and move on. I thought she had finally let it go when she left, but it's not out of the realm of possibility that, somewhere along the way to 'moving on,' she put a couple of bullets in the woman who set her up to lose."

"I suppose it's possible. I've learned over the years that *anything* is possible."

I figure I've probably gotten all the useful information I'm going to get from Cynthia, so I decide to switch gears and get off the topic of Sherry's death and end our lunch on a positive note. "How about some dessert? We have white-chocolate bread pudding and strawberry pie this afternoon."

"I think the cornbread was my food indulgence for the day. It must be loaded with butter."

"And sour cream," I say with a smile.

"Let me pay the bill and get back to the hotel. I still have some brainstorming to do and phone calls to make to figure out where we are going to go with the show given the recent turn of events."

"No bill," I say. "Lunch is on me."

"Thank you." Cynthia takes a last sip of wine, places her napkin on the table, and gets up from her seat. "I wish you luck, Halia. I hope the police can find out who killed Sherry, but if you beat them to it, even better."

"You're welcome." I stand up as well. "Come by again sometime, and we'll talk about more pleasant things."

Cynthia smiles in a way that makes it quite certain that a return visit is not likely.

I sit back down and watch as she exits the restaurant. As soon as the door closes behind her, I reach for my cell phone and dial.

"Yo," says the deep voice on the other end of the phone. "What may I do you for, Halia?"

"Hey, Jack. How are you?"

"Not bad. I figured I'd hear from you."

"Really?"

"Hutchins said you were on the scene at the Ashbury murder at that new hotel in Fort Washington. I know enough to expect my phone to ring if a murder happens anywhere in the vicinity of Halia Watkins."

Jack Spruce is a Sweet Tea regular, friend, and local police officer. I slip him the occasional complimentary slice of red velvet cake or banana pudding, and he is kind enough to give me a little inside scoop on the happenings at the Prince George's County Police Department.

"I can't say you're wrong, but strangely, I'm more looking to give you information rather than ask for it this time."

"Oh?"

"I just wanted to make sure that the police . . . that Detective Hutchins is aware that Cynthia went on a bit of an errand, in disguise no less, supposedly to score some drugs a few days before Sherry was killed." I know I told Trudy I wouldn't tell anyone, but when we parted company she hadn't made it 100 percent clear that she was going to notify the police about Cynthia's foray into the city and, clearly, they need to be made aware.

"Where in the city exactly?"

"An apartment complex called Brentwood Manors."

"Interesting. As far as I know we have not been told of Cynthia going there, but coincidentally, we've been working with the D.C. police department on breaking up a crime ring there for weeks."

"So Brentwood Manors is definitely a drug den like Cynthia said."

"Yes," Jack says. "But it's not just a drug ring we've been

after in that neighborhood. There's a weapons operation going on there, too."

"Weapons?"

"Yes, there's a guy there named Bruce—he's the one dealing drugs. And another guy named Sam—he's been dealing weapons . . . guns, knives, all sorts of ammunition and tactical gear. We tried to bust them just yesterday, but they must have gotten wind of police interest and shut everything down or moved it elsewhere. The apartments we've been watching were empty."

"So, given what you just said, it sounds like Cynthia may not have gone to Brentwood Manors to buy drugs—she may have gone there to buy a gun."

"Possibly. But at the moment, we have no way to prove what she purchased there."

"True. I guess I'll have to keep digging around."

"I'd tell you to let us do that, Halia, but I know I'd be wasting my breath."

"Probably so." I switch the phone to my other ear. "Thanks for chatting with me, Jack. Hope to see you in the restaurant soon. I've got a slice of pie with your name on it."

"I'll probably be in one day next week."

"Okay." I'm about to say good-bye and hang up, but then it occurs to me that there's one more thing I'd like to ask Jack. "Hey, one last question before you go."

"Shoot," he says. "Sorry, that was a poor choice of words given events of late."

"I stopped by the inn yesterday and talked to Trey McIntyre. We spoke for a bit in his room and he didn't tell me anything remarkable, but I did notice one thing—there's a door in his room that I assume, when unlocked, connects his room to Sherry's."

"Yes. We're aware of that. We're not completely incompetent, Halia," Jack jokes.

"Was it locked on Sherry's side the night of the murder?"

"Yes. It was locked when our team got there."

"Okay. Good to know. Thanks again, Jack."

I hit the end button on the phone and lay it down on the table. I start to get up to check on a few things in the kitchen when I see Wavonne looking at her own phone as she strides toward me.

"Wavonne, you know my rule. No phones when you're working. Put that away."

"I don't think you want me to do that." She hands the phone to me. "Hit the play button."

I take the phone from her and see she has some tabloid TMZ or Perez Hilton–type site up on the screen. I hit the play button and see a grainy, dimly lit video of someone, a woman, I think, slinking around the pool at the Willow Oak Inn. It was clearly taken after dark. I continue to watch and see the figure approach Sherry's sliding glass door, knock lightly, and let herself in. It's only when the figure is right up by the door that a light from the side of the building illuminates her face in the darkness.

"Twyla," I say.

"Yep," Wavonne replies. "Little Ms. Southern Charm has got some explainin' to do."

Chapter 31

"I hadn't seen you in over ten years and now three times in two weeks," Twyla says to me as I walk into the darkness of Dauphine.

"Maybe I'm just missing you," I say playfully.

Twyla laughs. "I find that hard to believe, Halia. Let me guess: You saw the video?"

"I suppose you'd also find it hard to believe if I said, 'What video?'" I say. "Honestly, I wasn't sure I'd find you here. I thought the police might have already brought you in."

"They've been here. I explained the whole thing to them, and they left."

"If you don't mind, I'd love to hear your explanation for being caught on tape slipping into Sherry's room on what one assumes was the night she was killed."

"I was filmed the night Sherry was killed, but I was not going into her room."

"What?"

"If you looked closely at the video, you'd have seen there is another room to the right of the one I went into. Sherry's room was at the end of the hall—there were no more rooms to the right of hers."

"So, whose room did you go in?"

"Trey's."

"Trey's? What were you doing in there?" I ask as the answer becomes obvious.

"That's not really any of your business, Halia, but I explained everything to the police, and I also told them I stopped for gas after I left his room. I dug up my receipt, and it's stamped with the exact time I filled up the Cadillac. Eleven twenty-seven. Sherry was killed only two minutes later. There is no way I could have been back at the inn that quickly. The gas station's a good fifteen minutes from there. And, if the receipt is not enough, there is probably security camera footage of me at the station or one of the cashiers would remember me. After all, I am a bit of a local celebrity, and my vintage Cadillac is not easily forgotten."

"Do you . . . or the police know who took the video? And why?"

"Halia, I've shared all I care to at this point, but if the police are convinced I'm innocent when it comes to Sherry's murder, I would hope that's good enough for you." She grabs a menu from the counter. "So why don't you leave the murder investigating to the police and sit down and have some lunch."

If Twyla's food was not so dreadful, I'd be tempted, but since that's not the case, I simply say, "Thank you, but I just stopped by to have a quick word. I need to get back to my own restaurant."

"You know," Twyla says to me as I turn to leave, "if you're still nosing around in the whole thing, maybe there is one thing you should know."

I twist back around and look her in the eyes.

"When I was with Trey in his room, he said something that was a little bit concerning to me. Before I left, I wished him good luck, and he said he didn't need it. He said he was not worried about winning . . . even if he had to 'play dirty.' I distinctly remember him saying, 'If other contestants are playing dirty, why shouldn't I?' When he said this, Sherry was the only other contestant left in the competition. I can only assume he was talking about her when he mentioned 'other contestants.'"

"Interesting."

"Isn't it?" Twyla says. "By 'playing dirty' I thought he meant hiding her olive oil or switching out her salt with sugar. Murder certainly did not come to my mind."

"For Trey's sake, let's hope murder did not come to his mind either," I reply as I, once again, turn to leave and hurry toward the door to get out of Twyla's gloomy restaurant and back into the daylight.

Chapter 32

"It does smell good." Wavonne eyes the foil-covered plate in my hand as we walk toward the inn.

Twyla's talk of gas station security cameras made me think about the cameras at the inn. There seem to be an awful lot of people, including her, who just happened to be in places with both security cameras and witnesses when Sherry was killed. Cynthia was in the monitored concierge lounge, Russell was in the monitored restaurant, and Twyla managed to be at the Shell station on Indian Head Highway when Sherry met her maker. And my guess is that Russell and Cynthia were the only two who knew that the area by the pool was not under surveillance. It's just a lot of stuff that makes one "go hmmm," and adds credence to Trudy's theory that Cynthia, or any number of people, may have arranged Sherry's killing without actually being the one to pull the trigger on the gun.

"Let's hope it puts Mitchell in a good mood . . . or at least a persuasive mood."

After I left Dauphine I went back to Sweet Tea and prepped a plate of my butter-baked chicken, some mashed potatoes and gravy, and a nice serving of collard greens with some chopped bacon on top. I also packed a bag with some cornbread and honey butter and a slice of Momma's chocolate–peanut butter pie. I'm hoping my treats and a few kind words will help convince Mitchell to let me see the security footage of Cynthia and Russell. But I brought Wavonne along as a bit of an insurance policy in case the food does not do the trick. She's much better than I am at throwing on a little sugar to get what she wants, usually in a cleavage-revealing blouse and hot pants.

"Hello, ladies," Mitchell says as we come through the door. "To what do I owe the privilege?"

I smile. "Oh, nothing in particular." I set the plate on the counter in front of him. "We were coming this way and thought you might enjoy a few samplings from my restaurant. Once you open, maybe you can recommend it to some of the guests. I'm sure they will want to eat at Sunfish, but probably not every night."

"That's very nice. Thank you."

"You're welcome. It's my butter-baked chicken with a few sides." Wavonne sets a bag on the counter as well. "And that's my sour cream cornbread and a slice of my momma's pie. I hope you enjoy it."

"I'm sure I will. We had already planned to put Sweet Tea on our list of recommended restaurants in the area, but that doesn't mean I'm not going to indulge in every bit of this food."

"Glad to hear that." I move closer to the counter. "So how are things going here since all the commotion? I heard you haven't lost any bookings, even with all the press about Sherry."

"That's true. We expect a full house when we have the grand opening next month. I'm confident we'll be ready. Russell has a whole team of tradesmen working overtime to make sure everything is done by the tenth."

"Does part of that everything include getting cameras installed around the pool? It's unfortunate that they were not in place when Sherry was killed. The murderer would be behind bars by now."

"It's definitely on the list. I'm assuming the crew will get to it over the next few days."

"So, I'm curious. How do those cameras work exactly? Where is the footage stored?"

"It's all online. We get a live feed in the back and can call up any past video on the cloud."

"So, you have access to the footage of the concierge lounge and the restaurant when Sherry was killed?"

Mitchell looks at me quizzically. "Yes, of course. I pulled the footage for the police. Why do you ask?"

"Is there any chance I can get a look at the recordings?"

Mitchell dawdles for a moment before speaking. "Honestly, no, I don't think so. Not without authorization from Russell."

"Are you sure? I'd just like to take a quick look . . . make sure no one missed anything."

"I'd like to help you . . . especially after you brought me all this wonderful food, but I just can't. I could lose my job."

"Couldn't you lose your job anyway?" Wavonne asks.

"What do you mean?"

"I mean we *know*." Wavonne tilts her head at Mitchell. "We know what you've been doing behind that counter. If anything is goin' to get you fired—"

"How do you know about that?"

"Let's just say we're very observant and have eyes and ears everywhere," Wavonne decrees while I stand there dumbfounded. I have no idea what she's talking about. "Listen, you let Halia see the video, and I promise we'll keep the little tidbit of knowledge we know about you to ourselves."

Mitchell looks at us, clearly perplexed about what to do.

"Are Russell or Cynthia here?" I ask.

"No. They said they had a meeting in the city."

"So how would they find out that you showed Halia anything?" Wavonne asks, but doesn't wait for an answer. "I'll stay out here and be the lookout. You take Halia in the back and show her what she wants to see, and I'll give you a holler if they drive up."

Mitchell looks at Wavonne and then at me. "Fine," he says, and motions for me to follow him.

I scurry to the other side of the counter and walk behind him into a little back room. He sits down in front of the computer and starts moving the mouse around, pointing and clicking on folders on the monitor.

"Okay, here is the concierge lounge when the shots went off."

"There's no sound?" I ask, leaning in to get a closer look and seeing Cynthia taking a seat at the bar.

"No . . . I mean yes, there's no sound."

I stand behind Mitchell and watch the attendant pour Cynthia a glass of wine. She takes a sip. Then picks up her phone and starts tapping on the screen. A second or two later, she and the attendant are both clearly jolted by something, the first gunshot I assume. As Cynthia hops off her chair you see her flinch again at what must be the second gunshot. She and the attendant stand still as if they are waiting to see if there might be a third blast. When they don't hear anything more, Cynthia approaches the door to the main hallway with the attendant following, and they fall out of view.

Mitchell does a little more pointing and clicking. "This is the restaurant."

I lean in even closer this time as Russell and the man he's talking to are farther away from the camera than Cynthia. This footage is not as crisp as the previous one, but I can tell that Russell is giving the man he's talking to—or more likely yelling at—a good shakedown. I watch as Russell yells and gestures with his hands until he suddenly stops all motion and begins looking around with a puzzled expression on his face.

"That's the first gunshot going off," Mitchell says.

Neither he nor the man he's talking to have time to do much more than look confused before Russell twists his head from left to right, trying to figure out where the second sound is coming from. They remain still for a few seconds, waiting to see if there is a third boom. When it doesn't come, Russell seems content to get back to scolding the man about whatever he was dissatisfied with before the shots went off.

"Keep in mind, the restaurant is in a separate building from the hotel, so I'm guessing the noise wasn't as loud over there as it was here," Mitchell says, coming up with his own explanation for why the two gentlemen didn't find it necessary to immediately go investigate the noise. "Is that all you wanted to see?"

"Yes. Things seemed to unfold just as Cynthia and Russell said," I say, although Cynthia didn't mention that she was tapping on her phone right before the shots went off, which makes me wonder if she was texting whoever actually did kill Sherry, giving him or her the final go-ahead to move in for the kill. "There's no way for the date and time on that film to be altered, is there?"

"I'm not an expert, but all the film uploads to a cloud run by the security company as it records. My guess is the only way the date or time could be altered would be if it was done by someone at the security company."

"I guess it doesn't matter, considering Russell and Cynthia also have witnesses corroborating their whereabouts when Sherry was killed. And I, myself, saw Cynthia coming out of the lounge right after the gunshots." I make my way out of the office with Mitchell following. "I'm not sure I've learned much more than I knew an hour ago, but it's nice to see actual proof that Russell and Cynthia were where they said they were at the time of the murder. Thank you for your help, Mitchell. And you can be confident that your secret is safe with us," I assure, even though I have no idea what his secret is.

"Nothing good on the tapes?" Wavonne asks as I step out from behind the counter.

"Maybe a little something."

"What?"

"Cynthia was texting on her phone . . . or doing something on her phone just before the first shot went off. We know she didn't kill Sherry, but I'm wondering if perhaps she was in contact with whoever did."

"You couldn't see anything on her phone screen?"

"No. Honestly she could have been checking the next day's weather, for all I know."

"Or checking Facebook or her e-mail . . . or watching YouTube." Wavonne looks at her watch. "You ready to go?"

"Not just yet," I reply. "Let's swing by Trey's room. I want to ask him about Twyla . . . why he didn't tell us she came by his room before Sherry was killed. By the way," I ask Wavonne as we start down the hall toward Trey's room, "what was it that Mitchell was doing behind the counter that could have gotten him fired?"

"Hell if I know."

"What? You said you knew what he was doing."

"Last week I told Marvin that this is my natural hair, and the other day I told the clerk at Macy's that I'd never worn the dress I was returnin'. What's your point?" Wavonne says. "Most people have done something at work that would get them fired if anyone found out. I figured Mitchell was most people. The worst he could do was call my bluff. And it—"

"Shh," I say. We're approaching Trey's room and, a little further down the hall, I see a beam of light coming from the one next to his. "That's Sherry's room. Who's in there?" I whisper to Wavonne as we creep toward the door, which is ajar by a foot or so.

Wavonne presses her back against the wall to the right of the door and cranes her neck around to take a quick peek into Sherry's room. "It's Angela."

"Angela?" I say quietly, more to myself than anyone, questioning what she would be doing in Sherry's room. Then I figure if she's up to something nefarious, she wouldn't have left the door open. So this time I say her name more loudly. "Angela?"

"Yes?" She comes to the door and opens it fully. "Hello."

"Hi. We were about to pay Trey a quick visit, but then we saw that someone was in here. I guess we were curious."

"Mitchell let me in earlier. I leave with Sherry's body in the morning, and . . . I don't know, for some reason I just wanted to see where it all went down. I've been in here thinking of my sister's last moments."

Angela takes a seat on the sofa, and Wavonne and I sit down with her. I can tell she's been crying, so I put my arm around her. I wish I had some kind words to offer but nothing is coming to mind. My first instinct is to say, "It's going to be okay," but it's not really going to be okay. . . . I imagine nothing is ever really okay again after something like this. But even if I can't think of anything to say, I figure Wavonne and I can sit here with her for a little while, maybe make her feel less alone.

I'm not sure how long we'll be here, so I shift around on the sofa and try to get a bit more comfortable, and that's when I notice something on the carpet over by the desk, which sits against the wall right next to the door that joins this room to Trey's. "Excuse me for just one second." I get up and walk over near the connecting door. . . .

And there it is, plain as day. One little pink crystal that

must have been missed by the police and the cleaning crew. As I bend down to pick it up all I can think about is the pink Himalayan salt mask that Trey was wearing the night Sherry was killed.

"Wavonne, can you stay here with Angela? I'm going to pop next door and see if Trey is in his room."

Chapter 33

"Trey," I call. I've been outside his room for a few moments.

After asking Wavonne to stay with Angela, I hurried into the hall and started knocking on his door. I can hear him moving around in there, so I knock again, a little harder this time.

"Hi," he says after swinging the door open and removing some headphones from his ears. "Sorry, I had my earbuds in."

"No problem. May I come in?"

"Um . . . sure." Trey opens the door wider and steps aside to let me pass. "What can I do for you?"

I decide to get right to the point. "What you can do for me is tell me why, after Sherry was killed, you were over by her side of the doors that connect both of your rooms."

"What? What are you talking about?"

"I was just in Sherry's room, and I found a little fleck of Himalayan salt on the floor by the joining door. As far as I know, you were the only person in her room at any time in the recent past with little pink crystals on his face. And if I recall correctly, you said you had just finished putting on your beauty mask—"

"Sports facial."

"Sorry. You said you had just finished applying your *sports facial* . . . your *pink* sports facial when the shots went off. Which means, if you're telling the truth about when you put the mask on, you were over by the connecting door in Sherry's room after she died. But I guess it's possible that this little bit of evidence you left on the carpet could be from when you went to see her shortly before she died, too."

Trey looks back at me with a dumbfounded expression on his face.

"Yes, I know you paid her a quick visit before she was shot. I also know that Twyla was in your room the night Sherry was killed. Funny, how you didn't share any of this information with me when I stopped by yesterday."

"I didn't think it was relevant." He's trying to come across nonchalant, but I can tell my revelations have made him anxious. "So, I went by Sherry's room for a few minutes the night she died. I just wanted to have a quick chat and wish her luck. That's nothing the police don't already know. Just like every area of this property, except for apparently the pool area, the hallway is on camera 24/7, so they have me on tape going into her room the night she was killed. The camera also shows that I was only in there about five minutes. Word is they have Cynthia going in and out of there, too."

"Yes. I heard she's a premurder visitor as well. Sherry's sister told us that Sherry mentioned both of your visits to her on the phone that night," I say. "Was Cynthia's visit before or after yours?"

"Before."

"How long was she in there?"

"I don't know. The only reason I know about her visit at all is because the officer I talked to happened to mention Cynthia was on camera while going into Sherry's room a few minutes before me. He just let it slip while he was questioning me. He didn't say how long she was in there, but it couldn't have been too long, because she was gone when I got there."

"So, I'm guessing when you were caught on camera visiting Sherry before she died, you did not have your beauty . . . sports facial on?"

"No. Like I said, I had just finished applying it when the shots went off. And you saw me with the mask on when we both went into Sherry's room after she was killed. Why would it be a surprise, or in any way incriminating, that a small speck from the mask was on the carpet?"

"Because of where it was . . . so close to the connecting door. I have a vague memory of you going into the room behind me after the shooting, but then you fell out of my line of sight, and Mitchell was in front of me, so I'm sure he didn't see you either. Who's to say that, while we were distracted by the heinous scene on the bed, you didn't slip back against the wall and relock the connecting door from Sherry's side?"

"Relock? Who's to say that I ever unlocked it to begin with?"

"Is it not possible that you somehow distracted Sherry and unlocked the connecting door when you stopped by to see her before everyone met in the lounge to toast Vera? Then, after the shooting, when all attention was being paid to Sherry's dead body on the bed, you discreetly hung back and relatched the bolt?"

He looks at me very strangely, and I can't tell if it's because I've hit the nail on the head and described exactly what he did, or because he just thinks I'm freakin' nuts.

"While you may not have had enough time to kill Sherry, exit through her sliding glass door, reenter your room from the pool area, and emerge in the hallway right after Sherry was killed, you could have . . . just *maybe* you could have been able to pull it off if you used the connecting door."

"I can't even follow everything you just said. I certainly couldn't have actually done any of it. 'Exit.' 'Reenter.' 'Emerge.' You sound like you're providing commentary on some sort of rat's maze competition."

"Maybe so," I say, and begin to wonder if he's right. Perhaps the little salt particle fell off his mask while he was just standing there taking in the awful scene with me. Maybe one of the officers stepped on it and tracked it over by the connecting door or . . . or who knows what. I'm not sure what else I can ask him that will prove he either did or didn't relock the door, when it occurs to me that perhaps, instead of *asking* him something, I should *tell* him something. If Wavonne's bluffing worked on Mitchell, maybe a little of my own bluffing will work on Trey, too.

"You know what? Come to think of it," I say. "I remember hearing a click behind me after I walked into Sherry's room. I didn't think much of it at the time. . . . Any sound that wasn't a gunshot wasn't terribly bothersome at that point. But, in retrospect, that was you relocking the interior door, wasn't it?" From the way Trey is looking at me, I can tell I've really struck a nerve this time. "Wasn't it?"

He's quiet, but I can tell from his expression that he's guilty—he did relock the door, and suddenly I'm fearful. If he relocked the door, then he must have killed Sherry. Why else would he have unlocked it? He would have only done it for quick access to her room so he could murder her. What's to stop him from doing the same to me?

"Wavonne and Angela are right in the next room," I say, taking a few steps back toward the main door.

He senses my angst and smirks. "You honestly think I killed Sherry?"

I take a few more steps back. "Your face gave you away, Trey. When I said I heard you locking the door, something in your eyes changed. I have no doubt you relocked that door after Sherry was killed . . . after *you* killed Sherry." I put my hand on the doorknob and turn it, getting ready to make a quick exit and scream for the girls in the next room if I have to.

Trey is staring at me. He appears amused by how anxious I suddenly am. "You're right about me unlocking the interior door when I went by to see Sherry before she was shot. I'll give you that. And you're right about me relocking the door after she was killed. I even used a tissue to make sure I didn't leave any fingerprints. It's the part in between the unlocking and the relocking that you have wrong."

"Oh?"

"I *did not* kill Sherry. The whole using-the-connecting-door thing to commit murder would have been a pretty stupid plan when you think about it."

"How so?" I ask, my hand still on the doorknob.

"It was just by chance that I was able to get in there after Sherry died to reengage the lock. I got lucky with Mitchell being able to open the room and not know enough to keep us from going in there with him. There was no guarantee that the police wouldn't have been the first to open the door, cordon off the entire room, and not let me or anyone in. And that would have left an unlocked door between my room and Sherry's and made me the prime suspect. If nothing else, over the past couple of days, I hope I've shown you that I'm smarter than that."

"If you didn't kill her, why did you unlock the door from her side earlier in the evening?"

"If I tell you, will you promise to keep it between you and me? I didn't kill anyone. I swear. But what I did do was probably not exactly legal either."

I let my hand go from the doorknob and feel my body loosen up just a bit. "If you can convince me you didn't kill Sherry, then yes, I'll keep whatever you tell me private."

"When I stopped in to see Sherry the night she was killed, I did unlock the connecting door, but only so I could get back in the next morning when she went to the gym."

"Why?"

"Because I needed to retrieve something." Trey sits down at the desk and opens the drawer, which helps further ease the tension in my body. If he were going to kill me, I think he'd stay on his feet. "A listening device." He pulls what looks like a ballpoint pen from the drawer and tries to hand it to me.

I approach him carefully and take the pen.

"It's a voice recorder. You press the little clip to turn it on. I laid it on Sherry's desk while I was in there before Vera's little send-off in the lounge. I set it to pick up anything she said in her room for the rest of the night. I only unlocked the door so I could slip in her room and retrieve it in the morning."

"What were you listening for?"

"I'm certain that when they had their little late night rendezvous, Russell was tipping her off about the next day's challenges, which gave her time to plan and memorize recipes. We didn't get to shop for many of the challenges. Often, we were just given a basket of ingredients or a set time limit to raid the *Elite Chef* pantry and told to make do. More so than anyone, Sherry always seemed to know exactly what she was going to make. We'd get a theme and a basket of ingredients, and she'd go right to work. The rest of us would need some time to collect our thoughts and figure out what we were going to make. And often, our quickly thought-up ideas didn't work out too well. I figured if I could bug her room, I could get a leg up, too. If she was playing dirty, why shouldn't I?"

I think about what Twyla said earlier about Trey telling her that he was not the only one playing dirty. I also think about the most recent challenge and how, before she ultimately decided to prepare a version of my cheese nips, Sherry

seemed totally "ready-set-go" to make a Monte Cristo immediately after she had drawn her assignment from the chef's
hat—she had not needed to take any time at all to figure out
what she was going to make. I can't imagine she had any way
of knowing which ticket she'd select, but perhaps Russell let
her know what was on all of them, so she could make plans
for every possible scenario.

"I was just looking for some information . . . to level the
playing field for the last challenge. I didn't *kill* anyone."

"Cynthia told us that, to keep things fair with the other
judges, Russell wasn't briefed on the challenges." As I say
this I realize it was naive of me to believe Russell was kept in
the dark about anything that had to do with his own TV
show.

"I'm sure Russell knows everything there is to know about
what happens before, during, and after tapings."

"You're probably right." I look down at the listening device. "So, if this pen was in the room when Sherry was killed,
it should have picked up any voices or other sounds that happened just before Sherry was shot, right?"

"I've already listened to it. If there was anything that
would actually help the police identify the killer, I swear, I
would turn it into them, but there's nothing useful on it."

"Can you play it for me?"

Trey flips open the laptop on his desk and extends his
hand, gesturing for me to return the pen. I give it back to him
and he connects one end of a thin cable to the top of the pen
and the other to his computer. He does some pointing and
clicking with the mouse, an audio file appears on the screen,
and he uses the mouse to drag the cursor or whatever to a
certain time on the recording.

"This is about five minutes before she was shot. All you
hear is the TV running in the background, and at one point,
Sherry sneezes a couple of times."

I try to listen carefully, and like he said, I hear the television running in the background. Then, also just like he said, I hear Sherry sneezing. For a few more minutes there is nothing but background TV noise. Then Trey makes a dramatic pointing gesture toward the screen, and that's when you hear the first gunshot and then the second.

"And that's it," Trey says. "You don't hear anything after the gunshots until you hear Mitchell calling for Sherry from the hallway."

I'm about to ask him to play it again when there's a knock on the door. "What are you doin' in there, Halia? I'm startin to think Twyla isn't the only old maid that's got a thing for Trey."

Trey gets up and opens the door. "Hi, Wavonne."

"Hey," Wavonne says, and looks past Trey at me. "How much longer you gonna be? Angela stopped cryin' about ten minutes ago, and now she won't stop talkin' about what she calls her 'career.' If she wasn't in mournin' I'd explain to her that 'scented candle consultant' is not a career. We need to get outta here before I have to buy some vanilla-scented nonsense. She's been—"

"I think I'm about ready to go. Does Angela need a ride back to her hotel?"

"Nah, she said she'd take an Uber," Wavonne says. "So, did you find out anything new?"

I look at Trey and remember my promise to keep his secret if he could convince me he didn't kill Sherry. Then I look back at Wavonne. "Sadly, no."

"Well, let's go then," Wavonne says. "I'm supposed to meet Marvin at Oyamel for Hora Feliz in an hour . . . two-dollar tacos and free chips and salsa."

"Okay." I turn back to Trey. "But one more thing. Twyla?"

"What about her?"

"Her sneaking in your room via the patio door is all over the Internet. Why didn't you mention that to me the last time I came around asking questions?"

"Twyla told me earlier that night that she was going to come by my room after the competition. She said she had some intel she wanted to share with me that might help me win this thing. I have no idea why she used the patio door instead of coming through the hallway. But, when she got here, all she did was give me a few recipes for some of the tired dishes she serves at her restaurant. I wasn't interested in them, but I thanked her for them anyway, and then I hinted for her to leave. But she just kept lingering, making small talk. Eventually, I told her that I needed to go to bed, and that she should go. She finally left about fifteen minutes before the gunshots went off."

"I appreciate the backstory, but that doesn't really answer my question about why you didn't share anything about her visit with me earlier."

"I had let her paw me all day. I figured it was harmless enough and that letting her flirt with me might help with any judging she was going to do. But I didn't want anyone to know she was in my hotel room. I had a . . . a one-night *thing* with a forty-something woman I met at a club a few years ago. To this day, my friends still call me Giggo . . . short for Gigolo. And they ask me, 'How's Maude?' 'Are you going to bed Maude again?' 'Don't you have to go pick Maude up from her hip replacement?' Her name wasn't even Maude. That was just the best old lady name they could come up with. Twyla has to be sixty-something. If I've yet to live down a hookup with some forty-year-old lady, I can't imagine the repercussions of people thinking I was getting it on with Twyla. No offense."

"Why are you looking at me when you say, 'no offense'?" I ask, slightly horrified. "Twyla's got almost twenty years on me."

"Oh . . . no reason." Trey stumbles for words. "Some women . . . no matter how old . . . or *young* . . . don't like it when guys talk about age."

"Nice try," Wavonne says to Trey before turning to me. "Come on, Maude. Let's go before all the tacos are gone."

Chapter 34

"So, nothing from Trey? Really?" Wavonne asks as we head down the hall toward the lobby.

"Not exactly. But I agreed to keep what he told me quiet."

"Not from me though, right?"

I laugh. "He mostly just wants me to keep it from the police, I guess. I'll fill you in, but the short of it is I don't think Trey is our killer." I'm about to tell Wavonne about the listening device when I see the back of a police officer in the lobby. "Jack?"

"Halia," Jack says with a smile. "Why do you always seem to appear when there's trouble? What are you doing here?"

"I might ask you the same question."

"I'm here with Hutchins. He's in the back office talking with Russell and Cynthia."

"Really? Has there been a new development?"

"You might say that." Jack looks around before he says anything further. "The pool guys found a gun under one of the lounge chair cushions—it was a match for the gun used to kill Ms. Ashbury."

"Really?"

"And that's not all." Jack lowers his voice even more. "It's registered to Cynthia and we found some prints on it."

"Cynthia's?"

"Russell's."

"Wow. That would be some pretty damning evidence if Russell didn't have a solid alibi at the time of the shooting."

Jack is about to respond when Cynthia emerges from the back office with Detective Hutchins. I see Russell still in the back room on his phone.

"Yes," I hear Cynthia say. "Russell put the gun in the desk drawer by the sofa. I wasn't sure, but I figured we would not be able to take it into the museum the next day, so I asked him to put it away. That was the last time I saw it."

"And no one other than the two of you knew where it was?"

"I suppose one of the maids could have opened the drawer. . . ." Cynthia lets her voice trail off. "Wait a minute. You know what? Vera and Twyla were in line with us at museum Security, and I remember saying something to Russell about how it was a good thing we put the gun in the desk as we clearly would not have been able to enter the museum with it."

"Did they have access to your room?"

"Vera came by later that evening," Cynthia says. "She was alone in the living area for a few minutes while I was taking a call in the bedroom. I suppose she could have taken it then."

"Okay, we'll follow up on that," Detective Hutchins says. So far, he has not seen Wavonne and me, and I suspect it might be best if we keep it that way.

"I think Wavonne and I are going to skedaddle," I say quietly to Jack. "It was good to see you."

He nods at me and Wavonne, and we head toward the door.

"So I guess Cynthia's story about going into the city to buy drugs, rather than a gun, checks out. Why would she have gone to Brentwood Manors for a gun when she already had one?" I ask Wavonne once we've stepped outside.

"Beats me," Wavonne replies as we approach the car. "Do you think Vera may have taken Cynthia's gun?"

"I guess she could have, but I just don't peg her as a murderer. I think I'll try to get to her before the police . . . warn her that they'll be asking questions about what she was doing in the living area of Cynthia's suite when Cynthia was in the bedroom."

"Okay, but drop me off at home first. I'm already running late," Wavonne says. We're in the car now and she's got the visor down, using the mirror to put on some blush and mascara.

"Let me give Vera a call. If she's nearby, maybe you can just come with me, and then I'll take you home." I see Wavonne pull a little glass bottle from her purse. "Can you not spray that perfume in here? It gives me a headache and makes me sneeze." The word "sneeze" is barely out of my mouth when something occurs to me. "You know what?" I ask Wavonne as she puts the perfume back in her purse and reaches for some lip liner. "Sherry had to have been asleep when she was killed. Or we would have heard screams when the murderer came into her room, right?"

"Yeah. So?"

"I don't think people sneeze when they're asleep. Do they?"

"I don't know. I don't think so."

"So, it probably wasn't Sherry who I heard sneezing on the recording Trey shared with me. It was probably the killer."

"What recording?"

"It's a long story, but Trey had a recording device in Sherry's room when she was killed, and someone can be heard sneezing a few minutes before the shots went off."

"And Vera had been sneezing all day."

"And, as we now know, she both knew where Cynthia's gun was and had time to take it." I lean back in the car seat and run a possible scenario through my head. "What if she snuck in through the sliding glass doors, sneezed a couple of times while she poked around for a bit, looking for something perhaps or maybe just getting up the nerve to pull the trigger, before she killed Sherry?" I let out a long, cheerless exhale. "Maybe I misjudged Vera. Maybe she is, in fact, a murderer."

Chapter 35

Wavonne and I step inside Dauphine and I'm a bit shocked by what we encounter: *noise*. I hear voices and the clanking of dishes . . . and the patter of feet. The restaurant has been so desolate the last two times I've been here, it's surprising to see it busy. It's still dark and dated, but it's decidedly less gloomy with actual people at the tables eating and chatting and laughing.

We take a few steps forward, and my eyes catch sight of Vera at a table near the infamous salad bar. I called her as we were leaving the inn. She said Twyla had invited her to try the restaurant, and she was on her way there when I called.

"Hey," I say when I reach her table. She stands up and gives me a hug. "How are you?"

"I'm okay. Though the bar for 'okay' is a bit low these days. Any day someone isn't murdered down the hall from me or I'm not brought into the police station for questioning is a good day at the moment."

"No more Bigfoot sightings, I hope?" Wavonne asks.

Vera tries to smile. "Thankfully, no. How are you guys?"

"We're fine. We were just over at the inn snooping around a little. I had a good chat with Trey, and I'm pretty sure he's in the clear, but I got word of a new development in the case just before I left, and I wanted to talk to you about it."

"Okay. Sure."

"Detective Hutchins and one of his officers, Jack Spruce, were there as well, and Jack told me they found the gun used to kill Sherry."

"Really?"

"Yes. The killer shoved it under the cushion of one of the loungers by the pool," Wavonne says.

"Does finding the gun bring the police any closer to determining who killed Sherry?"

"Maybe. That's what I want to talk to you about." I pull my chair in closer to the table and lean toward Vera. "They traced the gun back to Cynthia but just as the owner. Her prints were not on the gun. But, get this, Russell's were."

"But Russell was in the restaurant when Sherry was killed, right?"

"Yes. Unfortunately, that's where you come in. While the gun belonged to Cynthia and Russell's prints were on it, neither one of them could have been the one to actually use it on Sherry. And . . . well . . . I'm afraid, because of that, you might find yourself being taken in for questioning again."

"Me? Why?"

"Apparently, you had both knowledge of where the gun was and an opportunity to take it."

"I did?"

"Cynthia said you were in line with them at museum Security, and she mentioned the gun being in the desk drawer. She also said you were in her room before everyone met for your little send-off party in the lounge, and while you were in there you had some alone time in the living area and could have taken the gun."

"Oh my God! I didn't take anyone's gun, and I sure as hell

didn't kill anyone. But they are going to arrest me, aren't they?!"

"No," I say. "I'm sure they will want to ask you more questions, but they have nowhere near enough evidence against you to make an arrest."

"This is unbelievable. Yes, I only now have a vague memory of Cynthia mentioning the gun before we went into the museum, and I did go to Russell and Cynthia's room, but Cynthia's gun was the last thing on my mind. I went to their room to convince Cynthia to let me have a redo . . . a second chance, which I thought I deserved . . . which I *still* think I deserve." Vera puts her hand to her head and looks down at the table. "I can't believe it. I stay in my room instead of venturing out into the hallway when an active shooter could be on the loose, and it ends up making me a prime suspect for murder."

"So, take me through it," I say, really wanting Vera to not be the killer. "What were you doing exactly when the shots went off?"

"I was just trying to relax after a bad day. Everything had been comped for us at the inn, even the minibar, so most nights I'd been treating myself to some pricey chocolate before bed. Some nights it was a Toblerone . . . other nights it was a Hershey's bar. The night Sherry died, it was a KitKat. I'd barely gotten it unwrapped when I heard the gunshots. As soon as—"

"Wait . . . wait," I interrupt. "Let's be more precise here— how long was it after you took the candy out of the minibar that you heard the gun? Minutes? Seconds?"

"Definitely seconds. Less than ten I would guess."

"You're sure?"

"Yes. I opened the minibar, grabbed the KitKat, and sat down on the bed. Like I said, I had barely gotten it unwrapped when the shots went off."

"Then I think you have an alibi."

"What? How so?"

"I'm guessing you have the same type of high-tech minibar in your room that Wavonne and I had in ours. If so, it records when something is taken out of it. If the system at the inn has a record of you removing something from the mini-bar a few seconds before Sherry was killed, there is no way you could have shot her. You couldn't have taken something from the bar and then gotten out of your room, past Trey's room, and into Sherry's to shoot her in ten seconds."

"No . . . no, I couldn't have done that," Vera says, and her mouth upends into something resembling a smile. "Oh, Halia, I could kiss you!"

I laugh. "I'm glad I could help. And even happier that we can prove you had nothing to do with Sherry's murder. But now, I'm still no closer to knowing who actually did kill Sherry." And I don't say it out loud, but I wonder who was sneezing on Trey's recording. *Maybe people really do sneeze in their sleep?*

"When Cynthia said I was in line with them at Security when they mentioned the gun, did she say Twyla was there, too?"

"Yes. She did mention Twyla being in line with you, but it sounds like Twyla didn't have access to the gun. She was never in Russell and Cynthia's suite," I say, before having a sudden recollection. "Or was she?" I turn to Wavonne. "When we first got to the inn after filming at the museum, we ran into Twyla in the lobby, remember?"

"Yeah. She had come from the hallway where all the rooms are. She said she had just changed her clothes and re-touched her makeup."

"Right. At the time I assumed she had a room at the inn like the rest of us and freshened up in there. I only later learned that she had never taken a room."

I've seen Twyla puttering around the restaurant since I got here, but up until now, I have purposely managed to stay off her radar. I really didn't want to talk to her, but I'm now finding myself with some questions for her. I start waving in her direction and finally catch her attention when she looks up from wiping a table.

"You're becoming one of my regulars, Halia," she says.

I smile. "Yes, it does appear I just can't stay away."

"Shall I get you and Wavonne menus?"

"No thank you. We just came by to chat with Vera, but while we're here can I ask you something?"

"Somehow, I suspect you're going to ask me *something* regardless of my answer."

I smile again, this time a little more uncomfortably. "The day we were filming *Elite Chef*, when Wavonne and I ran into you in the lobby, you said you had just changed clothes and redone your makeup."

"Yes. I remember."

"Where were you coming from? Where did you change clothes and what not? You didn't have a room at the inn, right?"

"Russell gave me the key to his room. He let me use it to get ready for the rest of the taping."

Vera's eyes meet mine in a "Well, isn't that interesting?" sort of way. I'm about to ask Twyla a few more questions now that I know that Vera was not the only one who had both knowledge of where the gun was and access to it, when the kitchen door behind Twyla swings open and a large man walks out into the dining room. Large is actually an understatement. He's massive—probably about six feet, seven inches tall with a big beefy build, long shaggy curls, and a beard that could give Grizzly Adams a run for his money. He's wearing what must be the uniform of Twyla's kitchen staff—black pants and a button-up purple shirt—the shirt is Mardi Gras–

themed with big flowers, jester masks, and beads all over it, but I can see how, from a distance, it could look like a Hawaiian shirt.

"Look," I say to Vera, and signal for her to turn around. "I think we may have found your Bigfoot."

Chapter 36

The first thing I hear when Vera looks over her shoulder is a gasp. "That's him! That's who I saw in the woods behind the pool. That's Sasquatch!"

"What?" Twyla looks at me. "What is she talking about?"

"That man." I point at the large man who is now switching out some platters on the salad bar. "That's what . . . *who* she's talking about. Who is that?"

"That's Malcom. He's one of my line cooks."

"Wasn't Malcom the name of the bartender you fired? The one who was running a scam with Sherry?"

"Yes, and that's why when I agreed to hire him back, it was for a job in the kitchen. I was not going to have him handling cash or credit cards."

"Why would you hire someone back who stole from you the last time he worked here?"

"Honestly, Halia, I'm done answering your questions. If you're not going to order—"

"You know what, Twyla, I don't think you're done answering my questions"—I take in a long inhale and try to soften my tone—"unless you'd rather the same questions come from the police. Why did you rehire Malcom, and why was he prowling around the grounds of the Willow Oak Inn the night Sherry was killed?"

Twyla returns my gaze but doesn't say a word.

"I've got Detective Hutchins on speed dial, and it's starting to seem quite possible that you pilfered Cynthia's gun when you were in her room changing clothes and then arranged for Captain Caveman back there to use it to kill Sherry at the exact time you would just happen to have a rock solid alibi." I stand up from the table. "Unless you can convince me otherwise, I've got a phone call to make."

"Oh for Christ's sakes." Twyla grabs a chair from the table behind us and plops herself down in it. "You have quite the imagination, Halia, and I guess what you said is plausible, but that is *so* not what happened."

"So, what did happen? Do you expect me to believe your line cook, who had a score to settle with Sherry, was in the woods behind the inn the night of the murder, and you, who also had a score to settle with Sherry, knew nothing about it?"

"Of course I knew about it. He was in the woods at my instruction. But he certainly did not kill anyone."

"You're not making any sense. Why was he in the woods then?"

"Malcom is the one who got the video of me going into Trey's room. He needed a job and I needed someone to get the footage for me, so we made a deal."

"Why did you ask him to film you going into Trey's room?"

"If you hadn't noticed, Halia, things around here were not exactly going well. Channel Four canceled my cooking segments and business here has been slow for a *long* time. And my *staff* . . . do you know what my staff has been calling me lately?"

"Twyla the Hun?" Wavonne asks.

"No."

"Grandma Gumbo?"

"What? No!"

"The Soggy Beignet?"

"Shut up, Wavonne!" I say.

"Well, that's what Nicki says they call her. They also call her—"

Twyla does not let Wavonne finish. "Some of my cooks and servers didn't know I was in the pantry, and I overheard them calling me . . . calling me the 'old gray mare.' They said something about how they were not sure how much longer they would have jobs . . . that my restaurant might close soon, and maybe it's time for 'the old gray mare' to go off to the glue factory." She leans forward in her chair. "I had to do something . . . *something* to revitalize my image and this restaurant. I figured a scandalous public affair with a much younger man was just the ticket."

"I talked to Trey. He claims there was no affair."

"Of course there was no affair, but the general public didn't need to know that. Viewers would see all our flirting during the episode we did together and, once it aired, I would accidentally-on-purpose leak the footage of me sneaking into his room to one of those trashy tabloid sites. But then the murder happened, and I figured it was best to just deny being there at all and keep the footage to myself."

"So how did it leak?"

"Once I realized I could prove that it was Trey's room, not Sherry's, that I was entering in the video, and that I had an alibi at the time Sherry was killed, I told Malcom to shop it around. The *Elite Chef* Murder, as the press has dubbed it, is all over the news—the video of me sneaking into what everyone assumed was Sherry's room got me a few million dollars' worth of press. So half of America thought I might be a murderer for a little while—half of America has also now heard of Twyla Harper and Dauphine. Look around—we have not been this busy in years. And Channel Four wants me to start doing my segments on the news again. Not too shabby for an 'old gray mare,' eh?"

I lay my forehead on my hand. "My brain hurts," I say. "So, all of it—you fawning all over Trey while we filmed at the museum, you sneaking into his room from the back door, your line cook who looks like a giant from a *Harry Potter* movie lurking in the woods—it was all to get press for Dauphine?"

"Pretty ingenious, huh?"

I so want to say, "Wouldn't it be easier to just serve decent food in a restaurant that doesn't look like a funeral home?" But instead, I just respond with, "That's one way to look at it." I shift around in my chair and let this all sink in. "I've done a lot of investigating over the past few days, and so far, all I've determined is that sometimes people want to be perceived as stupid, sometimes wives arrange for their husbands to cheat on them, and sometimes people go to absurd lengths to get publicity. I haven't identified a killer, but I guess I've learned a few things about the human condition."

"So basically," Wavonne says, "you've determined that people are nuts."

"Yes, but I guess I pretty much already knew that. I mean I live with you and Momma, don't I?" I jibe. "Honestly, I have no idea where to go from here. So far, all my poking around and questioning has only proven who *didn't* kill Sherry." I turn to Twyla. "Thank you for all the information. It's great things are picking up here. I'm happy for you." Then I switch my attention back to Wavonne. "Let's go. It's getting late, and I'm tired."

As I get up from the table I realize that "tired" doesn't begin to describe how I feel. "Exhausted" would be more accurate, or maybe "beat" is the right word. At this point, with no identified killer and no more leads to follow up on, I feel *beat* in more ways than one.

RECIPE FROM HALIA'S KITCHEN

Halia's Pineapple–Red Pepper Jelly

Ingredients
3½ cups chopped fresh pineapple
1¼ cups canned pineapple juice
½ red bell pepper, chopped
2½ cups sugar
1 tablespoon lemon juice
Grated zest of 1 lemon
2 tablespoons cornstarch
2 tablespoons water
Pinch of salt and black pepper

- Using a few quick pulses, finely chop pineapple and red pepper in a food processor.
- Add finely chopped pineapple, juice, red pepper, sugar, lemon juice, and lemon zest to a large saucepan and bring to a low boil. Then reduce the heat and stir mixture over low heat for 30 to 40 minutes until a jam consistency is achieved.
- Mix water and cornstarch and add to simmering mixture along with salt and black pepper while continuing to stir for 3 to 5 minutes.
- Remove from heat and let cool for 45 minutes.

For a delicious biscuit spread, spoon cooled jelly over a square of softened cream cheese and serve.

Chapter 37

I don't take baths very often, but tonight I soaked in the tub for a good half hour just trying to wind down after such a long and frustrating day. I just dried off and slipped into some pajamas. I'm lying on the bed, thinking about turning on the TV or picking up the book on the nightstand, but I can't seem to silence my mind. I keep mulling over everything I learned during the past few days. Trey and his recording device. Cynthia plotting to keep her husband out of their bed. Russell's prints being on the gun that killed Sherry. Twyla faking affairs with men thirty years her junior. Vera and her late night KitKat bar. Maybe none of them played a role in Sherry's murder. Maybe someone completely unknown to me killed Sherry. Her sister did say she was always scheming for a quick buck. She probably had a long list of people other than Twyla who she stole from.

I think about my motley crew of suspects for another minute or two and then decide to forget them and both the TV and my book, and just turn out the light and go to bed. I flip off the bedside lamp, and I've barely gotten cozy under the covers when I hear Wavonne click on the TV in the living room. Momma's a little hard of hearing, so I'm guessing it's still at the volume Momma had it when she watched it last. I know I'll never get to sleep if I don't go out there and tell Wavonne to turn it down, so I throw the covers off and step out of bed.

"Wavonne, can you turn that down, please?" I say, poking my head out of my bedroom door.

"Sorry," she calls back, and I see her reach for the remote and lower the volume.

"What are you watching?" I can't see the TV that well from down the hall, but something about the characters on the screen or just the look of the show seems familiar to me.

"*Nappily Ever After* on Netflix. It had barely gotten started when the gunshots went off at the inn."

"So that's the same movie you were watching at Willow Oak?"

"Yep."

"I thought you said the hotel didn't have Netflix."

"It didn't. I just streamed it to the TV from my phone."

"The wonders of technology," I say. "Keep the volume down, would you, so I can get some sleep?"

"I think I'll just turn it off. I'm tired, too." Wavonne picks up the remote again, presses the power button, and the TV screen goes dark.

"Ah . . . silence," I say, walking back to my bed. "Silence," I say again as the gears in my brain start turning. "Silence!"

Wavonne overhears me on the way to her room. "Are you havin' a stroke or somethin'?"

"No. In fact, I think I may have figured out . . ." I go quiet, deciding I want to keep my revelation to myself for now.

"Figured out what?" Wavonne steps over by my bedroom door.

"Nothing," I say. "What time is it?"

"I don't know. About eleven thirty." Wavonne turns on her heels toward her own room. "'Night, Halia," she says before looking over her shoulder and giving me a knowing sneer. "Good luck with that *nothin'* you just figured out."

As Wavonne closes her bedroom door, I get up and do the same. Then I pick up my phone from the table. It's really too late for me to be calling anyone, but Jack does a lot of shift work, so he's probably a night owl. I find him in my contacts and hit the call button.

"Halia? Is everything okay?" he asks.

"Yes. Fine," I say. "Sorry to call so late. Were you up?"

"Yes. Just watching TV."

"Oh good," I say. "I wanted to ask you a quick question."

"Shoot . . . argh . . . sorry, poor choice of words again."

"Actually, it's an *interesting* choice of words considering my question."

"What do you mean?"

"The guys you were looking to apprehend in Brentwood the other day. One of them . . . the one who sold guns . . . Bruce?"

"No. Bruce is the drug guy. Sam is the gun guy."

"Sam then. You said that, in addition to guns, he sold all sorts of weapons and other paraphernalia, right?"

"Yep. Word is if you can hurt someone with it, Sam can get it for you. Why do you ask?"

"I guess I'm just curious if he sells one item in particular."

"What? What item? What are you up to, Halia?"

"Nothing," I say, and I realize this is the second time in just a few minutes I've lied using the word "nothing." I'm definitely up to something, or more accurately, *on* to something . . . better yet, on to *someone*.

Chapter 38

"It just worked out—a meeting with the Mellingers sort of fell into my lap this morning," I say to Detective Hutchins as we approach Sunfish. We've parked the car and Wavonne is walking along with us. "I finally started to figure things out late last night and, first thing this morning, I got a call from Trudy saying that Russell and Cynthia would like us to come in for a conference. She said they are gathering everyone from the last taping to talk about how they are going to wrap up the whole competition and crown a new Elite Chef. I guess they want me and Wavonne involved in some respect."

"And you're not going to tell me what you plan to share with the group beforehand?"

"Now, how much fun would that be for either of us?" I ask, appreciative of the detective accompanying me to this meeting, but still annoyed with him for telling Cynthia and some of the others not to talk to me. "I believe you told Cynthia I had a . . . what did you call it?"

"A Columbo complex," Wavonne says.

"Yes. A Columbo complex. If I'm going to be pegged as someone with a Columbo complex, I may as well make things as dramatic as possible, right?"

Detective Hutchins looks at me with something between a smile and a sneer before holding the door to the restaurant open for me and Wavonne.

"We're going to have a runoff between Vera and Trey and include some sort of memorial tribute to Sherry in the episode," I hear Russell telling Twyla, who's seated to his right at one of the tables. Cynthia is to his left, and Vera and Trey are at a neighboring table.

"We had planned to shoot some of the final episode at the Museum of American History, but given the circumstances, we decided . . ." Cynthia's words fade when she catches sight of the three of us, but it's the detective she speaks to. "Detective Hutchins," she says. "What brings you here this morning?"

"Ms. Watkins asked me to accompany her."

"Really?"

"What's going on?" Russell stands up. "Detective Hutchins, we've done our best to cooperate with your investigation, but we've told you all we know. At some point, we have to get back to producing the show and getting this restaurant and the hotel open."

"We're all very sad about Sherry's death," Cynthia chimes in, "but—"

"Are we all very sad?" I ask Cynthia. "*All* of us?"

"What do you mean? Of course we're all sad that Sherry was killed . . . horrified really, but—"

"Frankly, I doubt whoever killed Sherry is terribly sad that she's dead."

"Well, by *all*, I meant everyone in this room. To my knowledge, everyone in this room has been cleared of killing her."

"Everyone in this room *was* cleared of killing her. But last night, I was able to patch a few pieces of this Sherry puzzle together, and I'm afraid that's no longer the case."

There's a shift in the energy in the room after I say this, and everyone, including Cynthia, is silent.

I walk over to the table where Vera and Trey are seated and stand behind Trey, but I direct my words at Cynthia. "We know it was your gun that was used to kill Sherry, and as far as any of us know, Trey had no knowledge of you having a gun in your room. And even if he did, he didn't have access to it. So, we can cross him off the suspect list." I move over to Vera and put my hands on her shoulders. "Vera's minibar recorded her removing a candy bar seconds before we heard the gunshots, so that's a second person we can take off the list." I shift my gaze toward Twyla and Russell. "And security footage from a gas station miles away from the inn shows Twyla filling up her Cadillac when we heard the shots. And Russell is also on camera meeting with a contractor when the blasts came from Sherry's room. But, here's an interesting little morsel of information that, after really giving it some thought, I'm virtually certain is accurate." I think of my "Columbo complex" and take a brief pause for effect. "Sherry wasn't killed when we heard the gunshots."

"What?" Russell asks.

"You're talking crazy," comes from Cynthia. She's trying to remain composed, but I can tell that I've unsettled her.

"If anyone knows I'm, in fact, *not* 'talking crazy,' it's you, Cynthia."

"She's gone mad," Cynthia says to everyone. "Why would I know anything? I was in the lounge with the attendant when Sherry was shot. I'm even on camera in there when the gun went off."

"Yes, that was great planning. It was quite smart to make sure that you not only had a witness but were also on film away from the scene of the crime, at the time we all *thought* the murder happened."

"What are you talking about, Ms. Watkins?" Detective Hutchins asks.

"I'm talking about Cynthia shooting Sherry."

"I did not shoot Sherry!"

"Oh yes you did. You just didn't do it when we all thought you did."

"I think it's safe to say you've lost all of us, Halia," Wavonne says.

"Well, let me try to find you." I lean against the table behind me and steady myself. "It all started to make sense when I thought about how Cynthia went to Brentwood Manors in a disguise . . . in a rented car on a little 'procurement' escapade."

"I told you why I went there, Halia. I'm not proud of it, but I went there to purchase some pills, which I later got rid of. It had nothing to do with Sherry."

"That's half true. You did go there to purchase some pills, among other things, but you didn't get rid of them, and it had *everything* to do with Sherry."

"What do pills have to do with Sherry?" Detective Hutchins asks.

"Cynthia slipped one or more of them in Sherry's glass of champagne the night she was killed . . . to make sure Sherry would be asleep when she came in to shoot her." I turn to Cynthia. "With your history of addiction, it would be hard to score any strong sedatives from a legit doctor, so you had to find an illegal source, which is half the reason you went to Brentwood Manors. I'm not sure what you got from Bruce—that is the name of your supplier, right? Apparently, he's known to be dealing in virtually any drug known to man—meth, cocaine, Percocet, OxyContin, Rohypnol. But whatever you got from him, you used it to spike Sherry's drink."

"She did pour and hand out the champagne that night," Wavonne confirms. "I remember because I was annoyed that she didn't fill my glass very high."

"It makes even more sense when you think back to Sherry, who I'm told was known to be a late night partier, being the first to leave Vera's little send-off gathering. Her sister also said that most nights they generally talked for an hour or more. But the night of her death, Sherry cut the conversation short because she was so tired—she wasn't tired, she was drugged with whatever Cynthia scored at Brentwood Manors."

"Even if she did drug Sherry, how does that explain how she was in two places at once?" Detective Hutchins inquires.

"I'm glad you asked," I respond. "That brings me to the second reason Cynthia went to Brentwood Manors. I got a little inside intel that Bruce was the go-to guy in that neighborhood for drugs, and that another fellow, by the name of Sam, a few doors down, was the go-to guy for weapons. And we have it on good authority that Cynthia went to see both of them."

"Why would Cynthia go to the weapons guy if she already had a gun?" Wavonne asks.

"Because this Sam fellow did not just deal in guns. He dealt in all sorts of weapons and what I guess you'd call accessories. I had to think on this one hard, but last night it came to me when Wavonne shut off the TV, and I was enjoying the quiet. It occurred to me that, in addition to guns and knives and all sorts of ammunition, Sam may have also sold the one thing that made everything make sense." I do another pause, because, well, let's face it, they're fun. "I'm quite certain that Sam sold, and Cynthia bought from him, a silencer."

"A silencer?" Vera asks.

"Yes. Sometimes called a suppressor. It's like a muzzle—it significantly reduces the noise a gun makes when it's fired—perhaps so much so that it would sound like little more than a sneeze to someone on the other side of the wall in a neighboring room." I turn to Trey. "You did say in passing that you thought you heard Sherry sneezing through the wall shortly before she was killed." I refrain from mentioning the truth—that Trey heard the sneezing sounds on an illicit recording device because, one, I promised him I would not share that information with the police, and two, I'm sort of embarrassed that I didn't insist on sharing it with the police immediately. If I had, unlike me and Trey, surely Detective Hutchins and his team would have been able to recognize the sounds of suppressed gunshots for what they actually were, and we could have wrapped all this up much sooner.

"Um . . . yes," Trey says. "I thought I heard her sneezing about five minutes before Sherry was shot, but you're making it sound like . . . like she was actually being shot when I heard what I thought were sneezes?"

"This is still not making any sense to me," Detective Hutchins says.

"Oh, it was a complicated scheme all right," I reply. "And it took me a while to figure it out, but in addition to my quiet time last night, something else Wavonne did tipped me off to Cynthia's exploits."

"Does this have anything to do with you dragging me out of bed at midnight to show you how to work the TV?" Wavonne asks, referring to me goading her out of bed after I talked with Jack last night.

"I didn't ask you to show me how to *work* the TV, Wavonne. I asked you to show me how you *synced* your phone to the TV like you did when you watched Netflix at the inn a few days ago. But, to answer your question, yes, you teaching me how to remotely control the television with your phone helped me figure this whole thing out." I start walking around the room as I speak. "This is how I think it went down: Cynthia went to see Sherry shortly after we finished filming for the day. While in the room, she synced her phone to Sherry's TV. At some point she unlocked the patio door. Then, while we were all gathered in the concierge lounge, she drugged Sherry.

"Shortly thereafter, Cynthia returned to Sherry's room via the unlocked patio entrance, found Sherry asleep on the bed, and shot her, using a suppressor to quiet the noise. Cynthia then quickly snuck back into her room via the patio, only to immediately leave it again through her other door and head down the hall to the concierge lounge. There, she sat down and got a glass of wine from the attendant. She took a casual sip from her stemware before she picked up her phone and began to remotely control the television in Sherry's room.

"With a few touches of her finger she raised the volume of the TV as high as it would go and blasted the sound of recorded gunshots. She'd been counting on the inn's top-of-the-line Bose Surround system, and it didn't disappoint. The fake gunshots sounded completely authentic . . . perhaps even louder than actual gunshots. This is when we all thought Sherry had been shot, when, in actuality, at this point she already had two bullets in her. There was so little time between when Sherry was really shot and when everyone thought she had been shot, it didn't occur to anyone to question the timing. Cynthia executed her plan so quickly that any early time-of-death indicators, like body temperature or skin color, didn't blatantly not coincide with the moment we were all led to believe Sherry was killed. Sherry was, in fact, dead before Cynthia raised that glass of vino to her lips."

"That is quite a work of fiction you've come up with," Cynthia says.

"I don't think it's fiction at all," I reply. "In fact, I'm willing to bet anything that, when the detective here gets a warrant and checks your phone records, we'll find out you linked your phone to Sherry's TV and remotely controlled it just before the noise of bogus shots came from her room." I'm using Wavonne's bluffing strategy again. I actually have no idea if Detective Hutchins can get such a warrant or if this level of detail would even be available via phone records, but I figure Cynthia probably doesn't know either.

My words make Cynthia shudder, and there is a look of complete and utter guilt on her face.

"I know you did it, Cynthia," I say. "But honestly, I'm still not quite sure *why* you did it. You didn't seem to care that Russell was having an affair with Sherry and, per Trudy, you would be very well taken care of if he divorced you. I know you enjoyed the privileges of being Mrs. Russell Mellinger but, as long as you were taken care of financially, I can't imagine it was worth murder to stay married to Russell."

"Well taken care of?!" Cynthia both asks and exclaims at the same time. "We had an airtight prenup. Even if I could prove that he was cheating on me, if we divorced, I'd barely get a pittance."

"Trudy said you would get eighty thousand dollars a month," Wavonne says.

"Like I said," Cynthia replies. "A pittance."

"On what planet is eighty thousand dollars a month a pittance?" I ask.

"Do you have any idea how much it costs to look like this at sixty-two years old?" Cynthia questions, and I'm quite certain everyone in the room gasped more at the fact that this stunning woman before us is sixty-two years old than when I accused said woman of murder. "The dermatologists? The plastic surgeons? The beauticians and makeup artists? Do you have any idea how much it costs to charter a private jet? How much it costs to own and maintain seven homes? You can't even rent a villa in the South of France for a summer for eighty thousand dollars. Eighty thousand dollars would not even cover my country club membership. My God, on eighty thousand dollars a month, I might have to . . . have to"—she can barely get the words out—"have to fly . . . fly *commercial*."

Cynthia seems to be completely unraveling at this point. "That little bimbo thought she was going to take my place. I was all for her taking *this*"—she gestures toward Russell next to her—"off my hands a few nights a week, but if she thought she was going to take my place as his wife, she had another thing coming."

"Boy did she ever," Wavonne says. "Two things. It was two bullets, wasn't it?"

A little side eye from me prompts Wavonne to shut it, and Cynthia continues.

"I have put up with *this*"—Cynthia eyes Russell again and her absolute disgust with him shows in her face—"for thirty years to have everything I have and intend to have until my dying day. There was no way I was going to cede my houses and my clothes and my cars and most important, my money, to some Mary-come-lately. But that little Sherry outsmarted me. She led me and *everyone* to believe she was a simpleton, and if there's one thing I've learned about this"—she looks at Russell and refers to him as "this" yet again—"it's that he'll sleep with anything with firm breasts and a nice pair of legs, but he's only truly attracted to women with some smarts. I always made sure to choose his little playthings carefully."

"Choose his playthings?" Detective Hutchins asks.

"Yes, I set my husband up with other women. Get over it," Cynthia responds. "But only as distractions to give me a night off here and there. I was careful to not choose wife material. The stupider they were, the less chance of Russell having anything other than the most primal interest in them." This is the first time tonight she has referred to her husband as "Russell" rather than "this." "And Sherry gave us all the impression that she was the stupidest of the stupid. But it turns out, little Ms. Oops-I-Forgot-And-Used-All-The-Cheese was not so daft after all."

"So she did sabotage me?" Vera says.

"Of course she did," Cynthia replies. "That girl was scheming from day one. I just wish it had not taken me so long to figure that out. We were almost two weeks into filming . . . about the time she said something about Benjamin Franklin being the first president of the United States, that I began to wonder if anyone could really be as dim-witted as she was making herself out to be. Once I really gave it some thought I figured out how smart she actually was. But it wasn't until I realized that she had manipulated Russell into giving her advance notice of the challenges that I knew she was trouble."

Trey sends an "I told you so" look my way.

"We did an exotic seafood challenge last week. Each contestant was given a basket with a unique seafood item in it. We tasked the contestants with preparing espardenyes, gong gong, whelks . . . all sorts of oddities most people, even experienced chefs, had never heard of. Moreton Bay bugs, lobster-like things from Australia, were in Sherry's basket. All the other contestants were near-clueless about what to do with the ingredients given to them and needed a lot of time to formulate a plan. But Sherry set right off preparing a rather complex Moreton Bay bug curry with mangoes. A few days earlier she was totally prepared with a recipe for a strawberry-almond cobbler when the gang was tasked with making sugar free desserts. She had clearly gotten Russell to tip her off, and if Russell was playing along, I'm sure he eventually figured out she was no dummy either. And that's when I was done for—I can compete with youth and beauty—I can't compete with youth, beauty, *and* brains." Cynthia turns to Russell. "You fell for her, didn't you? I have put up with you for thirty years and then you go and fall for the first hot young thang that isn't dumb as a doornail."

From the way Russell is looking at her you can tell she pretty much has it right.

"You killed her?" Russell asks, anger rising in his voice. "You killed my Sherry?"

"Oh no," Cynthia yells back at him. "You do not get to be mad at *me*! I'm the one that should be mad. I gave you the best years of my life, and you were ready to throw me out like yesterday's garbage with an allowance not fit for a pauper. That's right, I heard you on the phone with the divorce attorney last week, and that's when I knew I had to do it.

That little hussy was going to take everything away from me if I didn't . . . if I didn't kill her."

"I think you've pretty much taken everything away yourself, Ms. Mellinger," Detective Hutchins says, walking toward her. "I'm sure you know that you're going to have to come with me."

Cynthia doesn't resist when he reaches for her hands and cuffs one and then the other. He gives her the usual spiel about her right to remain silent and her right to an attorney before grasping her elbow and leading her toward the exit.

"I'm sorry, Vera," Cynthia says on her way out. Detective Hutchins allows her to stop as she continues talking. "I never meant for you to be implicated, but when things started to turn in your direction it was a convenient way to throw them off my trail." She swings her head around to look at Russell. "It should be *you* in handcuffs. If you had just gone to smoke your stupid cigar like you do every other night instead of meeting with that contractor in here, you'd be the one being hauled off to the police station, and I'd still have your name, and your money, and your properties—I'd have it *all*, without having to put up with you."

"What are you talking about?" Russell asks, now looking more confused than angry.

"Why do you think I asked you to put the gun in the desk before we went to the museum? I could have just as easily done it myself, but then it wouldn't have had your prints on it. If you had just been off smoking your cigar around this secluded property with no cameras and no witnesses when I shot Sherry, like you were supposed to be, you'd be the man whose prints were on the gun that killed her and you would not have had an alibi. Combine all that with a love affair gone bad, and I suspect you would have had a very hard time proving your innocence."

Russell appears to be completely speechless, as if he's too shocked by what he just heard to say anything.

"Let's go," Detective Hutchins says, and gives Cynthia a little tug.

The rest of us hang back and watch as he takes her outside and out of sight. We remain quiet while exchanging glances. Just when I think no one has any words to share, Wavonne pipes up, "This isn't going to affect me and Halia being on TV, is it?"

Epilogue

"I finally figured it out. Last night. When I was switching out the box of baking soda in the refrigerator," I say to Momma and Wavonne as the three of us try to wrap up dessert preparations for the day. "Buttermilk!"

"Buttermilk?"

"That's why Sherry's biscuits rose, and Vera's waffle didn't." I wait for one of them to ask me to elaborate, but both of them seem far more interested in the cakes Momma is popping out of their pans than my cultured milk revelation. "They both used the expired baking powder, but Sherry's biscuits came out nice and light while Vera's waffle was a mess. Remember?" I ask Wavonne.

"I haven't stayed up nights thinkin' about it." Wavonne says this with a "because I, unlike you, have a life" sort of inflection. "But, yeah, I remember. Fluffy biscuits." She pats me on the behind and then looks at my bustline. "Flat waffles. But what's buttermilk . . . and your pear-shaped figure have to do with anything?"

I let Momma finish laughing at Wavonne's little quip before I continue.

"Way back when, Grandmommy taught me that you could

substitute baking soda for baking powder as long as you added something sour or acidic with it. Sherry must have used both baking powder *and* baking soda in her recipe—the recipe I went over with her certainly called for both. Her adding buttermilk to the mix was enough to activate the soda and aerate the biscuits even if the baking powder was bad."

"Makes sense," Momma says while filling a pastry bag. "I never trust dates on anything. I always check my baking powder . . . put a little in a spoon, pour some water over it, and make sure it fizzes. If it doesn't bubble, I throw it out regardless of the expiration date on the package."

"I guess that's why these look so good," I reply, watching her work her dessert-making magic. She's piping a layer of vanilla custard over freshly baked sponge cake, and, now, Wavonne and I will go behind her, arranging a mix of fresh berries over the custard. Momma will then add a second layer of cake, pipe on another coat of custard, and Wavonne and I will do our thing with the berries a second time.

"Berries are always better in the summer," Momma says, keeping an eye on Wavonne and me as we top the cakes.

"They do seem to be brighter or sweeter or something," I agree as I try to delicately arrange some strawberries on one of the cakes. When I reach for some blueberries, one of my servers steps into the kitchen.

"Halia. There's a Vera Ward here to see you."

"Tell her to come on back."

A few seconds later Vera comes through the kitchen door, and I walk over and give her a hug.

"Hey, girl," Wavonne says.

"Hey, Wavonne."

"Momma," I say. "This is Vera. She was one of the contestants on *Elite Chef*." I turn to Vera. "And this is my mother, Celia Watkins."

"You're the one who got the raw deal with the cheese and the baking powder?" Momma asks.

"Yes. That would be me. But it all worked out. . . . Well, not for Sherry, of course."

"Hate to break it to you," Wavonne says. "But it didn't exactly work out for you either. Sherry screwed you out of a possible win, and you ended up a murder suspect."

"True," Vera says. "But the tide has turned."

"Really?" I ask. "How so?"

"Russell called a meeting with me and Trey at the inn, which is finally open . . . like *really* open. I figured he was going to talk to us about taping a final challenge and that I might still have a chance at winning. It's been two months since Cynthia was arrested, so I figured he was ready to start moving on without her."

"So, what happened? Is there going to be a final cook-off between you and Trey?"

"No."

"No?"

"Russell said, with Cynthia's trial pending there are legal issues involved with airing any of the episodes that we taped. He said he wasn't sure if the season would air at all, and he didn't want to spend a bunch of time and money to film a final challenge that may never make it to the screen."

"What?" Wavonne says. "I may not get on TV?"

"You may not. . . . We *all* may not. And, if the season ever does make it to air, it won't be for a long time."

"So no one gets crowned Elite Chef?"

"Yes and no. No one, neither Trey nor I, will win the official Elite Chef title, but Russell agreed to split the more tangible components of the competition. Trey will be the executive chef at Sunfish and I, get this, am fifty thousand dollars richer."

"Fifty thousand dollars?!" Wavonne calls. "Drinks are on you tonight. Hell, drinks are on you *every* night."

Vera laughs. "I don't know about that. I sunk it all back into my business. Vera's Fried Chicken and Doughnuts Food Truck is officially in the black. The startup costs really drained me, and I thought I might have to close the whole thing down. But now, with some fresh capital, I'm ready to peddle my fried chicken and doughnuts all over town."

"Congratulations! That's wonderful!"

"Thank you. I just wanted to stop by and share the good news. Who knows how things would have turned out if you hadn't agreed to help me the day after Sherry was killed."

"I think you would have been fine either way, but if you want to throw a little credit my way for helping you keep your business, I'll gladly take it."

"I'll be parked on Twelfth Street in the city near Metro Center this week. I hope all of you will come by for free fried chicken and doughnuts." Vera reaches for the door. "And thank you again for everything. I'm so glad it's all behind us."

"Now that all that nasty solving a murder business is over, and you have some extra time, maybe we can get you over to the CVS to meet my pharmacist. I was there yesterday and still no wedding band," Momma says after Vera leaves the kitchen. "Maybe you can pretend you have asthma and get an inhaler prescription from your doctor."

"I'm not making up an illness to try and snag a date with your pharmacist, Momma."

"Because you have so many other suitors beatin' down your door?" Wavonne jibes. "Because you'd hate to give up all those lonely nights watching *Friends* reruns, and the four black people that were on that show over the course of ten years."

"There were more than four, Wavonne. Aisha Tyler was on there. And Gabrielle Union. And there was that waiter . . . and that self-defense instructor . . . and the guy at the tanning salon. And that neighbor who sang 'Morning's Here'—"

"If you bein' able to name every black character on *Friends* is not testament to you needin' a man, then I don't know what is," Wavonne decrees. "And the guy at the tanning salon was Puerto Rican."

When I realize I do know all the black characters on *Friends*—the black man who played Chandler's boss . . . and I think a black woman played a different boss, and there was the black nurse, and Ross's divorce attorney, and I think the black nurse again—I start to think that maybe Wavonne is on to something. "Maybe you're right," I say. "No one, no non-sad, nonpathetic person should know this much about a twenty-year-old sitcom." I look at Momma. "So, asthma, you say?"